D1345443

a30118 014753697b

Antonia

Antonia

by

BRENDA JAGGER

HODDER AND STOUGHTON
LONDON SYDNEY AUCKLAND TORONTO

 First printed 1978. ISBN 0 340 22712 5. *Photoset and printed in Great Britain for Hodder and Stoughton Limited, Mill Road, Dunton Green, Sevenoaks, Kent, by Lowe & Brydone Printers Limited, Thetford, Norfolk. Hodder and Stoughton Editorial Office: 47 Bedford Square, London WC1B 3DP.*

To Philip

1

THE EMPEROR GALBA invited us to dine and, although he didn't like women in the way men are supposed to, he looked hard at my sister-in-law, Corellia. Naturally, my father would have preferred the old gentlemen to look at me but there are hundreds of faces like mine and Corellia had always been unique. Her hair was the colour of antique gold, yet her eyes were dark and slanting and her mouth, ever since childhood, had smiled secrets which had got us all into trouble. She was tall and slender and altogether lovely but, having known her all my life, I was used to her and she made no impact on me any more. My brother, Clarus, had known her all his life too, but he'd been away from home a long time—studying abroad and doing his stint with the legions—and when he came back six months ago he'd forgotten all about her beauty and was so wounded by it that no one else would do. There'd been a lot of scandal in her family and they hadn't much money left, but Clarus had threatened to fall sick and die if he couldn't have her and father, surprisingly, had given his consent.

They had kept me well away from the palace while Nero was alive but, like all legendary places, it fell a little short of my imaginings. I had entered the park—those scandalous 125 acres Nero had stolen from the centre of Rome—expecting, if not enchantment, at least the memory of it, lingering like a fragrance in the air. But Galba—who didn't believe in fragrance and frivolity—had locked enchantment away, just as he'd turned off the machinery that operated Nero's revolving dining-room and brought perfume and flower-petals showering down from the ivory ceiling. He'd put out most of the lamps too, so that hurrying through the long, painted rooms leading to the heart of the house, one couldn't really see the encrustations of precious stones, the gold inlays, the statues with emeralds and sapphires in their eye-sockets and pearls around their marble throats. One saw nothing but the pale light, illuminating no more than a corner of Nero's famous party-room, and because Galba had shut off the heating system too, and very few of the braziers were burning, we had hurried towards that light, eyes straining through the gloom, feet and fingers already nipped with cold, to a meal which would have covered Nero's chefs with shame.

In his time, only six months ago, the room would have been full of actors and harlots and charioteers, helping him to squander the 2,200 million sesterces Galba had pledged himself to recover. But now the contrast couldn't have been more marked. Nero had been young and glamorous and crazy. Galba was old and mean and sly, and although moderate men like my father expected a great deal from him, he was well into his seventy-third year and whatever he was planning to do one felt he'd have to be quick about it.

He was my mother's uncle, her closest living relative, and, having been brought up to revere him as the holder of high office, a consul and a former governor of Aquitania, Greater Germany, Africa and, until very recently, of Tarragonian Spain, it was no more than my duty—and very much to my advantage—to adore him now that his Spanish Legions had proclaimed him emperor of Rome.

He was squat and square with a bald head and a prim, tight-lipped mouth. An uncomfortable man, stiff and stern, who barked out questions and commands and stared rudely through his watery blue eyes, looking for the flaw in one's argument or the mudstains on one's sandals. And, like all my mother's family, he never for a moment forgot his aristocratic lineage, that unbroken line of illustrious men which went back to Rome's foundations and, according to Galba, even beyond that. It had pleased him, since becoming emperor, to trace his pedigree, and consequently mine, through deepest antiquity to Pasiphae, the Cretan Queen, and to Jupiter, the father of the gods himself. And although I didn't mind having such grand relations I couldn't help thinking—knowing quite well that no one cared a fig for my opinion—that Galba himself looked very much like any other aged senator, nodding off between the courses and being nudged into wakefulness by the two men who never left his side—Laco, his new Praetorian Prefect, and the consul Titus Vinius, that suave, secret man who tonight had looked, not at Corellia, but at me, assessing my worth as Galba's great-niece and wondering if there was anything in it for him.

I'd heard a great deal about these two, none of it very good, and in spite of all my mother had to say about Galba's brilliance, I suspected, along with a great many other people, that the reality of his power lay at least partly with Laco and Vinius. Galba had the great name and the great reputation—for one couldn't replace Nero with just anybody—but Laco and Vinius had the energy, the greed, the ruthlessness, to keep him where he was. And perhaps they, more than anyone else in Rome, were uncomfortably aware that, at seventy-three, he couldn't be expected to last much longer. No one knew if they could survive without him but their prospects, like ours, would depend largely on the man he appointed as his successor.

Galba, whose interests were not domestic, had no children, no one, really, except my mother, to call his own, and since my brother Clarus had been judged too young—and Galba hadn't taken to him anyway—his choice of an heir would have to be made outside his own circle, and would have to be made soon. He had singled no one out as yet but since he first came to Rome at the start of the winter, both Laco and Vinius had been constantly drawing young men to his attention, making promises, doing deals with ambitious families, trying to cut each other's throats, for whoever gained control of Galba's heir held the future in the hollow of his hand and Laco and Vinius were equally determined to be that man.

The meal was far from magnificent. Galba was using Nero's gold plate but the food could easily have come from his camp kitchens, while the servants, trained by Nero's butlers to be graceful and discreet, to adorn a meal as well as serve it, seemed embarrassed by the dishes they were putting before us. The cup in my hand had amethysts set below the rim and a delicate tracery of golden acanthus leaves carved all around them, but the wine inside it was young and sour and if it had a name I hadn't heard it before.

I was the youngest woman in the room, and probably the richest, but no one took any notice of me. All the men, except my brother Clarus, were busy proving to Galba that they were as serious and sober and straitlaced as he was himself, while Clarus was fully occupied in gazing at his wife. She looked at me once or twice across his head, raised her eyebrows and heaved a sigh, and I knew she was bored too. She'd been quite willing to marry Clarus, for a single girl of twenty with a small dowry will take anybody she can get, and considering her mother's reputation she'd been lucky to get anyone at all. But none of us had been brought up to expect this sort of thing from marriage, and my brother's devotion was a surprise and a burden to her. So much of a burden that I knew how glad she'd be if my father, who was going out to Judaea at the end of the month, decided to take Clarus with him.

There was a very good chance of it. Father, because of my mother's new imperial connections, had been chosen to deliver messages from Galba to the army in Judaea, and although he'd really wanted the governorship of Germany, which had gone to Aulus Vitellius, we all realised he was setting off on a mission of great delicacy and importance. After Nero's suicide in June the Empire had been at the mercy of any man of senatorial rank who commanded an army and had the courage to use it on his own behalf. There had been several of them, ambitious provincial governors with everything to gain, and perhaps I'd been surprised when my old uncle Galba had not only been the first to declare himself but had managed to get most of the others out of the way. Men who could be bribed or blackmailed had been dealt with accordingly, men in distant, difficult places like Britain had not been considered dangerous, but the governors of Lower Germany and Africa and the Commander of the Praetorian Guard here in Rome had all been assassinated at lightning speed and Galba's men put in their places. Laco himself had taken command of the city garrison, Aulus Vitellius had gone to Germany, much to my father's chagrin, and there remained now only the Eastern question to settle, the matter of the great General Vespasian who had gone, with a large army, to impose Nero's will on the Jews, and who must absolutely declare for Galba if the new regime was to survive. Vespasian, who was brilliant and terrible and dangerously popular with his troops, couldn't help knowing that Galba was only sitting in Nero's chair because his legions had put him there, and it was vital to dissuade him from using his own legions for the same purpose. My father, a man of integrity and charm, was being despatched post-haste to deliver the bribes, the veiled threats, whatever it was likely to take, and a few days behind father on the road there would no doubt be another messenger, someone with no integrity at all, coming to put a knife between Vespasian's ribs if father's mission failed.

The meal ended but there was no entertainment after it, no exotic dancing-girls, no lute-players, none of the sparkling conversation and the tricky, intellectual games Nero had enjoyed. There was just Galba, reviewing his dinner guests as he reviewed his troops. I was taken up to him hopefully but although I resembled my mother and he was supposed to have been fond of her at one time, his weak, light eyes passed over me without interest.

"Good. Good," he said, and then, realising that something

more was required, "Yes—we will keep your face in mind." And I stepped back, feeling like a new recruit who has asked for promotion out of turn.

But my effect on others was more immediate. The consul, Titus Vinius, from his place beside Galba, smiled at me in the way I detested, undressing me so thoroughly with his eyes that I wondered if he was considering me for himself, while Laco, the man who had murdered the commander of the guard and would have been called a criminal had he not been on our side, got up and took my arm, apparently wishing to present me to someone. His hand was hot, the pressure of his fingers unpleasant, but I had been brought up to respect power and, in any event, simple duty to my family—to our estates which in times like these could so easily be confiscated—required me to be more than polite.

"My dear young lady," he said, brimming over with false, after-dinner cordiality. "There is someone I want you to meet—a very dear friend of mine, recently returned from exile—Piso Licinianus. Obviously you will know the family and its tragic history. So many worthy men lost—but we must hope for better things in the future. Piso, my dear fellow, this is the young lady we spoke of, Lucilius Antoninus' daughter, Antonia. Piso—Antonia—a propitious meeting, I feel sure of it."

A cold hand took mine and I saw a man of about thirty, a pale face, pale eyes, a mechanical smile. He was meticulously dressed, correct in every detail, as returned exiles always are, and he told me, without any delight in his voice, how delighted he was to meet me, and held my hand just long enough to let me know that Laco had asked my father's permission to make this introduction and that my father had agreed. I was neither alarmed nor surprised, for this was always happening to me. I had one of the biggest dowries in Rome and rich expectations not only from my father but from childless relatives as well, and all my life, long before I was old enough to understand it, people had been showing me their sons and brothers and nephews, singing praises to which I no longer listened since it was my father, not I, who would eventually decide. And this Piso was just one of a crowd. I understood perfectly what Laco was about. Piso was his new candidate for imperial adoption and if he could marry him off to me, a member of the imperial family, then it would make everything that much easier. The husband of the emperor's great-niece couldn't be passed over and through him Laco could destroy his rival, Vinius, and rule the world. And since my father naturally wanted to get me settled before he left for Judaea I thought he'd be very likely to consent.

Behind me Corellia was all interest but Piso took no notice of her. Dutifully he kept his eyes on my face, seeing not Antonia but Galba's relative, a Sulpician lady, the most marriageable girl in Rome, and, beside all that, Corellia's beauty counted for little. He spoke a few commonplace phrases, and although I found him pompous and unattractive, I understood how hard it is for these ambitious, penniless aristocrats, returning from exile to a city they barely recognise, to claim their places in a society which is always slightly embarrassed by them and would really like them to go away again, or at least try not to make a fuss when they find strangers living in their ancestral homes. And I felt sorry for him.

"My dear boy," my father said, the warmth in his voice telling me my future had already been decided. "I remember your father and your brothers—such a loss—such a sorrow—you must dine with us." And as the invitation was being given and accepted, a new arrival swept into the room, someone from the glittering past who knew these halls better than any of us.

"Otho," Corellia breathed, her voice naked with admiration, and as everyone craned their necks to look, Vinius—Laco's arch enemy—rushed forward and threw an arm warmly around Otho's shoulders, declaring with that one gesture that this was the man for his money, the man for whom he intended to win Galba's favour and an empire with it. And I wondered how I would have felt if, instead of Laco, my father had decided to back Vinius and that in place of this stiff, humorless, sexless Piso, they were offering me Otho?

He was thirty-seven years old—only a little older than Piso—and he was beautiful. His glossy black curls were arranged, like Nero's, in the kind of artistic disarray that took hours to achieve, he had glittering black eyes and a wide, warm, challenging smile, and he brought so much glamour into the room with him, so many of the wicked enchantments of the past that every other man suddenly looked stodgy and pale and dull. He had been one of Nero's boon companions in the old days. They'd run riot together, designed a whole, intricate, scandalous system of good-living all their own, and had quarrelled only when they'd both fallen in love with the same woman, the beautiful and unlucky Poppaea, who had finally married Nero and then been kicked to death by him one night when she was pregnant and he, perhaps, had remembered too clearly how she'd once preferred his best friend. Otho had been sent away, packed off in disgrace to govern Lusitania, in the hope that he'd make a mess of it and lay himself open to prosecution. And, having nothing to hope for from Nero but an uncomfortable death, he'd been one of the first to join Galba's rebellion and was now back in Rome, still managing, after an absence of ten years, to get himself cheered by the Praetorians. The city garrison had adored Nero's crazy generosity, and all his splendid wildness, and Otho was just like him, the same dash and swagger, the same inexplicable charm that excited men's imaginations so that they'd risk far more for him, just for a smile and a colourful turn of phrase, than for a man like Galba who could win battles and govern nations, who was serious and responsible and really far more worthwhile. Galba was not popular with the soldiers. He was too proud, and too mean, to pay them a proper bounty, to buy their loyalty as Nero used to do, and that being the case he needed Otho, and would be a fool to hesitate.

"That's a man," Corellia breathed into my ear, "that's a man I could really—" But Clarus was instantly at her side, pressing against her and shielding her from Otho's view, for Corellia's mother—my aunt Fannia—had been a feature of Nero's court in her day, and Otho would be sure to remember her.

"I think we should leave now," Clarus pleaded, and so urgent was his despair that my father yielded to it and we left, Laco and Piso walking a little way with us down sombre corridors that had once blazed with the light and echoed with the music of a man who had been not quite a genius and not really an emperor at all. Galba had snuffed out the candles but not quite all of the magic and Corellia, avoiding Clarus' hands in the dark, was sure that Otho would light them all again.

"I shall look forward to seeing you at your father's house," Piso murmured awkwardly and I knew, because I was making the same effort, that he was trying hard to mean it. I smiled and followed Corellia, who had gone sighing out into the night, so utterly consumed with longing for Otho—or someone very like him—that she had forgotten Clarus altogether and, later on, would be able to offer him her passive, uncaring body and hardly notice him. And all the way home I heard him whispering to her, "My darling, I won't go to Judaea. I won't leave you," blissfully unaware that she had drifted too far away from him to care.

2

On the day Piso was to dine father had the household up at daybreak, creating such a stir that it was hard to think of him as a man who controlled the destinies of at least 2,000 slaves on our properties up and down the country and an army of freedmen and clients whose affairs he considered very much his own. We had moved for the winter to our house on the Esquiline, not because anyone liked it but because it was an ancient mansion of the Sulpicii—my mother's family—and she felt it her duty to occupy it for at least a part of the year. My grandparents had lived here and their grandparents before them and since their tastes had been simpler, their resources possibly smaller, my father fretted—on this great day—for the circular dining-room overlooking the river at our villa across the Tiber and the spectacular emptiness of the house he'd recently bought and extensively improved near the Temple of Diana.

"One can breathe there," he'd told my mother hopefully all through the summer, but she'd only smiled, and on her return from our estates in Toscana in October, she'd had them open up this large but somehow oppressive house, standing, full of its own importance, among decaying streets that should long ago have been pulled down, a heavy, antique jewel surrounded by scraps of base metal at which my mother disdained to look but which caused considerable inconvenience to the rest of us. My mother was at home here, surrounded by the busts of her ancestors and the memory of their achievements, completely unconcerned by the inadequacy of the servants' quarters and the badly-placed kitchens, but my father, who paid a great deal of money for his chefs and thought it only right to make things easier for them, spent every winter in consultation with his architects, buying new stoves, enlarging bedrooms, augmenting the water supply, suggesting major improvements my mother usually rejected, until it was a relief to us all when she finally succumbed to the first spring breezes and consented to close the house up again and move on.

My mother was a lady of the highest nobility, my father less noble but extremely rich, and although they had been married for a very long time, he was still decidedly in awe of her. My father's family had concentrated on acquiring property, and had tended to avoid public life, seeing it as a bad risk, but my mother was connected with the Sulpicii, the Metellii, the Cornelii, the Livii, with an impressive array of consuls and censors, commanders of armies and governors of key provinces, with so many generations of rank and privilege that my father, for all his millions, could never quite manage to feel worthy of her. And I suspected that, on her side, she could never rid herself of the idea that he had done very well to get her in the first place.

She was, in her way, a beautiful woman, but because I looked like her it was not a kind of beauty I admired. She was tall with tapering hands and feet and smooth black hair coiled into a neat chignon at the nape of her neck. She was elegant and aloof, with the high-bridged nose of the Sulpicii and sharp, black eyes that saw through walls and into the minds of defiant children, and no one ever approached her less than cautiously. She was an uncomfortable person, like her uncle Galba, and my strong resemblance to her, and the growing realisation that people were often careful with me too, had started to worry me of late.

She had borne my brother Clarus twenty-two years ago in great pain and then, two years later, after a series of miscarriages, had managed to bring me into the world. But after that she had considered her duty done and had become so untouchable and so chaste that, like the goddesses of ancient Greece, it was as if she'd found the power to renew her virginity by bathing in some enchanted stream. And yet, although I'd known for years that my father often slept with one of our freedwomen and sometimes indulged himself with a fashionable courtesan, I understood that he was entirely devoted to my mother. The only ambition he had was to make her proud of him and, having failed to win recognition from either Claudius or Nero, he was going out to Judaea—risking his life—simply to prove to her that he was capable of such great enterprise. And, perhaps, like Corellia, she would be glad to see him go.

"What a pity he can't take Piso with him out East too," Corellia said wickedly, later that morning when she came to plague me at my work. I had been asked by my father to choose a dinner-service for the evening meal and, in busy consultation with the man who looked after our gold and silver plate, I turned Corellia's remark aside, refusing to let her see my disappointment. Ever since that night at the palace she had been indulging herself with her dreams of Otho, sighing and giggling and making love to him in her imagination so that Clarus was in a sulk and her mother—who was living with us just then—was in despair.

"I hear Otho's going to marry Nero's widow," I told her, but she only laughed, for she had never been a good marriage prospect like me and, being my Aunt Fannia's daughter, knew all about mistresses and the glory some of them could achieve.

"And who's going to marry you?" she said and just as I began to snap that nothing had been arranged about that yet, my father called me to his library and repeated to me the familiar words, "Antonia, dear child, a most interesting proposition has been made to me concerning you."

It wasn't the first betrothal he had arranged for me. At the age of seven he'd promised me to my ten-year-old cousin, my uncle Marcus' only child, who had died at fourteen, bequeathing me his place in my uncle's will, and then, five years ago, there'd been a young Cornelius whose face I couldn't now remember and who had been sent into exile by Nero before the marriage could take place. A year later a brilliant and fluent gentleman with a well-established place in the Senate had asked for me as his third wife and had been accepted, and then refused, when it transpired that his pedigree was not up to my mother's exacting standards. And, just last year, there had been a young Metellus, handsome and sophisticated and closely related to my mother, highly acceptable until I realised he was a practising homosexual and chose to object. My mother would have swept my objections aside, seeing them as an insult to her clan but my father had promised never to force me and when she saw that for once he meant to stand firm she spoke some sharp words to me that still rankled between us. But my victory had been short-lived for she'd amused herself, ever since, by raising strong and unshakable barriers between me and the male sex as a whole.

But Piso was different. As a direct descendant of Pompey the Great and Marcus Crassus, who had once ruled the world with Julius Caesar, his breeding was immaculate. He was a serious young man, with nothing known against him, and, in any case, since Laco hinted that the matter had won Galba's approval, not even my mother could be anything but very well pleased.

My father was full of his easy, warm delight—glad for my sake, for I was twenty and it was high time something was done, and relieved that mother showed no signs of making a fuss.

'You'll do well," he kept on telling me. "You'll do well. The young man is destined for high office—Galba has singled him out most particularly—naturally I can't divulge the details, even to you, but you'll be delighted, over-joyed. And apart from that, he really is a very pleasant fellow—so unpretentious, so open—I can't remember when I've taken such a fancy to anyone."

But I had to go to Corellia's mother, my aunt Fannia, for the information I wanted. She knew nothing against him but then, what was there to know abut him at all? Nothing but a trail of disaster. His father and his brother had been executed by Claudius, another brother by Nero, the rest of the family sent into exile, and she really couldn't tell them one from the other. She'd heard that Piso himself had been married for several years to a woman called Verania or Verginia or Vipsania, something beginning with a 'V' anyway, but, like all returned exiles he was finding old associations and old marriages cumbersome, and was anxious for new ones.

"He'll value you," she told me. "He'll value you for the dowry you bring and for your family connections—you can believe me—he'll value these things enormously. All men do, but an exile even more so. It's exactly what they dream about, all those years, on their little islands or wherever the emperor chooses to send them. All they want to do is to get back in the mainstream of things, and the right kind of wife to go with it. Don't worry. You'll be important to him. You're Galba's great-niece, a Sulpician lady with your mother's pedigree and your father's fortune. He won't do anything you don't like. He'll spend years being grateful and after that you'll be used to him and won't care what he does. Come, I'll lend you my pearls tonight and show you how to arrange them in your hair. The maids never get it quite right—but I'll make you beautiful."

Fannia, unlike Corellia, was kind, and when she came into my room with her pearls and her ornate silver box of cosmetics I put myself entirely in her hands, knowing her taste to be perfect. Corellia was twenty, Fannia just thirty-five, and in the distance one couldn't always tell them apart but at close quarters the resemblance ended. Corellia was often harsh and impatient, prone to fits of temper when she threw her mirrors and vases about and ended up in a heap of hysterical tears, but Fannia was so warm and easy that one tended to forget the scandals of her past and how her tarnished reputation had made it so difficult for Corellia to get a husband. Fannia herself had been married five or six times and I had first known her as the wife of my father's younger brother, a woman already twice divorced and bringing with her a little daughter, Corellia, about five years old. Her union with my uncle had been brief and stormy but he'd kept Corellia with him for a while after they parted and then, when he remarried, had handed her over to us, to be looked after whenever Fannia—who had become one of the ornaments of Nero's court—was too busy to do it herself. Fannia had had lovers and adventures, had spent her own money and her husbands' money, had got into debt and into trouble, and now, still bewildered and very nearly bankrupt by Nero's downfall, she was taking refuge with us, exploiting us as father had always feared. It wasn't that he disliked her—for no red-blooded man could ever do that. He was simply worried about what mother would say. But there were distinct advantages to mother in having a noblewoman of Fannia's undoubted refinement and good taste about the house. Fannia could arrange mother's pearls too, far better than any of the maids, she could interview unwelcome guests and settle tedious domestic disputes, and so, although mother sometimes sighed and let father believe Fannia was a burden she bore only for his sake—since he'd consented to the ridiculous marriage in the first place—no one but father was deceived and Fannia stayed on.

Dinner that night, like everything mother arranged, was superb without being in any way ostentatious, and I noticed, with annoyance but without surprise, that the new and very beautiful gold plate I'd asked for, had been replaced by the antique silver of her choice, dishes that had served generations of patrician statesmen with cool eyes and crisp voices just like hers, and goblets that had held the wine of victory and, just now and again, the brew of death.

Piso arrived at exactly the hour named, immaculate in a synthesis of white lawn with no jewellery but the gold ring on his hand, and if I hadn't been warned that he was coming as a prospective bridegroom I would never have suspected it. He did what was required of him as a guest but he did it stiffly, addressing his stilted remarks mainly to my father, and it wasn't until Laco swept into the room, full of his toothy camaraderie, that he remembered the role he'd come to play and turned, briefly, to me. His mouth smiled and told me I looked very well, but his eyes were uneasy and I knew I wasn't in his mind at all.

My mother's food, as always, was light and elegantly presented, the sauces loving, not disguising, the flavour of the birds from our own coops and the fish from our ponds, and she'd arranged the couches in such a way that conversation was easy and yet we were far enough apart to breathe our own air.

Luxury, in all our houses, was displayed with immense discretion—uncluttered space, muted splendour—so that it took a few moments to notice that every painting and every statue was a masterpiece, every elegant twist of ivory and every stem of silver had a history, or that the mosaics, commissioned by a very famous Sulpician indeed, were beyond price. And if this was too subtle for Laco, who seemed a man of direct appetites, I suspectd that Piso immediately recognised the wine as twenty-year-old Falernian and knew that the goblet in his hand may well have touched the lips of the Emperor Augustus or the tragic Agrippina—Caligula's mother, Nero's grandmother—who had won the friendship and caused the downfall of another ancestor of mine.

He'd know too, as any sensible man would know before proposing marriage, exactly what my fortune consisted of, how much of it was in land and how the remainder was invested, and it seemed his purpose here tonight was to show my father his sound financial brain—how well he'd take care of my capital—rather than to present himself to me as a lover. Even Corellia, in her sea-green gown with strands of gold and coral in her hair, sat neglected by everyone but Clarus, and when Piso turned from my father he addressed my mother, far more at ease with her than with me. She was wearing white silk with a cameo on her shoulder, one large, perfect pearl on her forehead and another on her hand, as elegant and pale as the atmosphere she'd created, and I understood that this was what he admired and what he wanted me to be. He wanted—not Antonia—but an untouchable aristocrat, a woman like my mother who was always obeyed because she never questioned her right to command, a woman to whom all doors were open and who, by lifting her cold eyebrows, could strike terror into the hearts of anyone who dared question the rights of a returned exile like himself. And because I could do those things too, because part of me was like that and he'd never ask to see the other part, perhaps I'd be able to live at peace with him. Perhaps—but I'd been engaged too many times before to think about marriage until it happened, and there was no point at all in deciding whether I liked his smooth, dark hair and his uneasy eyes—in deciding whether or not I wanted him to touch me—when the matter might never arise.

I had a few moments alone with him just as he was leaving and, having been informed that my father had consented and that I was not unwilling, he said the things men say on such occasions, and which I had heard several times before.

"You and I are strangers, Antonia—I'm very much aware of it. You must be aware of it too and I beg you not to feel any alarm. I hope—very sincerely—that you will feel able to give me your trust—that you will rely on me in all things. Believe me when I say I will do my utmost never to offend you."

It was adequate, in fact it was spoken like a gentleman, but it wasn't enough and he must have known that. My first fiancé—my cousin—had pulled my hair; my second, the young Cornelius, had held my hand and kissed my cheek; while my third, that distinguished gentleman of the Senate, had at least been honest, for, as the acknowledged protector of a well-known actress, he'd never pretended that his interest in me went beyond the financial. And the homosexual Metellus, in many ways, had been the best of all for he'd been light and quick-witted and had made me laugh. But Piso was cold and tense, trying far too hard, and I wondered if he'd been happy with his wife and was sorry to part with her.

When they had all gone I stood for a while in the garden with my father, happy to have a few moments alone with him while he explained to me the things I already knew.

"I intended to leave Clarus at home to look after things here while I'm away," he said. "But now we've found Piso I don't see the necessity for it. I shall speak to the emperor tomorrow about your betrothal and, if he consents, I shall ask him to take the auspices at your wedding in the spring, whether I return or not. Piso will do everything that is required until then. I have complete faith in him and your mother tells me she will feel quite easy—quite easy, which means a great deal to me. And so Clarus can come with me to Judaea. It will do him good."

He sighed his pleasure, a man well content, and when he asked me, "You do like him, don't you, Antonia?" I said, "Yes, I think he's a good man," because he had little enough in his life to make him truly happy and I didn't want to spoil this for him. He put an arm around my shoulders and I leaned against him, loving him when he was himself, good and straightforward, a dependable, simple man unfettered by the woman—my mother—who made him despise his own goodness and strive instead for success. But, although she had already gone to her chaste bed, a nymph locked away in her shrine far beyond the sweaty lusts of mortal men, she was never out of his thoughts for long.

"Your mother likes him," he said, his voice suddenly hesitant as if he had spoken a sacred name, "And I—well—you know how delighted I am. I want you to be happy, Antonia, and I know I can place you in his hands and know that whatever happens to me you'll be safe—cherished—as I have always cherished your mother."

"Oh no," I said. "Hardly as much as that," and he sighed and took his arm away, for this was an old argument, an old demon, and neither of us could win.

He sighed and took a few nervous paces up and down. "How hard you are. How hard. Youth, I suppose, is like that. But let me say this, Antonia—my dear daughter—I am leaving on a long journey from which I may not return, and I would travel lighter if I knew your mother could depend on you not only for the support but for the affection that—in her weakness—she needs."

And, put that way, the sore patch of resentment that always built up inside me when he talked of her melted away and I put my head on his shoulder and made him all the promises he required—made them sincerely, although I knew it wouldn't matter whether I kept them or not for, either way, she would complain about me when he came home.

"Yes, well then," he said, "run along now, you have an exciting time ahead of you and you need your rest."

He walked with me a little way through the house but when I reached the passage that led to my room he patted my cheek and walked on, towards the atrium and the street beyond. He was going out into the night, as he often did, for his wife's door would be bolted against him and, although I loved him more than I loved anyone else, it was none of my business where he slept. I only hoped she was beautiful and kind and knew how to make him smile.

My urgent thought pursued him. "Father, don't go to Judaea." But before my unspoken plea had ended I heard Corellia's voice from the next room, tinged with the beginnings of hysteria. "Can't you leave me alone, you dreadful boy," she shrieked. "Must you keep on pinching and pawing me—my head aches and I feel sick—and if you've got me pregnant I'll never forgive you." And I opened my door and went quickly inside, for there wasn't much time left now for me to sleep alone. Quite soon, in the spring, Piso would share a bed with me, doing his nightly duty so as to give my family no cause for complaint, and for just an instant I didn't think I could bear it. But, as the waiting maids undressed me and took the pins out of my hair, the feeling passed. The chain of circumstances had kept me single for too long and I needed a husband. Piso would take me away from my mother and he wouldn't embarrass me—as my brother Clarus embarrassed his wife—by demanding a passion I couldn't feel. His love-making would probably be as well-mannered as the rest of him and, in any case, if Galba wanted it, I really had no choice.

3

Father and Clarus left ten days later, just before the arrival of those disquieting despatches from Germany which would have prevented them from setting out at all.

Mother said goodbye to father in her room, one of the rare occasions he was allowed inside, and he came out to join Clarus with tears in his eyes. But my brother was feeling too sorry for himself to have any pity to spare and he just stared sullenly and shuffled his feet. He had asked me the night before to keep an eye on Corellia and I'd told him bluntly, "Be unfaithful to her. She'll think you're a fool if you don't enjoy yourself when you get the chance. She's too sure of you." But he'd looked at me like an enemy and said spitefully, "It's all right for you. You're a cold fish, just like mother. I don't envy Piso—but he's a cold fish too. You'll do well together." And I had no reply because we both knew Corellia wasn't to be trusted and, more than that, she liked me better than she liked him, and he was jealous.

They left, and the house spread relaxing arms around us, telling us that now there were no more men to impress we could leave our hair uncurled, dine when it suited us or not at all, come and go as we pleased. My mother went back into her private apartments and closed her door even more firmly than usual, for not even my father's timid knock would disturb her now, while Corellia floated about from room to room on a high tide of bliss, chanting, "I can sleep tonight. I can really sleep. No pinching and pleading and sulking and no waking me up to apologise. I can sleep." "Nonsense," Fannia said reprovingly, taking Clarus' part because he'd just lent her some money and because the maids were listening, but Corellia rounded on her furiously and they launched one of their famous scenes, with Fannia weeping and asking what she'd done to deserve such a daughter, and Corellia screaming and stamping and smashing whatever came to hand. Usually, after one of these explosions, my brother took her out and bought her something or, if her tantrum had exhausted her too much for that, he sent for her favourite jewellers and silk-merchants to come and display their wares for her at the house. But it was a scene she couldn't play by herself and she soon recovered her good humour. She spent the whole of that first afternoon of liberty in her bath, a sea-nymph basking among the green-veined marble fittings, while her attendants massaged perfumed oils into her skin, painted her toe-nails and smoothed every hair from her body, preparing her for her solitary couch as she'd never bothered to do for my brother. And the next morning she had the bloom of a new-born rose.

"Let's go out," she said. "Let's get dressed up, Antonia, and see what we can see. I've had the most fantastic sleep and now I'm more wide-awake than I've ever been in my life. Even the sky looks a different colour."

And so, because I knew she'd go without me and do something stupid if I refused, we went out to Mars Field to watch the young sparks racing their chariots and the soldiers on parade, and while I tried to be dignified—a credit to my upbringing and my expectations—she allowed men she hardly knew to lounge beside her litter and treat her, not as my brother's wife, but as Fannia's daughter, a plum only too ripe for the picking.

"Don't look so prim," she told me, rich laughter bubbling in her throat, "I won't go to bed with any of them. It's just such fun to let them think I might."

But even so, I was glad to get her home and glad too, to be able to distract my mother's attention when, during the evening, two separate messages were delivered which sent her, chuckling and gloating, into her room.

"What fun," she told me when I looked in to say goodnight. "And how strange men are. Last year when I was a single girl without a dowry no one would come near me but now, with Clarus' fortune behind me, suddenly I'm beautiful and desirable and all sorts of other nonsense too. Look—young Verginius Tullus has written asking me to meet him somewhere, to talk about old times, he says. And that's interesting, because last winter when Fannia was trying so hard to marry me off he was the one who got himself such a reputation as a wit by working out those famous five hundred ways of avoiding dowerless girls and their mothers. Don't you remember? It was the top joke of the season. They all laughed themselves silly at good old Verginius—and at me. I wonder if he's forgotten that I was his inspiration—his Muse? Shall I agree to meet him and remind him?"

"Be careful," I said. "Very careful—for your own sake. It may be gratifying to pay Verginius back—but is it worth it?

Clarus could divorce you and return your dowry out of his monthly allowance. And you wouldn't like it if you had to start peddling it—and yourself—around town again."

She tossed her head, full of her warm, rich laughter, her eyes sparkling with mischief and defiance.

"You're quite right, Antonia." she said. "Perfectly right. In fact you're always right—just like your mother. You're quite famous for it." And, still smiling, she shrugged herself down among her pillows and dismissed me with a yawn.

Life, as it always seems to do, wove itself into a pattern so that the old routines were replaced by new ones and the spaces left by my father and Clarus were soon filled. My mother continued to rule the household with a firm but almost unseen hand, her power so absolute that she seldom needed to show herself. She expected to be obeyed, was mildly astonished when—just now and again—someone forgot or misunderstood, and since she treated her children very much as she treated her servants, I often writhed with them under the lash of her sarcasm and her immaculate justice. She rarely punished. She simply obliged me, or anyone who had earned her displeasure, to admit she was right and, in the face of so much perfection, there were many times when a beating would have been easier to bear. "Hit me," I'd once yelled at her but it was a request I never repeated for her disdain had been a crucifixion in itself and now I merely gritted my teeth and thought about escape. If I'd been a slave perhaps I would have run away, although our slaves never did so, but I was free-born, my only escape route was marriage, and there were moments of bitter frustration when any man would do.

Piso's betrothal ring—a plain band of gold which my mother thought tasteful and Corellia paltry—had been placed on my finger a few days before father left, and although he came now every day to prove how much he valued his connection with our house his main concern was not with me at all, but with my mother. She was fifteen years his senior, passionless and spotless as a drift of mountain snow, a woman who couldn't even be imagined in terms of desire, but perhaps because he too was cold and fastidious and lived his life strictly in accordance with the rules, he was only really at ease with her. Corellia and Fannia embarrassed him, whereas I, just a younger version of my mother, hardly counted at all and their friendship—at first just a pin-prick in my side—soon grew into a devouring sense of outrage which I couldn't always contain.

"She'll manipulate him," Corellia murmured, "just like she manipulates your father. Poor lamb—every time you ask him for anything he'll have to come and check with her first. You'd better not move into that house on the Aventine, he'll wear himself out having to dash up here ten times a day."

And although I told her to mind her own messy affairs and leave mine alone, and that if anybody manipulated my husband I'd make sure it was me, I couldn't even convince myself.

"The best thing you can do," she said unwisely, "is to have lots of babies. That's the one thing she can't do for him and while she's busy choosing their doctors and teachers and taking them into the country to get away from your father, you can slip out of the back door and start enjoying yourself. Just so long as the eldest son has a long pale face and a stiff neck like Piso no one is going to look too closely at the rest. Don't despair." But anger—in my case always swift to kindle—deserted me and instead of slapping her face as I'd intended, I turned and left her, worrying her, because she never really meant to be cruel.

Marriage was still my only escape yet Piso—who didn't mean to be cruel either—was thrusting me deeper into my trap. Closing my eyes I looked down the future and saw myself exchanging boredom and frustration for adultery, mistaking it for love, and I saw my mother's cool eyes searching me out, her pale mouth telling me I was worthless, ridiculous, that I had disgraced them all, and I knew I couldn't stand it. Our engagement—entered into with imperial approval—was beyond my power to break, but I was my mother's daughter and no one would set me aside. If Piso wanted an arrogant, commanding woman to lean on I'd make sure he leaned on me. I'd do battle with my mother and convince her, somehow, that she'd have to make do with my father. And feeling rather better—forgetting the bad news from Germany and the growing unrest among the troops in Rome—I went and forgave Corellia, for no matter how grim my future seemed, hers was likely to be far worse.

Her dream of Otho had sustained her through the month of December but now, with Clarus and father out of the way and mother engrossed in her immaculate flirtation with Piso, dreams were no longer quite enough. Her beauty, which had frightened marriageable men away when she'd been poor and hampered by Fannia's soiled reputation, was now bringing her the admiration, the fun, she'd always craved and, like a great, golden butterfly, she took to the winter air as if it held all the warmth and fragrance of May. At first she wanted no one in particular, just men falling at her feet, promising love when she knew quite well all they wanted was sex, men who trembled when she allowed them to touch her hand, her shoulder, the tip of her breast, who made themselves ridiculous with their pleading or, occasionally, their abuse. Men making fools of themselves, sending her messages and presents, running risks because most of them had wives too, men to whom she made promises and kept waiting in secluded corners of the park in the rain, men who could be easily handled, who aroused her lazy cruelty, and a few who intrigued her because she knew they were dangerous and capable of forcing her when all tenderness failed.

"I never felt beautiful before," she told me. "I always knew it, but I never really felt it until now. Not even with Clarus because, well, he's so besotted with me that I never really trusted his judgment."

But quite soon the edges of flirtation became blurred and she no longer knew herself what was allowed and what forbidden. She gave her wide, luscious mouth to one man, her breasts to another, let herself be half-undressed, half-possessed, confusing and frustrating herself until she was as miserable as she'd been before. And then, one night, in the winter-garden of a house across the Tiber—a heated room full of exotic plants and caged birds where we'd gone to drink rare Greek wines and eat oriental confectionery—she met a member of Otho's suite, a young man called Marcus Camerinus, and all her confusion vanished in a blinding flash of certainty and acknowledged desire.

Neither my mother nor Piso would have permitted me to attend that wine-tasting had they really understood it, but Piso accepted my mother's ruling on all things and, since the fabulous winter-garden, that indoor forest of spiky foliage and savage blossom, belonged to her cousin—the mother of that young, homosexual Metellus I'd almost married—she had seen nothing against it.

"Give my cousin Aurelia my regards," she'd told me, but the lady Aurelia was unrelated to my mother in spirit, for she was fond of young people, liked to see them enjoying themselves in their own way, and, far worse than that, her sympathies—which had once belonged to Nero—had now been transferred entirely to the man who had been Nero's friend and the lover of Nero's wife—Otho. Galba was an evil she was prepared to tolerate for a while. "Let the poor old miser live out his span, it can't be long," and it was no secret that she was looking forward to a future made up not of Piso's sensible cautious policies and his good intentions, but of gaiety and good-taste, of Otho and his own incomparable brand of *savoir-vivre*.

"There's far more to him than one imagines," I heard her murmur to someone behind me. "One sees the charm and the beauty and most people are too dazzled to look beyond it. But he was an excellent governor of Lusitania—ask anyone who served under him—and the Praetorians adore him. And is it any wonder—?" And as her voice faded to a whisper, followed by a little, artificial tittering and some honest laughter, I knew she was comparing him to Piso and asking her listeners to tell her what chance Piso could possibly have against a man like that?

Otho was not there himself but Aurelia's garden-rooms were full of his supporters, young men who had done their military service in Lusitania, or held junior magistracies there, and who, having been at ease with Nero, now looked to Otho to restore the kind of world they knew. None of them had anything to hope for from Galba and, as I watched them lounging among those exotic plants, sipping the unusual vintages Metellus had brought back from his travels abroad, occupying themselves solely, it seemed, with the arts of conversation and gracious living, I knew that Piso—for whom life was duty and detail and hard labour—could never come among them as anything but an intruder.

They were elegant and beautiful—these Othonians—in a way that had less to do with height and colouring than with meticulous grooming, the way they had curled and burnished and perfumed themselves and draped their fine, lawn garments with a flair my father and brother—and Piso—could never imitate. And watching them closely, as they chatted and smiled, full of abrasive wit and studied grace, it was easy to forget that many of them—like Otho himself—spent every penny they possessed, or could borrow, on personal display and would go home tonight, in all their splendour, to some attic flat in the Subura or to a family mansion where everything but the walls themselves had long since gone under the auctioneer's hammer.

I had been brought up to despise such men, to know that my fortune must not fall into their hands, but Corellia, who had no fortune, had no barriers either and when Marcus Camerinus smiled at her across the room with admiration and enquiry—'You're beautiful. Are you available?'—her answering smile brought him immediately to her side.

He was tall with an easy, athletic build and a mouth that always had a smile hovering at its corners. He had Otho's mop of artistically untidy black curls, something of Otho's dash and swagger, and he was so obviously the kind of man about whom I'd been warned, irresponsible, insubstantial, a man for whom life is a game but whose pleasures require a woman like me to pay the bills, that I stiffened and felt my eyes turn cold. Aurelia, who certainly knew better and so perhaps hadn't quite forgiven me for rejecting her son, brought him over to meet me on some pretext or other but, although he was too well-trained to neglect me, paying automatic court to the pearls around my neck and the whispers he'd heard about the size of my dowry, his eyes slid over me and fastened themselves on Corellia.

He had a gold wine-cup in his hand studded with amethysts, gold bracelets around his lean, brown wrists and a fortune in oriental fragrance moving in the air all around him, but I knew he owned nothing but his wits and the chance of birth that had made him a nobleman. There would be a heavily mortgaged estate somewhere in Italy, or an estate long since disposed of to pay the debts of a feckless father, a feckless elder brother, so that he—the beauty of the family—had had to make his own way in the world, attaching himself to men like Otho who might one day, as emperor, have lucrative appointments and rich marriages to bestow. And if Otho failed—and, as my father's daughter, I was in duty bound to hope he did—then there'd be a wealthy woman somewhere, some richer version of my aunt Fannia, who would buy his permanently smiling mouth and his glossy curls.

"I was in Lusitania for six months as a military tribune," he started to tell me, but as soon as Aurelia moved away he turned to Corellia and although they didn't speak, didn't touch, what passed between them was so intense that I couldn't stand it and, deserting my post, leaving my brother's wife to her fate, I moved away. There was nothing I could do about it here—nothing they could really do about it here either—yet their hot signals seemed to strip me naked too and I wondered, "Could I ever feel like that? Do I want to feel like that? Or is it better to feel nothing like my mother, so that at least one can't be hurt?"

My host—my former fiancé, Metellus—came and spoke a few easy words to me, making sure I had what I required, and then passed on, leaving me with a group of quiet women who knew my mother and could be relied upon to entertain me. I drank a wine that was light and subtle, tasted caviare from the Black Sea and cakes full of mysterious eastern flavours I couldn't identify, and brooded, with a dismay I refused to call comic, on the sorry fact that Metellus did not regret me in the least. He had married yet another cousin of ours, a girl with a smaller dowry but a much easier disposition than mine, and watching her as she laughed and flirted with Otho's young men, knowing how unfettered she was by Metellus who was always a delightful friend if only occasionally a lover, I wondered—bleakly—if I had been wrong. He would have treated me with the same exquisite consideration, would have given me the same freedom he required himself, so that I could have discovered, at my leisure, what sort of woman I really was. And yet I had pleaded with my father quite frenziedly, unable to explain the strength of my feelings—unable to admit I wouldn't marry a man who could never love me because I wasn't even sure love existed, or that I wanted it if it did—but hanging on with grim determination until at last he'd gone to my mother and told her he wouldn't force me. She had sent for me then, coldly furious, and I heard her voice coming now through the damp heat of Metellus' garden, and the steamy odours of his plants. "Your preoccupation with the physical aspect of marriage amazes me," she'd said scathingly. "You must be well aware that the vast majority of husbands have sexual involvements with which a wife need be in no way concerned. A civilised man can be relied upon to ensure that his wife never suffers the least embarrassment—and in return a sensible woman, a woman of taste, chooses to ignore such matters altogether."

But I was hard and stubborn too and in the end, for reasons I still couldn't name, I'd exchanged Metellus, who was gay and warm and easy, for Piso who was stiff and cold and could never love me either. Metellus' passion was still given to willowy young men like himself but would that have been harder to bear than Piso, who wanted only to do the right thing and needed my mother to tell him what it was? How could I live with him? How could I bear to see myself growing daily into a more pefect copy of my mother? How could I lose myself like that? And yet, who else could I ever be? I had my mother's pale oval face, her sardonic eyebrows, the same cutting edge to my voice. Yet in me these things had always been a defence. I'd armed myself with my mother's weapons first of all to fight her and then, seeing their usefulness, to subdue all those girls who were jealous of my money, and men like Camerinus who made me feel ill at ease, so that when they laughed at me it was only behind my back, never to my face. Had my mother's manners hardened around me, crushing out of existence that fragment of myself I know to be different? And did I really want that fragment to survive? Did I want to take the risk of being different, of emerging from my mother's world to one where I didn't know the rules and where I'd have to fight for my place? Wasn't it easier to be the lady Sulpicia's daughter, the great heiress, Piso's aloof, stainless wife, than to step out alone and be Antonia, a girl who could make mistakes and who could get hurt? I had alway known my life didn't belong to me. I had been born to take my mother's place when she vacated it, to be the guardian of part of my father's wealth, taking it with me as a dowry when my family chose to ally itself to another but bringing it back with me if that alliance was dissolved. The men I served were not lovers and husbands but my own kin, my father and brother, and I had no right to complain about the personality of any husband who suited their purposes. I knew it—understood it—accepted it—yet that night, in Metellus' over-heated rooms, I had to remind myself that it was necessary.

Corellia sighed all the way home that night, and she staggered through the next few days like a sleepwalker, coming alive only in the afternoons when she went off alone in her litter and returned, sometimes barely in time for dinner, with a glaze over her eyes that nothing could penetrate. She had no appetite, no peace. Her hands burned, her head ached, she had no concentration, nothing in her mind but her grim determination to get out of the house somehow, anyhow, whenever she could, to see Camerinus.

My brother Clarus had touched neither her emotions nor her sensuality. She'd found his devotion irritating and his love-making offensive, and had borne both with an ill-grace, but Camerinus had broken down all her defences, releasing sensations she hadn't believed in, so that this discovery of herself as a sensual woman knocked her off balance, destroying what little caution she possessed and convincing her that no other man in the world could do these things to her. Passion chained her to him, made her submissive and silly and ready to do anything he asked, and so obsessed was she in those early days, so utterly a prisoner, that I was afraid to interfere.

I was Clarus' sister and I should have stopped it. I should have gone to my mother, or to Piso, and had them take action on Clarus' behalf. But I didn't. I wondered, instead, what Clarus would want me to do and, if he came home at all, what he would hope to find. Would a letter from my mother, informing him of his wife's infidelity, really help him on his way or make it easier for him to face up to danger and discomfort? Would it help him to die a braver death? She was only doing what everyone, including Clarus himself, had expected of her, and if he still wanted her when he came home, so long as the matter was not made public he could pretend to her and to us, if not to himself,that he didn't know about it. But if my mother once took a hand and exposed Corellia to the world as an adulteress he'd no longer have that choice and so, rightly or wrongly, I kept it to myself.

Their passion would end, would be forgotten soon enough by Camerinus at any rate, who had his way to make in the world, and I tried to forget it too, to tell myself that if this shameful exhibition was love then I was glad to be without it. But one night as I stood briefly alone with Piso in the hall, waiting while they brought torches to light him home, I swayed much closer to him than I'd intended and, held by some demon of curiosity, didn't move away. For a moment he was puzzled but, like all who have been poor enough to need patronage, he was quick to see what was required of him and, putting a firm hand under my chin, he tilted my face and kissed me on the lips, performing this function as correctly as he did everything else. His body never touched mine, just our mouths locked politely together, his hand without a tremor on my neck, and although he even lingered over it, giving me full measure, it was a duty to him and an embarrassment to me. I'd never met desire but I recognised its absence.

4

GALBA HAD PLEDGED himself to recover the 2,200 million sesterces Nero had given away and the matter filled his whole mind. "The Praetorians," people murmured to him hesitantly, for his old man's temper was unreliable. "The despatches from Germany. Is there news yet from Vespasian?" But his prim little mouth remained tight shut, his watery blue eyes seeing nothing beyond those tantalising columns of figures, and throughout that long winter, when even the festival of the Saturnalia took on something of Galba's greyness, he sat in a corner of Nero's beautiful golden house, his toga huddled around him against the cold, totting up figures and underlining totals with all the satisfaction of a careful housewife.

The men of the city garrison had never liked him. They were Nero's troops, accustomed to his lavish hand-outs, and they'd taken it badly when Galba, having robbed them of Nero's bounty, refused to replace it with one of his own. He'd told them bluntly that the opportunity of serving their country was bounty enough and, since they were slack and lazy and there wasn't a fit man among them, they could think themselves lucky to be paid at all. He promised them nothing but tighter discipline and extra duties, a return to the old days of stern leadership and severe punishment. He'd lick them into shape, one way or another, make soldiers of them again, and when he boasted that he'd never found it necessary to buy loyalty, it may have sounded well in his ears, and ours, but I imagine the troops thought him a fool.

Otho would pay them, there was no doubt of it—in fact it was rumoured he was paying them already and facing bankruptcy as a result—and the news of Galba's meanness—and Otho's promises—spread outwards from the Praetorians to all the other soldiers in Rome, the men Galba had brought with him and the men Nero had collected here in readiness for his Eastern campaigns, and, in their turn, they spread it farther still until the word was carried to Africa and Asia and Germany and the wilds of Britain. "He's a mean old bastard, lads. He's not the man for us."

Dangerous talk, especially since those legions in the Eastern and Northern provinces knew nothing of Galba and, unless induced—bribed—to do otherwise, would prefer to follow their own commanders, Vitellius in Germany, Mucianus in Syria, Vespasian in Judaea and Otho here in Rome who, without even the title of commander had the Praetorians eating, quite literally and very expensively, out of his hand.

A difficult situation, but the answer was not far to seek. If Galba—who must eventually adopt somebody—could be persuaded to adopt Otho then at least the city garrison would be satisfied, and Vespasian and Mucianus and the others would think again before taking on the mighty prestige of a united Rome. But the succession seemed to interest Galba not at all, and although Vinius was constantly drawing his attention to Otho, and Laco brought Piso to see him every day, nothing could distract his stubborn mind from those squandered millions, Nero's gold which he was determined to track down, no matter how long it took, no matter how much it cost.

The money, of course, had gone to entertainers, loose women, informers, dissolute young aristocrats, sword-fighters, poets and musicians, a butterfly collection of glamorous people who had drifted with Nero on his summer breeze and were ill-equipped now to survive the cold of this long, Galban December.

"Find them," Galba said. "Drag them before me." But most of them had no money left and, as it was decreed that their property must be confiscated and sold for the benefit of the imperial treasury, the city was turned into a vast market-place where houses, slaves, horses, jewellery, toilet articles, pots and pans, anything that would fetch a few sesterces, came under the auctioneers' hammer. Families were turned out into the street to watch while their houses were stripped bare and the doors barred against them, while others scattered as at the approach of a foreign invader, clutching bundles of whatever they could salvage and running for their lives. Within days there were no rooms to rent anywhere in the city, while existing rents doubled and trebled, leading to fresh evictions so that people were driven to camp out in the parks and under the colonnades of public buildings, shivering, and in some cases, dying through the rain-soaked winter nights.

There were a few suicides, men and women who, rather than face ruin, stabbed themselves on their own thresholds or slashed their wrists in the Neronian manner, but the imperial freedmen continued to seal doors and cart goods and chattels away, leaving so many houses for sale that half of them could not be sold at all and the rest were given away at a fraction of their real value. There were some men, undoubtedly, who got rich, snapping up these empty houses for a song and holding them until the wind changed, but my mother condemned such speculation and, in her alarm at seeing thousands of sesterces a day wiped off our own properties—from our tenements in the Subura to our ancient house on the Esquiline—she almost questiond her uncle's wisdom and was indisposed for a day or two when Piso called.

But for my Aunt Fannia the situation was immediate and grave, for Galba's net, thrown very wide, had caught her too. She had been a star of Nero's court, one of the few to survive his friendship, and he had given her many presents over the years, casual gifts of emeralds and horses and little love-nests at the sea, and serious gifts of cash in payment for services she wasn't prepared to name. But money danced over her hands like flecks of sunlight and she had nothing to show for the fortune she had frittered away. Fannia—timeless and joyful as the May blossom—had made no investments, acquired no solid assets. She had bought jewellery and given it away to a casual lover, lent money to friends who lost it and borrowed more, spent staggering amounts on perfume and wine and parties which had faded in her memory like a drift of smoke.

Where had it all gone? "On living," she said vaguely when an imperial freedman came to ask her what she'd done with it all. "Just on living." But, although she opened her lovely eyes wide and gave him her slow, lingering smile, not a muscle moved in his face and he flatly, insultingly, refused to believe she had nothing left to sell.

"Nothing but myself," she told him, still amused because he was only a freedman—a clerk—and she wasn't prepared to take him seriously, "And perhaps you can tell me how much I'm worth?"

But the glance he gave her in reply told her she had no value at all in his eyes, and faced with this open rudeness from an inferior, she hesitated and finally understood her peril.

"If that is a joke, madam," he told her stiffly, "may I remind you that I am here on serious business? I will call again in three days' time and I suggest you make a list of everything you possess—the rings on your fingers, the silk on your back, the linen from your bed—neglect nothing, however small, however personal. And we will consider it together. A figure of 400,000 sesterces has been set beside your name—an equestrian fortune, I admit, but what is that to you, madam? Come now, you have swallowed far more than that many times over. The emperor is showing not only restraint in your case but magnanimity. You should thank him. But I really must advise you to do everything in your power to see that the full total is realised. Ten per cent will be returned to you on completion of the sale—ten per cent, madam, if I may remind you, of 400,000 sesterces. In three days then. Good morning."

In her first panic Fannia turned to my mother, playing on her position as Clarus' mother-in-law and mentioning the possibility of a scandal, but my mother, who was too sure of herself to care about that, hid firmly behind father's absence, declaring that, much as she'd like to, she couldn't dispose of 400,000 sesterces without his consent.

"If I could only ask him?" she murmured. "But where can I find him?". And Fannia, who was no fool, went down into the city to see if credit was still to be had, and just what she'd have to do for it.

"You shall have my pearls," she told me. "They're the only decent things I have left and I'll dissolve them in old Falernian and drink them down like Cleopatra before I'll see them put up for auction. They're my wedding gift to you. I forget who gave them to me but I must have cared about him at the time, otherwise I wouldn't be so attached to them—anyway, they're yours and you'd better take them now and wear them before that pompous oaf comes back and starts stripping the lacquer from my toe-nails. Yes—take them—I know they should go to Corellia but her position's not much better than mine—the way things are working out for her she'd probably end up selling them—or giving them away. And I wouldn't like that."

I went to my mother and let her see how angry I was but my voice, cutting through the muted fragrance and the cool twilight tints of her chamber, sounded rude.

"Why don't you give her the 400,000 sesterces? She's desperate and you can afford it."

Her lips parted in the small, delicate smile of power I knew so well. "Your father—" she said, barely glancing at me, as if no other explanation was required, but, although my palms were sweating and my mouth dry—with rage and with fear too—I was determined to stand my ground.

"Nonsense. Father would give you that amount ten times over and not even ask you why you wanted it."

She nodded, still smiling. "Indeed he would."

"Well then—?"

She made a gesture which said 'Run along, child, don't worry me with your foolishness', and, my feet suddenly turning awkward and my body feeling heavy beside her airy presence, I made the kind of clumsy, emotional appeal she could always demolish, and blurted out, "I thought you were fond of her?"

One eyebrow raised itself in a pointed arch of surprise. "Fond of her—? My dear girl, my feelings for Fannia have no relevance at all to the matter in hand. She came to me not for affection but for 400,000 sesterces—not even a business proposition since she admitted freely that she saw no possibility of ever paying them back. I may be fond of a great many people but even your father's assets would suffer if I took it into my head to give each of them 400,000 sesterces whenever they asked for it. It's an equestrian fortune, Antonia. Are you aware of what that represents? It's the capital on which many worthy men of the middle classes bring up families. With 400,000 sesterces and the right connections a man can build himself a very decent career, yet Fannia would spend that amount on moondust and be absolutely amazed when it was all gone. You must know that it's quite out of the question. We are the guardians of our wealth—just as others guarded it for us—and we have a great responsibility towards the people we employ and those who depend on us. Fannia is not one of our people and I can't help her. I told her so, and she understands."

"Do you realise what will happen to her if she doesn't pay?"

"Oh yes," my mother's smile was bright and her eyes as hard as stone, "I know exactly what will happen to her. She'll survive. She always does."

"You can't be sure."

"Oh, but I can. Perhaps you don't know her quite so well as I do. Fannia has lived all her life from one crisis to the next. She enjoys it. Calm waters bore her. She needs a storm, and she's not really quite so worried about herself as she pretends. She'll find someone—you, very likely, if you held your own purse strings—to take pity on her. She always has. It's her one talent. She broke her parents' hearts, neglected them and made them ashamed, but she smiled at them as they lay dying and they left her all their money. She drove her husbands to despair with her criminal behaviour, but all five of them paid her debts when they parted, and she'll go to see them now, one after the other, with her begging bowl. She's done it before, and she can repay them with a coin they evidently still enjoy. Adulteress, bankrupt, unfit mother, parasite—yes, we're all fond of Fannia. Nero was fond of her. I believe he wrote a poem for her once, praising her inventiveness in what he called the art of love. And Otho knows her too, and Vitellius, the new governor of Germany, has sampled her delights, so she has excellent connections. She'll survive. Many women would have died long ago, simply of shame, but Fannia won't do that. You should take care, Antonia, not to associate yourself too closely with her. Your great-uncle, the emperor, is certainly not one of her admirers and if he adopts Piso he will not accept you as a daughter-in-law unless your reputation remains completely stainless. Fannia casts a shadow and if you fall under it you could lose a great deal. How galling, if Piso becomes emperor and marries someone else. Think of your own position. I really don't know who else there is for you to marry."

Her light voice, her air of mild amusement, mild exasperation, stripped the years away from me, filling me again with my childhood rages which led me so easily to play into her hands, to be ill-mannered and disobedient, to earn, in fact, the punishment she was preparing. But this time I clenched my hands behind my back and said, as coldly as I could, "If you won't help her for her own sake then think of Clarus. Surely her disgrace would reflect on him? Corellia is, after all, his wife."

And with the words still hovering between us I knew I had fallen into a trap.

"Yes," she said quietly, "Corellia is his wife. But for how long? I have been thinking about that a great deal lately, and perhaps I should say a word to you on the subject. In the interests of domestic harmony it is necessary for you to be fond of your brother's wife—whoever she may be. Think of her not as Corellia, or Aemilia, or Julia, or anyone else, but simply as a sister-in-law to whom courtesy is due. Your brother married in haste and his present union will hardly last—in fact, we never intended that it should. His second choice will be wiser—more conventional—and out of loyalty to him, when he dismisses Corellia you must do the same."

"Why?" But I wasn't asking how she expected me to forget a girl I'd known all my life. I was asking why she'd allowed the marriage to take place at all, and then, suddenly, I didn't want to know the answer, didn't want to hear her tell me how she'd used Corellia, cold-bloodedly, not seeing her as a real person at all but because in some obscure way it suited her plans for Clarus. I didn't want—absolutely couldn't bear—to hear that once again she'd been right.

Her fine, pointed eyebrow rose again, telling me how inadequate I was, how naive. "Surely," she said, "you must know how unhappy your brother has been with Corellia—and that it could never be otherwise? Naturally, we pointed this out to him and just as naturally he didn't believe us. But he believes us now and no doubt he'll listen to us the next time. Don't misunderstand me, Antonia. This situation could never arise in your case. We could allow Clarus to commit this folly knowing that, as a man, he could come out of it with his reputation unscathed. Far better, we thought, to let him marry Corellia and then divorce her—for we knew she'd give him ample cause for divorce—than to have him pining away for her, or, worse still, to have him seduce her and be obliged to put up with all kinds of unpleasantness and impertinence. Marriage was the right answer, I'm convinced of it. A man can survive these things and learn from them, but a girl is invariably ruined and if you ever formed an unsuitable attachment them obviously we'd put a stop to it at once. But Clarus will emerge from this a wiser man, I'm sure. Now then, dear, you must have noticed all those people waiting to see me when you came in. They won't go away, you know."

She lifted her thin hand very slightly, a gentle command we had all been trained to obey, and as her maids sprang forward, one to hand her a list of some kind, another to show me out as carefully as if I'd been a stranger who couldn't possibly know the way, I followed without protest, because I was a stranger and there were times when I rejected her with all my heart. Would I ever sit like this, a goddess in my holy place, playing cold games with other people's lives? And yet, in her eyes, her motives were sound. What she did was for Clarus' good, my good, and all that was wrong about it was that I didn't believe she cared about us at all. Corellia was not a good wife to my brother. In her better moments she tormented and scorned him, and now she had betrayed him altogether. But my mother didn't really care about his pain and his disillusion. She welcomed them because they were the tools she needed to persuade him into divorce and remarriage, not necessarily to someone who could love him, but to a girl who could bring money and prestige into the family. And, since we needed neither, I wondered why? What did it really matter, unless, having no emotions of her own she resented ours, seeing them as a threat to the good order she prized above everything else. Her own marriage was seen, by outsiders, as an immense success. She was a spotless patrician lady, untouched by scandal, adored by her husband, devoted to her children, and did she feel threatened on her high, lonely perch because we wanted something else, because I enjoyed Fannia's warm humour and my brother loved her giddy daughter? Did she resent us because, like father, we were imperfect flesh and blood? And would I have to go on watching my father trying to please her, resentful in my turn because, in one small corner of my mind, I wanted to please her too?

I had failed in my mission, but the thought of Fannia scurrying about the city in that chill January wind haunted me and, dressed in white with a cameo at my shoulder, looking as much like my mother as possible, I went up to the palace to find Piso. Basically he was a decent, well-meaning man and if I got to him first perhaps I could persuade him to do something for Fannia. He had no money but he could talk to Laco, who could talk to Galba, and, having studied the methods my mother used to intimidate my father, it seemed the right moment to try my hand. But when I arrived something had happened, or was about to happen, that would reduce Fannia's 400,000 sesterces to a mere drop in the ocean of our troubles.

There was outward calm. Laco and Vinius were at their places, one on either side of Galba, whispering to him, glaring at each other, while Piso stood, stiff and tense, at Laco's side and Otho lounged, perfectly at ease, just within earshot. His black eyes rested quizzically from time to time on Vinius, reading the signs and making light of them, a gambler who can lose just as gracefully as he can win, but underneath his charm he was as nervous as Piso, and far more watchful. Something was in the air, something was coming, and the only one who seemed unaware of it was Galba himself—that careful old man huddled in his corner doing his sums, gloating over every sesterce that took him nearer his goal.

"There has been news from Germany," Piso said quietly. "Grave news." And it seemed, as I moved through those unheated, unloved rooms, picking up a whisper here, a grumble there, that everyone but Galba knew not only what it was but exactly what should be done to put it right.

The German Legions, restless and sullen since the murder of their governor—for which Galba had been blamed—were quite simply demanding a change of emperor. No one was surprised. It was what they had been predicting all along. Galba should have swallowed his pride and paid them to keep quiet, should have sent gold instead of an old reprobate like Vitellius as their new governor, a man who'd got out of Rome just one step ahead of his creditors and couldn't be trusted, now, to handle a situation like this. Everyone had known all along that this was bound to happen but, even so, panic was not far away, for if Germany defected then Britain and Belgica and Gaul would probably do the same, and could Galba defend us against these crack troops, and that dreadful horde of native auxiliaries? Did we even wish to be defended against men of our own nation, Romans against Romans? Civil war had happened before, but not in our time. Nero, his friends insisted, had committed suicide in order to prevent it, and could we now—any of us—allow it to happen? Mouths smiled and voices remained well-modulated, polite, saying the right things, but an unspoken plea came out of all our hearts. 'Do something. Don't let it start.' And eyes turned to Galba, willing him to look up from his account books, to take notice, because who else was there to turn to?

No names had been mentioned, the legions declaring themselves willing to accept any emperor the senate named, so long as it wasn't Galba, but we all knew that there had to be someone out there who meant the choice to fall on him, and we all wondered who it could be. Left to themselves the soldiers would have grumbled and run wild a little, there would have been insubordination, some violence, a few desertions, but someone was holding them together and making them dangerous, someone was out in front, offering them leadership and loot, and willing to take the blame if things went wrong. Vitellius' name was the first to spring to mind—the new governor, a man of senatorial rank every bit as noble as Galba—but he'd only been in the province since December, hardly time to win anyone to his side, and he wasn't thought to be that kind of man. Galba had chosen him in the first place because he'd judged him too mediocre to be dangerous, and Vitellius—heavily in debt and in all sorts of other trouble besides—had been grateful for the appointment. He'd thanked Galba with tears in his eyes and, since his abilities were really not outstanding, it seemed unlikely that he'd risk losing what he already had for a wild dream of empire. Vitellius, people murmured, would be content with the more obvious pleasures of life, good food and wine, obliging women, soft mattresses and no creditors pounding at his door—and, in any case, he lacked the energy, the fire, he wasn't bright enough. But still, who else could it be? No one else in the province had sufficient rank to be acceptable to the soldiers and no one was missing, every senator who should be in Rome was here, present and accounted for. No one had slipped out of town to join the German armies. Who else could it be? And if it was Vitellius, then who was behind him? He was no general. He'd need men to lead his armies, men to prop him up as Laco and Vinius propped Galba, and who could these men be? Legionary commanders, commoners, adventurers, anybody. And, if it was Vitellius, and there were such men working through him, could he control them?

Hushed groups of senators gathered in Nero's long, golden corridors or paced restlessly on his marble pavements, treading delicate blendings of shape and colour underfoot without looking down at them, trying not to whisper, not to worry, trying desperately not to regret an allegiance to Galba which could now prove fatal, trying to resist the temptation, not exactly to desert him, but to disassociate oneself slightly and wait to see which way the wind blew. At seventy-three Galba might have been willing to die for his principles but few people were willing to die for him. They'd accepted him largely because he'd been the first man on the scene, after Nero, ready to pick up the pieces, but he'd have to do something now, do something quickly, save us or sacrifice himself as a king should—he'd have to stop adding up those damnable figures and realise that bribery, not integrity, was the order of the day. He'd have to pay Vitellius, and everybody else, to keep quiet and then he'd have to buy himself an army—pay the troops their miserable bounty, so we could all rest easy at last.

Suddenly he looked up, his pale, peevish eyes going from face to face. He looked at Piso, and Otho and all his lovely, lounging young men—Camerinus among them—who seemed to think the impending crisis no more than a vehicle for their sparkling wit. He looked down at the rippling mosaics, working out their value and regretting, perhaps, that he couldn't tear them up and auction them off with everything else. He looked at the painted walls and the ivory ceiling, the carved, hanging lamps and the silver filigree baskets intended for flowers, not bills of sale and notices of eviction. He looked down at his figures, smiling, and then, getting to his feet, he nodded briskly, bidding us wait for the proclamation that was bound to be made.

He withdrew, taking Laco and Vinius with him, leaving his precious balance sheets unguarded, and Piso came at last to my side, as taut as a bow-string.

"He will name his heir today," he said, and I nodded, for what else could he do? The German Legions had demanded a new emperor, but perhaps they'd be satisfied with an emperor-to-be. And if, in the end, Galba was forced to step down, at least his successor would be a man of his own choosing, someone who owed everything to him and would be in honour bound to keep him safe. Otho, I thought. It had to be Otho, and everyone else thought so too. He was popular with the troops, popular with the people, he had the growing support of the senatorial and equestrian classes, he had flair and originality and enough administrative experience to make him useful as well as decorative. Admittedly, his debts were known to be staggering and he was still tainted by the dissolute atmosphere of Nero's court but he was the man the Praetorians wanted and although the German Legions didn't know him they'd heard his name and they'd soon find out he wasn't mean like Galba, that he'd pay them their bounty out of his own pocket if necessary and wouldn't ask them to do a great deal to earn it. He was the perfect front for Galba's cautious policies, someone to cheer in a parade, a brilliant cloak to cover Galba's shabbiness. He was the obvious, inevitable choice and, as Galba came back into the room, leaning heavily against Vinius, with Laco walking several paces behind, something like a sigh swept over the crowd, for this surely meant that Laco had been defeated and Vinius—and Otho—had prevailed.

They came slowly down the room, an old man's progress, Galba's eyes brimming with malicious glee and then, his hand still resting treacherously on Vinius' arm, he announced in his parade-ground bark that due to the worsening situation in Germany, due to this and that and the other, due to so many things that we knew he was spinning it out on purpose to torment us, he had decided to adopt Piso Licinianus, as his son and heir.

He began to give his reasons but I don't think anyone listened. Vinius, the imperial hand still on his arm, kept on smiling, adroitly concealing the venom that must have been devouring him, but I saw the colour drain from Otho's face and understood that he had gambled everything and lost. He had always lived precariously, balancing gaily on the edge of disaster, surviving—with grace—from one crisis to the next as Fannia did, but his debts now were so enormous that no private fortune could hope to settle them. Only an emperor could live in the style he'd set himself, but the choice had fallen elsewhere and now he'd either have to get out of the city before his creditors caught up with him, or do the dignified thing and put a dagger between his ribs. He stood, just for a moment, ashen-faced, ruined beyond all hope of recovery, and then, with a shrug and a smile, he tossed the despair out of his eyes and came striding across the room to Piso, warm with congratulations, bringing with him his friends, his hangers-on, his creditors, and the whole treacherous multitude.

A moment ago Piso had been a pompous nobody, dull as dish-water, but now—although everyone really believed Galba had chosen the wrong man—he was everybody's darling, the one they'd been secretly backing all along. Vinius and Otho withdrew discreetly, leaving the field to the victors, but Laco—Piso's puppet-master and probably mine too—was everywhere, back-slapping and hugging, roaring his triumph with the deep-chested noise of a rutting deer. And through it all Piso moved not a muscle. The news—dreaded, desired—had turned him to stone. They were paying homage to a statue, for the man was not really there at all, and I couldn't help wondering where he had taken refuge.

A public proclamation had to be made and instead of going first to the Senate House Galba decreed that since the soldiers were causing all the trouble he would take Piso to the Praetorian barracks and let them be the first to hear the news. There was to be no bounty. The soldiers were men, he declared, real men, and he wouldn't insult them by suggesting their loyalty was for sale to the highest bidder. Naturally it wasn't true—what they really wanted was discipline and the tough life they'd signed up for—but simply putting the idea into their heads was dangerous. The better element among them would resent it and the malcontents would use it to cause trouble.

"Soldiers need to be told what to do," he informed us flatly. "That's why they join the army in the first place. If I gave them the money they'd only squander it on cheap wine and cheap women and ruin their health—and then blame me for it, I shouldn't wonder. I've had dealings with soldiers for more than fifty years and the one thing I've learned is never to ask them to make a decision. Tell them what to do—once, out loud—and if they don't do it, let them feel the consequences. Nero turned the army into a greedy animal he could never fill, and the only cure for that is starvation. They'll thank me for it in the end."

And so, in his plain, purple-bordered toga, with nothing to distinguish him from any other elder statesman except his bald head and the fear he inspired in everyone around him, he stamped outside with his gift to the Praetorians—not the money they were expecting, nor the prince they were hoping for, but a new, young leader, someone who wouldn't pay them either because he valued his own integrity and was too scrupulous to question theirs.

"Yes, yes, to the barracks," everybody said, wanting to get it over with, and we rushed out of the palace in an excited huddle and then halted, unprepared for the driving rain and the lowering threat of the winter sky. Thunder rumbled in the distance and, as we hesitated, lightning tore apart the skirts of a cloud and the thunder moved nearer and became the drumbeat of an enemy crouching behind the hills.

"We cannot proceed," Vinius said, drawing his toga—of a much finer quality than Galba's—around his light frame. "A proclamation of such importance cannot be made in this inauspicious weather," and I saw his eyes meet Otho's significantly, conveying the need to play for time.

"Nonsense," Laco growled. "Let's get on with it."

But Vinius moved swiftly to Galba's side, smooth and persuasive, "No, no, we must take care. We are dealing with soldiers and is there a more superstitious breed of man? If we bring Piso to them in a storm someone will read the omens and tell them no good can come of it. Wait until the sky clears sir, I implore you. Let the storm blow itself out and take Piso to them in the calm that will follow. Appearances, sir—appearances—"

"Rubbish," Laco bellowed, knowing that if the proclamation was not made today it might never be made at all, for Vinius would do anything in his power to stop it and apart from the more obvious means—assassination, blackmail terror—Galba's mind, old and getting older, could so easily be changed. "I know more about soldiers than you do," he said, squaring up to the smaller man, his fists clenching and unclenching at his sides. "Soldiers don't give a damn about peace and good order. There's no money in peace. They want a good scrap and a good screw at the end of it. So take the lad to them now and let them see he's got the guts to read the omens to suit himself."

"Yes," Vinius said suddenly, almost to himself. "Yes, indeed. Let them see he doesn't believe in their gods—that he's above that sort of thing—yes, why not?"

But Galba cut them both short. This time he would make up his own mind and, having finally put away his sums, he was impatient of any delay. "Superstition be damned," he growled, "we will proceed at once. And anybody who makes a fuss about it—anybody who doesn't care to get wet—will be answerable to me."

And so they went, all of them, not wanting to go, not daring to stay, fearing the storm and the soldiers, yet fearing Galba too. And since his authority was immediate and he could punish them here and now, they followed him through the lashing rain, without even asking Piso what he thought about it all. They just took him with them and whatever superstitions or fears he had he kept to himself.

Otho appeared to follow the rest but as I went inside—the Praetorian barracks being no place for an unmarried girl—he appeared suddenly in the corridor, his face grey and grim again now that there was no one to see. Camerinus, Corellia's lover, was with him, just as beautiful in uniform as in his graceful evening clothes, and as they saw me they broke off their conversation and became—instantly—the easy, polished socialites I knew.

"My dear young lady—?" Otho said, the question in his voice telling me he couldn't quite remember my name, but Camerinus' mouth moved silently and Otho's answering smile dazzled all my disappointment away.

"Antonia," he said, as if the name suddenly enchanted him because it was mine, "What a great day for you. May I wish you every happiness? May I give you my congratulations?"

He smiled again, his warm, dark eyes touching my skin, quickening my pulse-beat and my heart-beat, so that beneath his gaze I was more alive, more myself, than I'd ever been before. And instead of making one of my mother's conventional replies I said, "Yes, you may congratulate me—if I may congratulate you on your courage and your dignity. I suppose I'm talking out of turn, but women are allowed to do that sometimes, aren't they? And it's sincerely meant."

Surprise took the easy charm from his face, briefly exposing the strain beneath it, revealing him as a man who could feel and fear like anyone else, and then, instead of the annoyance and the quick rebuff I'd feared, he moved so close to me that I could hear the breath moving inside his chest, feel the heat of his body, and I knew I would have to take care for I had never been so aware of a man in my life before.

"Thank you, Antonia," he said. "Thank you." And for an instant his hand rested on my cheek, a touch that almost asked a question. And if he had asked it—on that strange day, under that yellow, unquiet sky, with Camerinus looking on—who knows what my answer would have been. Certainly for him it would have been a piquant revenge—stealing a woman from the man who had stolen his future and using my money to keep his creditors at bay—and perhaps in the first bitterness of his defeat he even considered it, wondered if it could be done, but Camerinus was there, watching, his brown eyes full of the same wicked sparkle, thinking about my dowry too, and Otho turned to him with a short laugh.

"If you ever take a wife, my friend," he said, "then this is the kind of girl to choose—yes indeed—serene and calm and warm. A fatal combination, Camerinus my boy, believe me. You'll come to realise the value of a pearl when you've bruised your eyes once too often on those coloured stones you young men chase after so eagerly. Serenity, honesty, someone who won't send you packing and want her dowry back when she sees your first grey hair or when she knows damn well you haven't got the wherewithal to pay. If you can get your hands on a girl like this, Camerinus, you'll be a lucky man. And if her marriage was in my gift—well then, Antonia, what would you have me do, would you take a graceless young scamp like this and mould him, save him—you'd do it well, although he's not worth it."

He touched my cheek again and his teasing smile, which in any other man—in Camerinus—would have offended me, only drew me nearer to him, softening the sharp edges of me so that I no longer cared about Camerinus, nor about Piso who would be horrified to see me here, chatting indiscreetly with his enemies. When Otho smiled in that particular way all that mattered was Otho, and his magic was so intense that it was a relief—and a sorrow—when he moved on. For a moment I floated in a warm fantasy—Otho's kind of woman in Otho's world—but as he turned the corner, the dream faded and I knew that even if my father had chosen to ally himself differently and promised me to Otho in the first place, the engagement would have had to be broken now that his fortunes were at this low ebb.

I waited a long time for Piso and eventually he came, the heir to an empire, wet and bedraggled and desperately ill at ease, yet unable to confide in me because I was part of everything that Galba and Laco had done to him. I'd believed him to be truly ambitious but now I wondered if he was committing himself to this by no means certain undertaking simply to appease the ghosts of his murdered father and brothers. Perhaps he would really have preferred to stay quietly at home with the woman he'd married instead of being dragged about in the rain to impress the Praetorians who only wanted their bounty, and the Senate who would have accepted a monkey if Galba had sent them one. I felt sorry for him, but my sympathy—which had touched Otho—would not have been acceptable to Piso and so I gave him no more than a cool hand and a polite smile.

"You will wish to go home now," he told me and, overburdened as he was, he made arrangements for my escort and took me to my litter himself.

"You must take care," he said, but he didn't say why, didn't suggest he would be glad of a strong woman beside him. He said goodbye, faded away into a rain-lashed distance, and by the time I arrived at my door I had difficulty in remembering the exact lines of his face. Corellia met me in the hall, and perhaps until I saw the envy in her eyes I hadn't fully accepted the change in my own situation.

"Look at her," she shouted, as if she hated me. "Here she comes—a drowned rat—and she's going to be Empress of Rome."

5

A DAWN SACRIFICE at the Temple of Apollo. Galba shuffling his feet and feeling the cold, his attention wandering. Piso, very stern and straight-backed, concentrating totally on the matter in hand, determined to get it right. A dawn sacrifice heralding the fifteenth day of January, a day no different from any other.

I came to the palace every morning now, to smile at Galba who barely noticed me, to stand at Piso's side, moving, bowing, coming and going as Laco pulled the strings. His freedman attended me at first light, lecturing me all the way to the Palatine, telling me which men must be singled out, which topics must not be mentioned, which invitations I must accept and which refuse. But mainly I was required simply to be there, to show everyone that Piso—the imperial heir—had my father's wealth as well as my mother's prestige behind him, and that through them he had the means, if not the desire, to be generous.

The fifteenth day of January—cold, a bitter wind sneaking through the city, biting deep whenever it could—and I was late, delayed by a gigantic explosion of rage between Corellia and Fannia, a dreadful outburst which had required my mother's ice-cold interference to separate them and lay them prostrate on their beds. And when I arrived all that was left of the sacrifice was dismay, for the entrails of the sacrificial beast had promised nothing but disaster.

"The liver was quite misshapen," Piso told me gravely. "One of the lobes was missing altogether, and the rest of it was—grotesque. The gods are not with us in our present undertaking—offence must surely have been given—" And as he shivered—from cold? from dread?—I knew he was remembering how the earth had trembled slightly when Galba first entered Rome as its master, and that odd sound—bulls, people said, bellowing in anguish—when he first set foot in Nero's Golden House. And then there was Galba's own off-hand treatment of the immortals, the way he'd promised certain jewels to the Goddess Fortune as a thank-offering for his success, and then, when his success no longer seemed so miraculous, had decided they were too much for her and given them to Capitoline Venus instead.

"If immortal women are anything like the rest of us, she'll never forgive him," Corellia had said, laughing, and we'd amuse ourselves deciding what we'd do to him in Fortune's place, but to a superstitious man like Piso—who sacrificed reverently with his head covered at every turning point in his life—the enmity of a goddess was too terrible to contemplate.

"The omens will change," I murmured, not really daring to comfort him, "They always change," but he shook his head, telling me it made very little difference, for Galba, once again, as he'd done on the day of the storm, had decided to ignore all warnings. Someone had to go to Germany immediately to see what Vitellius was up to and to announce Piso's adoption to the soldiers, and if one awaited the good pleasure of storm-clouds and the organs of sacrificial beasts, one might not set off at all.

"The emperor states," Piso told me, trying hard to conceal his disapproval, "that omens, like figures, can be manipulated to mean whatever one wishes them to mean. He concedes they now indicate death and disaster but insists it could be Vitellius' disaster, not ours. The embassy is to go to Germany as planned."

He turned away from me stiffly, unwilling to say more because he considered it ill-bred to cause a lady even the slightest alarm, but I knew there was more to it than Vitellius. The Praetorians were still clamouring for their bounty, standing around in angry groups all day on Mars Field, drinking, grumbling, looking for trouble, waiting for someone to come along and set their frustrations alight. And what about Vespasian in Judaea, with an army of his own—seasoned troops in peak condition, equipped to take what they wanted if they could only make up their minds what it was? Nothing had been heard from my father. Did Vespasian know about the situation in Germany and the unrest here in Rome? And if he did, would it feed his own ambitions and show him the way to satisfy them? He had friends here in the city who would open the gates for him. And could one be sure of Otho, now that he had nothing more to lose? May he not already have pledged himself to Vitellius or Vespasian, promising Praetorian support in exchange for cancellation of his debts and the means to live once again like a gentleman?

It seemed likely—obvious—and if it was going to happen one had to prepare for it, survive it. Whispering groups formed again, as they had on the day of Piso's adoption, and as I moved among them, smiling and pretending not to feel the cold, I saw anxiety gathering on their faces as the dust was gathering all about them in those golden rooms where pleasure had retreated beyond the edge of memory. Galba, if nothing else, had set his seal on Nero's house and made it his own. The glorious marble pavements remained unswept, losing their colour beneath a layer of neglect, the silver was tarnished, and the unlit corridors hid their treasures in shadow, so that in this general fading, this loss of heat and light and care, the house itself seemed to mourn for Nero and to cower dangerously, like a resentful slave, before this new master, this mean, bald, scornful old man who had changed it from the architectural splendour of the age into a mere place of business.

I shivered, superstitious in my turn, for the house, if it could feel, would hate Galba for that, as a woman would hate him for the loss of her beauty—as the people he'd evicted from their homes hated him for his cruelty, and the soldiers for his meanness—and when my mind finally detached itself from this inanimate, ridiculous, menace, I had walked back to the room where Galba was sitting and Otho, even more elegant and luxurious in defeat than he'd been in success, was blocking my path.

"You're dreaming," he said, laughter in his smooth face. "And I won't even ask—although I'd dearly love to know—just who puts those stars in your eyes."

And once again, I was too enchanted to be dignified, to let him know, as my mother would have done, that if I dreamed at all it was only of doing my duty. And if I dreamed of a man then it could only be the one they had chosen for me. Instead I smiled, feeling again the warmth and lack of caution—the silliness—he inspired in me, wanting to be near him because he could laugh away the part of me that was stiff and cold—my mother's part—and help me to be different. I knew I couldn't keep him long. Laco would soon come rushing to separate us, or someone like that damned smirking Camerinus with his airs and graces would glide up with some whispered message and take him away, but—although I knew all about his debts and his adulteries, his criminal irresponsibility, that he was probably every bit as black as he was painted—his presence delighted me and I was grateful for it.

"The omens are unfavourable," he said. "Have you heard?"

I nodded. "Yes. They often are. Next time perhaps they'll choose a sounder beast."

His eyebrows flew upwards and he laughed—incredulous, pleased and just a little uneasy. "And what must I read into that, Antonia—dear Antonia? Are you merely sceptical, as I am, or could it be? —When you speak of choosing a sounder beast—?"

Suddenly his eyes were excited, such a young emotion in his sophisticated face, such a fierce thing, that it alarmed me. And then, just as suddenly, it was wiped away and he was suave and light-as-air, himself again.

"No, or course not," he said, answering his own half-asked questions. "But Antonia—the omens are really very bad. In Piso's place I'd feel very much inclinded to send you safely home. Shall I be very bold and suggest it to him? Would he be offended—or jealous?"

"Not jealous—certainly," I confided, amused and then saddened at the thought of it, and I saw Otho watching me very carefully, as if my reaction had more significance than I realised. And his eyes were excited again.

"Go home," he whispered and then, as other people surged around me, the naked, youthful emotion went out of his face and he was the man everyone expected to find, urbane, cynical, brushing the omens aside with a nonchalant hand. "My dear fellow—a man must think for himself—yes, indeed, reverence is due—but to be ruled entirely—" And as he chatted to this one and that, pleasantly and calmly as if he hadn't a care in the world, a freedman approached him from behind and whispered with the kind of false discretion that was intended to be heard, "The builders are awaiting your instructions, sir."

I saw Otho's jaw clench, his eyes close briefly, and then the slight grimace which could have been pain, was gone and he was saying to anyone who cared to listen, "Ah yes, of course. My memory! My dear fellow, what would I do without you to remind me—? I really must be off—and in this bitter weather too." He'd heard of a house, he told us, going cheap and he'd asked his builders to have a look at it and see what it was worth. He'd just learned that the fellow was already on the site and he'd simply have to dash off and hear the verdict for himself. He shrugged and shivered, managing to convey charmingly with those two gestures, that Galba was to blame not only for the flooding of the property market but for the bad weather as well, and although he went on talking about houses and what a bargain he hoped to be getting, he said it all in such a way that everyone understood it wasn't a builder he was hurrying to meet, but someone's wife. And he was barely out of the room before they started taking bets on who it could be. As he left he looked back just once, not at me but at Galba, his face naked again and, holding his expression in my mind, I felt sorrow, not surprise, when an hour later a man came running to say that a senator—he didn't know who—had been proclaimed emperor by a party of soldiers and was being carried shoulder-high to the Praetorian Barracks.

A party of soldiers, a handful, no more. Trouble-makers, fools, they couldn't get away with it. But they were heading for the barracks where more fools awaited them and if someone—Otho—jumped on a platform and began to promise them gold, they'd grab it without even asking where it came from. It had to be Otho. No one had expected him to take defeat lying down and everybody remembered now, when it was too late, how many times lately he'd been seen with Praetorian officers, and that for a ruined man he'd been laughing too loud, putting himself too much on display when he should really have been hiding his head in shame. And how else had he managed to stay in Rome and hold off his creditors unless the Praetorians had been behind him all the time, with drawn swords, making sure no one pressed him too hard? He'd done well to laugh, allowing us to worry about the threat of Vitellius when the danger was here, in our midst, and although most of the grim-faced senators and knights assembled in the palace that day, blamed Galba, feeling he'd created the danger himself by driving Otho too far, no one cared to say so out loud, for Otho was taking a desperate gamble and might not succeed. A handful of soldiers did not imply the entire garrison, and the senatorial party—who couldn't afford a second Nero—would do nothing to help him.

"He'll be dead by nightfall," someone said, "making a damn nuisance of himself to the very end," and, although he was my enemy—for if his coup succeeded he'd have to kill Galba and Piso, and certainly wouldn't make an empress of me himself—the thought of his head rolling in the gutter gave me pain.

It had to be Otho, and only Galba seemed unwilling to believe it. The danger had seemed to come from the North, from Vitellius who was still far away, and his stubborn, old man's brain hung on to the threat he'd grown used to and made light of this new menace. Otho indeed. He looked up, almost savagely, from his meticulous adding and subtracting and, from a safe distance, I saw his prim, tight mouth pronounce Otho's name with a sneer. Vitellius could be dangerous because he sweated and swore like a man, and could drive a racing chariot without caring about blistering his hands, Vespasian could be dangerous because he sweated too and marched with his men and had blood on his sword, but Otho was all perfume and curls and fine phrases, and Galba refused, petulantly, to take him seriously. "Let him play his games," he growled, " and when he's had enough let him come and try to talk his way out of the mess he's made. Yes—I shall enjoy that."

"Yes," Vinius said, his eyes unreadable, "I shall enjoy that too." And Laco, who was bursting to accuse Vinius of complicity in Otho's treason—for wasn't he Otho's friend, Otho's backer, hadn't he staked everything he had on Otho's future?—growled out an obscenity I hadn't heard since my childhood battles with my brother.

But reports were coming in thick and fast now, brought by one hysterical, malicious, well-meaning, lying, sane, unbalanced messenger after another. Otho had been proclaimed emperor by the entire city garrison. The soldiers had rejected him and killed him. He was being carried in triumph to the Capitol. He'd lost his nerve and fled the city. He was here, now, with an army at his back, to stuff Galba's arithmetic down his throat and take the things he had been denied.

"Barricade the doors," someone shouted, and someone else, "Out into the streets. Run. We're like rats in a trap."

But could we run? And where could we go? Suddenly the palace was full of people, strangers who had no right to be there, and outside the whole precinct was blocked solid by a shouting, struggling crowd—spectators? enemies? an assassin, perhaps, hidden among them, waiting his chance to get close to Galba? Who knew? Laco, standing beside the emperor he had helped to make, began to shout, a wordless, blustering noise, and gradually, from the chaos, it seemed they had remembered there were other troops in the city beside the Praetorians, and men were being sent to find out how much they could be relied on. And what of the cohort on duty in the palace precinct? Piso went outside and, standing on the shallow, marble steps, spoke to them in his cool way about loyalty and the obedience due to their rightful master. And when they'd shrugged their shoulders and refused to commit themselves—knowing that now there'd have to be a bounty from somewhere, and waiting to see who made the best offer—he came up to me and said in the same quiet tones. "Someone must go to the Praetorian Barracks to ascertain exactly what is amiss—one must know the extent of the problem before hoping to find a solution, and none of the other messengers have returned. So I must leave you for a while. I am persuaded that if you stay here—with the emperor, my father—you will be quite safe. And if the situation deteriorates then he will arrange for you to be looked after."

"Yes," I said, "Yes, of course." And he took a few steps away from me and then came back, closer than he'd ever been before, so that I could see the muscles clenched tight around his jaw and the pain in his eyes.

"You'll be all right," he said jerkily. "If things turn out badly lose yourself in the crowd and make your way home—and Antonia—if we shouldn't meet again—Antonia, we barely know each other—but if I am killed today, as I may be, there is a woman—Verania—my wife—she's at my brother's house—I think she would wish to bury me." And for the first time I took his hands, knowing he was a man who could love and suffer and that if I ever succeeded in piercing his shell we could at least be friends.

"Yes, I'll see to it," I told him as he walked away from me curiosity—which had kept me calm—deserted me and I was afraid.

Time passed and for those of us who remained with Galba it passed slowly. We stood silently around him, afraid to show him our fear, afraid even now, when professional killers threatened us, of his abrasive tongue and his sardonic stare, his hard, unforgiving nature that had refused to light Nero's lamps or pay his soldiers their bounty. And if he needed us—noticed us—he gave no sign of it.

"Old fool," someone murmured behind me, but we had sworn allegiance to him, old fool or no, and if he died today some of us would certainly die with him. I didn't expect to be killed deliberately, for there would be no profit to anyone in that, but a stray knife could easily pierce my side or a random blow tumble me beneath a maddened crowd and, because it had to be faced, I made myself think about it in detail, more than once, so that if it happened I would have a better chance of retaining a certain dignity. I was a patrician woman and whatever happened I wouldn't disgrace myself by screaming for mercy. But, just the same, watching Galba scan a column of figures and arrive gleefully at the total, it seemed to me an easier thing to die at seventy-three, certain of a place in history, than at twenty with nothing to remember at the end but the things one had never had the time to do.

Time passed, and since nothing was required of me, I took refuge in the stillness surrounding the emperor, drawn close to him because he alone, of the hundreds of people milling aimlessly—dangerously—all over the palace, seemed not to care. The air was thick with emotion, fear, anger, malice, eagerness to inflict suffering and curiosity to watch it done, but for Galba there was simply the job in hand and he seemed to feel nothing more than a mild impatience with the tumult around him. No one approached him too closely for no one had anything good to tell him. None of the messengers sent to interview the troops or to test the true mood of the city had returned, and there was nothing now to rely on but the shouted comments of the crowd who were still forcing their way into the palace precinct and into the palace itself, standing with the blank smiles and greedy eyes of a circus crowd waiting for the show to begin.

Time passed, and abruptly Galba arrived at a final total, put down his work and announced that the thing had gone far enough. Vinius, still smoothly at his elbow, had been advising him all day to stay in the safety of the palace, not to show himself, but Laco, in a roaring frenzy, intervened and the two men almost came to blows.

"You'd like that," he sneered. "Keep him here, out of the way, so Otho can have a free hand. You don't fool me. You don't fool me at all. You've been Otho's man from the start. Oh you're in this up to your neck—"

Laco, his face mottled purple and red, his massive shoulders heaving, strode forward his hand on his sword-hilt, his eyes too full of hate to see clear, and I felt my stomach lurch for if swords were drawn now—in this confined space, in this crowd—then few of us would survive the stampede. I looked desperately for a place to hide, something to climb, but Vinius simply lifted his arms and shoulders in a gesture of contempt—showing at the same time that he was unarmed—and Laco, side-tracked, turned to the crowd and bellowed. "Get out into the city and see things as they are. Don't give the bastard time to get organised."

They brought Galba his sword and his breastplate and he buckled them on with the slight grimace I often saw in my father when, in the heat of summer, he was obliged to change his tunic for a ceremonial toga. In his armour he looked squatter, older, than ever but at last he was ready and, because there was no other way of doing it, they put him into a chair and carried him out of the palace and through the frantic streets, his bearers and his escort besieged on every side by the mob who wanted not only to stare but to touch, pressing themselves against us like the waves of a greasy sea, their volume swelling so that soon it would go over our heads, drowning us in human bodies. Panic seeped into the corners of my mind and my lungs began to pant out their protest, anticipating that foul choking, and if I could have got away, lost myself in the crowd as Piso had told me, perhaps I would have done it. But there was nowhere to go and, as the bearers stumbled, gasping for air, and Galba, on his precarious perch, was almost lost, I got as close to him as I could and steadied his chair with my own weight, for he was, after all, my kinsman, a Sulpician and a gentleman, and I didn't want to see him grovelling in the dust. Behind me Laco was still blustering, for he was head and shoulders above the rest and could still breathe.

"Turn here. No, here. Cut them down if they won't give way." But the few soldiers who had come with us had neither the space nor the inclination for sword-play. They looked sheepish, resentful, as if they didn't really know what they were doing here at all when their mates were over at the barracks with Otho, collecting their bounty, and although they went on shouldering a passage through the throng and showed no signs of attacking us, I didn't think they'd help us much either. There was a moment when I closed my eyes and my head was full of pleading, for I didn't want to die, didn't want to feel pain, I wanted to go home, and I hated everyone who stood in my way. But then, what else was there to do but go on, and when I opened my eyes Piso was miraculously there, back from his fruitless errand, his hand, like mine, steadying Galba's litter, conscious of what was due to the old man—his emperor—who had been his father for five days.

The Forum was an ant-hill of heads without faces. Nothing stirred. There was no sound, just people, staring, waiting, and then, behind them, a noise in the far distance, clattering, pounding, growing, and, as sea-water is sucked away on a strong tide, the silent watchers were dispersed and the square was full of soldiers, Otho's soldiers now, come to earn their pay. Galba's bearers dropped their load and fled and even as the old man went sprawling to the ground a soldier was on top of him, pinning him down. His head cracked against the pavement and I thought he was unconscious—dead—and perhaps the soldier thought so too for he seemed to hesitate. But Galba's watery blue eyes suddenly shot open and his peevish little mouth barked out his last command. "Get on with it, man," he said and, as the blade went into his throat, it seemed that a pack of human hounds were at him, hacking and rending whatever bit of him they could reach. And watching it, I wondered why I was standing there so quietly.

Someone screamed beside me, a high, animal wail, a thin sound not like Laco at all, but when I looked Laco was lying dead, his mouth still open on a final shout, and Vinius was backing away shrieking, "No. No. I'm with you. I'm with you. Otho said I was not to be harmed." But they killed him just the same and, as the sword came red and steaming out of his gut, Piso grabbed my arm and began to run. I didn't really see much point to it—for they'd catch us, kill us—but no one seemed to block our way and my mind, floating beyond the rim of the real world, asked no questions. We ran towards the round, pregnant curve of the Temple of Vesta. I felt my feet on the steps, going up, up, to sanctuary I supposed, although that wouldn't stop them for long, and then Piso stumbled, choking, against me, blood spurting from his mouth and seeping through a ragged gash in his chest, and there were armed, helmeted men all around us. He fell dying across me, bringing me down to the ground with him, and as the marble step bit into my back, one of the soldiers hauled Piso to his knees and slit his throat like a sacrificial calf.

I started to scream, expecting to die too, but one of them, an officer I thought, although my eyes were full of Piso's blood and I couldn't see clear—dragged me to my feet, pushed me inside the temple and left me crouching there, retching and trembling, but still alive. And for a while I remembered nothing more.

The killing went on, and when it had burned itself out, what remained of the Senate rushed to kneel at Otho's feet and kiss his hand. The Forum was still foul with blood, with splinters of bone and severed limbs and the reek of death, when they carried Otho through it in triumph. But even as he entered Nero's golden palace and claimed it at last as his own, the news leaked into the city, and was quickly suppressed by the new-born regime—that far away in Germany, Vitellius—hearty, sporting gentleman that he was—had been proclaimed emperor too, by his legions, some days ago now, and that they would be bringing him to Rome ere long to make their proclamation stick.

6

My mother regarded the murders of Galba and Piso as a personal affront and so great was her annoyance at losing the rich appointments and splendid marriage Galba had promised that she refused, at first, to see that because of her connection with him, she could be in danger herself.

I got home somehow that dreadful day, creeping out of the Temple of Vesta with the early winter dark, and the feel of Fannia's warm arms around me and the concern in Corellia's eyes made me a child again so that I let them wash me and dress me, and wept without shame. Corellia, who had disliked me as an empress-to-be, loved me again now that I was just Antonia, nowhere near as pretty as herself, but as soon as they'd washed Piso's blood out of my hair and got me into a clean dress, my mother came and engaged me in what seemed, in my weakened state, to be mortal combat.

She was prepared to leave her uncle Galba's body to the carrion crows but Piso, who had only been a Caesar for five days and had shared every one of them with her, was another matter. She felt it to be her duty to recover his remains and give them a decent burial and had come to enquire just where they could be found.

"No," I said. "He wants his wife to bury him. He asked me to see to it." And when she dismissed this as childish nonsense I got up from my couch and shrieked that I'd promised him and that I'd find Verania if it was the last thing I ever did.

We stood for a long time facing each other in a bitterness that was not entirely about Piso, and when it seemed that neither of us would give way Fannia, amazingly, persuaded us apart and took my mother off to her room. I don't know what she said to her, but when mother emerged, looking cool and frail, she conceded that a man's dying wishes must be respected and, since I was too hysterical to be trusted with anything as important as this, she would find Verania herself.

"Was she in love with him?" I asked Fannia after she'd gone, and she raised her painted eyebrows and gave me the suggestion of a wink.

"Not in the way we understand it, darling. She's amused herself with these intellectual flirtations for so long as I've known her. She likes admiration Oh—don't we all—but your mother doesn't like desire—no, no, she doesn't want a man who undresses her with his eyes and swoons at the sight of her bare shoulder. With your mother, it's power. She likes a man who comes and tells her all the secrets of his heart, someone she can guide and mould so that the poor man ends by not being able to make up his own mind about anything. She doesn't want to be touched, she wants to be consulted. Yes—she's had a whole series of them—spotless relationships every one. Power—that's what it is. Poor Piso. No, she didn't love him, or want to go to bed with him—but if she could have given him your father's millions, or given your father Piso's pedigree and his beautiful manners, then she may have married her ideal man. And even then she wouldn't have wanted to go to bed with him."

"My father—" I said suddenly, sitting bolt upright, "Where is he?" For father, somewhere on his way to Vespasian, was carrying messages which no longer made sense, which could even be his death-warrant. But Fannia put her scented arms around me again and hugged me tight. She was a new woman today. Galba had threatened her with disgrace and even death, but Otho, a friend from the old days, wouldn't dream of asking her what she'd done with her money, and she wanted me to share in her good luck.

"Your father knows what he's doing," she said soothingly. "Just think—if he'd been here today he'd probably have got himself killed trying to do something heroic for that crabby old man. Because, you know, darling, Galba may have been your mother's uncle and very distinguished and all that, but he wasn't really our kind of man, was he? Your father's quite safe now—if he goes to Vespasian he'll be well received, because what possible reason could Vespasian have for treating him badly? And if he wants to come back to Rome all he has to do is wait until things calm down a little. I know he supported Galba but, darling, Otho won't kill him. He's not like that. Oh, I know there was a lot of killing today, but that was just the soldiers, you know—they get carried away and, after all, it's what they're trained to do. But once it's out of their systems they won't start it again unless Otho tells them to. And darling, he's a perfectly lovely person, he'll invite your father to dinner as soon as he gets back and they'll get along splendidly, because your father's a perfectly lovely person too. Otho doesn't bear grudges.

And really, darling, if he decided to kill all Galba's supporters he'd have to kill us all, wouldn't he? Everybody supported Galba yesterday and today everybody supports Otho. There's absolutely no reason to worry."

They cleared up the Forum. Verania, with mother's help, found Piso's body although she had to buy the severed head from an enterprising soldier who had recognised it and drove a hard bargain, and when the decencies had been observed, mother came home something of a heroine and a credit to us all. I'd barely known Piso. I could neither miss nor mourn him, but, for some time after his death my appetite disappeared and I was apt to come across him in my dreams, stiff and dead but standing upright, continuing to do his duty because no one had told him it didn't matter any more.

Vitellius still threatened us from Germany, but Germany seemed very far away. Nothing had yet been heard of Vespasian and, at least as far as Rome was concerned, Otho was supreme. Nero had come again in saner form to usher in an era of elegance and good taste, and mother—worried about father and Clarus and still very much put out at the blow to her expectations—decided that since we had no share in the making of this new age we would ignore it altogether. Ours was to be a house of mourning and she wondered, icily, who would dare criticise her for doing what was no more than the decent thing?

"You may do as you please," she told Fannia. "Your loyalties are your own affair. But as for myself and my daughter—and I rather think your daughter too since she is still married to my son—we shall remain at home in strict seclusion. I feel it is what my husband would wish."

But that very night Corellia, wearing an apple-green dress and my topaz bracelets, slipped out of the house after mother had gone to bed, just like father used to do, and next day didn't even trouble to hide the bruises on her neck and the dreams in her eyes.

I didn't know if we were in danger, but Fannia, who had bought a whole new wardrobe and a new pearl necklace on the strength of her friendship with Otho saw the future as a golden meadow where every flower had a jewel at its heart. "We can all have a perfectly lovely time," she kept saying and had such faith in Otho's good nature that she was undismayed even when my mother refused, on the grounds of ill-health, an invitation to dine at the palace. The freedman who brought the message went away smiling and that should have been the end of the matter, but later in the morning Otho—who was no longer a private person and couldn't come himself—sent a member of his personal suite to renew the request—Corellia's lover, Camerinus.

My mother, her mouth hard and a strange brightness in her eyes, announced that she was receiving no one, and was furious when she learned he had asked for me.

"You may inform the gentleman that my daughter is otherwise engaged," she told our highly excited butler, but I shook my head.

"No, mother. We can't do that—you know we can't. Whatever we may feel about it, we can't send a personal friend of the emperor about his business—and Otho is our emperor. There's nothing we can do about that, except try to survive. And he could make life difficult for us—or impossible. Mother—?"

My voice petered out, for I was saying such obvious things, things she should have been saying to me, and her attitude astounded me. She knew that Otho, with one word, could exile my father and brother, confiscate our property, strip us naked if he so desired, yet she, with her strict code of conduct, her implacable worship of hearth and home, was prepared to risk all that for one dinner-party. Had her feelings for Piso been stronger than she cared to acknowledge? Or did she, in some secret recess of her heart, want my father to die? Or was there something else, some aspect of her I'd never suspected which was coming to the surface now that she was alone and free for the first time in her life.

"How dare you?" she said, "How dare you remind me of my duty? How dare you even suggest that I could forget it? I am aware that this regime—for as long as it lasts—is something to which we must bow. But just the same I will not have a perfumed, painted gigolo strutting around my house demanding an interview with my daughter. I am worth more that that and so are you. And it strikes me that Otho's choice of a messenger is a direct insult to us all. If Otho wishes to see you, Antonia, then he will see you, but bear in mind it is only because he has already promised you and your dowry to one of his associates, as a reward for services rendered. And if he wants to see me it is only to show the world that Galba's own family bear him no malice. Well—you need a husband, and if Otho lasts you'll have to take the one he offers. But I see no reason to give in so soon. You will accept my judgment on this matter, since you evidently have none of your own."

But lately—since that day in the Forum when I had seen men

tear each other apart and Piso had fallen dying across my knees —my mother no longer seemed quite so terrible to me.

"No," I said, "I'm sorry. I don't want to see this messenger either, but to send him away can only give offence—and perhaps I'm a coward. Galba didn't care about dying. He'd had his life. But Piso didn't want to die. He was afraid, that last afternoon, and it was the only time I ever really liked him. Perhaps I never realised how easy it is for life to bleed away until I saw it happen to him. And I know, in that moment, he would have done anything to stop it—far more than accept an invitation to dinner. And so I think I'll see this messenger if you don't mind."

"I forbid you—" she began but then, meeting the answering chill in me and because she knew I was right, she said quickly, "Do as you please. I am fast learning not to care." And swept out of the room.

They had kept Camerinus waiting in the atrium and I received him there, needing the space and the impersonal atmosphere of that vast hall. He looked just once over my head to see if he could catch a glimpse of Corellia and then, resplendent in a brand new uniform and with an exact copy of Otho's easy charm, he made an official speech, telling me how distressed Otho was to hear of my mother's indisposition, how distressed, indeed, at the sorrow political necessity had put on our family as a whole, but that in view of the friendship he had once felt or was prepared to feel for my father, in view of civic harmony, in view of a great many other things I didn't listen to, it would give him pleasure to see me that night at his table. And when the graceful speech was over Camerinus leaned forward and said, "He really wants to see you, you lucky girl. You'd better come. I don't think any woman has ever turned him down yet."

Suddenly the tension of the last few days, the bitterness between me and my mother, Corellia, my own desperate anxiety for my father, pressed hard against every nerve in my body so that violence crackled inside me and, to my own amazement, I lifted my hand and struck his grinning face a stinging blow.

I heard my own gasp of dismay—for how could I forget myself and behave like this, like an actress, a hoyden?—but Camerinus, the courtier to his fingertips, had had his face slapped before and, after that first bare instant when he wasn't sure what had happened to him—because he hadn't expected me to behave like an actress either—he staggered back theatrically, rubbing his cheek with a gesture of exaggerated pain, not in the least offended because it was only a game like everything else and, having laughed his way through life for twenty-five years he saw no reason to stop now.

"My, my," he said. "Such emotion. I think you've broken my jaw—which is quite all right if that's what pleases you—just so long as it doesn't leave a scar."

I clasped my hands firmly together, clasped the whole of myself together, but I was trembling with humiliation—cold and sick with it—and I found small consolation in knowing that this man, this perfumed gigolo, would never understand what it cost me to stand my ground and give him my mother's unflinching stare.

"I should not have done that," I said. "But you spoke to me in a way I didn't like—which I don't expect—and must ask you not to do it again."

"No, no," he murmured, "I won't do it again. Is that the message you want me to take to Otho?"

I could have been really violent then and, as the words Clarus had taught me when we were children flooded my mind, I could have forgotten the freedwoman, who would certainly be hovering somewhere behind a pillar, to chaperone and report. But before I could disgrace myself again I heard a low, hoarse laugh behind me and Corellia, in a rainbow swirl of silk and dancing golden hair, walked past me as if I wasn't there, going to Camerinus like a moth going into the fire.

"Ah yes," he said, nothing more than that, and she had no answer. She just stood there, staring at him, her mouth half open, panting a little as she took in the air he breathed, bathing herself in his atmosphere while he began to undress her with his eyes, just as he'd done the night they met, removing each garment delicately, lingering on the sensitive places he'd discovered in her so that by glance and smile alone he was bringing her body to the point of orgasm. And I couldn't bear it. It was indecent, shameful—for, after all, Clarus was my brother—and, pushing past them I muttered "Have you no shame?" and almost ran from the room, "Then we'll see you this evening, madam?" Camerinus called after me, remembering that this was how he earned his bread, but with tears stinging my throat, I left Corellia to answer for me, angrier with her than with him, for he meant nothing to me and I'd always called her my friend.

I offered Fannia her pearls now that no one threatened to take them from her, but she wouldn't hear of it. "I've remembered now who gave them to me and I find I didn't care for him after all." And so I wore them that night in my hair, taking more time and trouble than usual, watching closely as my hairdresser wound the heavy coils high on the crown of my head, securing each one with a pearl cluster, because—and it was useless to deny it—I wanted to look my best for Otho. I had the maids set out a great many garments, the misty lilacs and cool lemons which suited my personality, but in the end I chose white silk with silver threads and seed pearls at the hem, and spoke sharp words when my dresser—a woman I'd inherited from my mother—suggested that Fannia's necklace, an intricate arrangement of pearl-studded silver filigree which completely covered the throat, was rather more than I could carry. I had lost weight since Piso died and, as my cosmetician—a girl I'd chosen myself—painted my eyes, and my dresser, standing behind me to hold the lamp, went on with her murmuring, "Surely, madam, isn't that shadow a little too mauve?—that line too long?—isn't it too Oriental?—too much?—" I thought the hollows under my cheekbones suited me and that the pale oval of my face, held between Fannia's jewelled collar and the piled-up coils of my hair, was not unattractive.

I got up feeling pleased, almost happy, and lingered over the tray of perfume they'd brought me, wanting something special to suit my mood. I wasn't beautiful but tonight I was elegant, someone who would be looked at and to whom exciting things could happen. But then Corellia swept into the room in a dress of bridal orange covered in gold embroideries with gold ribbons in the rich cascade of her hair, and I pointed to the phial nearest my hand and told them it would do.

I was still angry with her—still hurt—but she pressed her flushed cheek against mine and gave my arm a squeeze. "Don't be cross, Antonia. I know I'm a disgrace and I know you mind about Clarus—and so you should—but I can't help it. There's no point in promising to behave myself because I don't intend to. I love him so much, you can't imagine. Heaven knows, I didn't want to love him. I didn't want to love anybody because I knew I couldn't afford it. I just wanted—fun—I suppose, and something to remember later on. But instead I've got myself in this dreadful state and I know I'll suffer for it in the end. You can't know what he does to me. My bones just melt away when I see him and I go crazy. I'm not myself at all. I could eat him alive, I really could. And he'll go away soon. He'll have to go off to war to fight Vitellius, or he'll marry a rich wife. He hasn't any money and he couldn't marry me whatever happened. Oh,

Antonia, I'm in despair sometimes. When Clarus comes back, if he still wants me I suppose I'll have to go on being his wife—although your mother'll put a stop to it if she can. So my future doesn't look bright—Clarus and babies, or divorce and any rich old man Fannia can get to marry me. So don't be cross, Antonia. Let me have this. I adore him." And what could I, who had never adored anyone, say to that?

The palace was now everything I'd expected it to be. Otho had rekindled all of Nero's lamps and the dining-hall blazed with light and laughter and sweet music. The carved ivory ceiling sent down a gentle cascade of perfume and flower petals as it was intended to do, and beneath it, on Nero's couches with their gold and silver and ivory frames, lay the beautiful people Galba had chased underground, wearing the jewels they'd hidden away from his auctioneers, chatting airily about the frivolities he'd despised—poetry and philosophy, the body's ease and pleasure, and the art of love. Nero's chefs too had been brought out of hiding for the food had a poetry of its own, not just of taste but of shape and texture, each dish playing subtle and decidedly sensual harmonies on my tongue, delighting my eyes and my nostrils, filling my whole body with an eager curiosity, an urge to explore, telling me that pleasure was not a wicked thing but should be taken into the senses like a rare wine, with delicacy and imagination. And as the oysters and flamingo tongues and the piquant, savoury souffles of smoked fish and chicken livers were succeeded by fluffy pink clouds that tasted of wine and honey and almonds, I forgot words like 'duty' and 'family' and 'mother' altogether and surrended entirely to Otho.

Greek flutes and harps played dream-music from hidden alcoves and there were flowers everywhere, not just that constant butterfly-soft shower from above, but flowers banked high around the walls in elaborate arrangements, or strewn casually here and there, looking as if they had sprung naturally from the glowing, living mosaics. I looked for the corner where Galba had crouched over his accounts, but it was gone, concealed by a sunburst of blossoms, shades of yellow and amber and deep cream filling an ivory bowl, and the place where I'd last stood with Piso and promised to give his body to his wife had vanished too. A lamp stood there now, a slender, silver tree with candles growing as thick as leaves along its metal branches, and beneath it, basking in its glow, a rosy Venus bathed in a marble sea. Dancers with lithe, brown bodies entertained us between the courses, white-robed boys—the remnants of Nero's choristers

—sang in voices that pierced my heart, and then, as the fruit and sweets were taken away, a woman stepped quietly into the centre of the room, an actress of such beauty and notoriety that she needed no fanfare to command attention. And, as I stared eagerly at her long, supple limbs and her lovely, intelligent face—for she was a woman who had received my father's attentions and I'd long been curious about her—she gave us a sparkling piece of satire and, as a daring finale, spoke a few lines of one of Nero's love-poems.

Perhaps I'd dreamed of evenings like this, sitting in my mother's house listening as her friends discussed their ancestry and their assests, but could I really be a part of it? My arrival tonight had aroused some interest. One or two men had tried to make themselves pleasant, one or two women—the mothers of marriageable sons or the sisters of young men who needed a helping hand—had done the same, lovely, languid women, their reputations as blemished and their finances as chaotic as Fannia's, but noblewomen never the less who knew what a good prospect looked like. And when they looked at me, beneath their drooping, sleepy eyelids, they saw the little girl who had almost managed to marry Piso, the daughter of that dreadful woman Sulpicia who would be a problem in any marriage negotiations, and of the fabulously wealthy Lucilius, who knew how to hang on to his money and could be quite a pet when his wife wasn't looking. I didn't hear them whisper, but I knew what they were whispering about, knew that by tomorrow I could be betrothed again to some sophisticated man of Otho's choosing, someone who would really take me away from my mother, to this glamorous world where she wouldn't condescend to follow. And when I thought about it I felt a thrill that was part delight and part panic, for a man like that would expect me to be sophisticated too and could I really hold my own? Could I really stretch myself out, night after night, on these couches and be witty and flirtatious and original? Could I even think of anything at all to say beyond the serious topics I'd learned at home?

"You're not eating," Corellia said, but she wasn't eating either. She had spent the evening in a trance, her eyes clouded over, and it was only when Camerinus—who, as a member of the imperial entourage, had duties to perform—came across to her that her face, and her body, awoke. In a flowing, saffron-coloured synthesis with a sardonyx at the shoulder he looked extremely handsome. But then, all Otho's young men looked very much the same—careless curls that had taken hours to get just right, flashing smiles one had to practice before a mirror, polished nails and polished teeth and chins that were shaved three times a day—and, remembering the painful embarrassment of the morning, I had no welcome for him. He paused several times on his way over to us, a word here and there, a woman's hand on his arm detaining him, demanding the attention it was his job to give, but he arrived never the less and, putting a hand on the nape of Corellia's neck he said very distinctly, so that as many people as possible could hear him, "I'm burning for you."

Otho too looked as if he had it in him to burn for Corellia—if he'd been a little younger and had more time—but when the meal was over and individual conquests were being made, she was left to Camerinus and I was the one invited to join the imperial party and to feel, once again, the thrilling pressure of Otho's hand on mine.

"Antonia—my dear young friend—" he said, ending the phrase as if there were so many other things he would like to say, as if there was something just a little more than friendship between us. And although I knew he had no real personal interest in me and had very likely promised me to someone else—'My dear fellow, I shall place you on the list of consuls for next year and find you a rich wife'—his charm, undimmed by defeat, was so dazzling in his triumph that I couldn't resist it. He made me feel like a woman and whether it was true or not it did no harm to enjoy it.

He presented me, informally, a hand on my shoulder, to the people around him, to senators whose names I knew and of whom my mother did not approve, to Statilia Messalina, Nero's widow, who was going to be empress for the second time, it seemed, now that Otho had seen the sparkle in her eyes, and, rather daringly even for him, to that famous, fascinating actress who told me, by her warm smile and the knowing glance she exchanged with Otho, that her memories of my father were very tender indeed. And then, when he'd shown everyone how Galba's niece had forgiven him for murdering her uncle, if indeed she'd ever blamed him, he drew me aside into an alcove, one of Nero's intimate little corners designed for whispering secrets and making promises and telling lies, and murmured "There is something I must say to you."

We were not precisely alone for the curtains remained wide apart and there were soldiers and freedmen standing nearby, appearing neither to see nor hear but in fact doing both, yet his tone was so caressing that, in the scented, artificial twilight, I forgot this was the way he always spoke to women, and blushed.

"How charming," he said, enjoying my confusion far too much to let it pass by. "And how flattering—if I can still bring that colour into a pretty girl's cheek then perhaps I'm not so old—eh?—perhaps there's hope? Antonia—I'm sorry your mother is ill, and I'm sorry for other things too. You'll understand, I know, that I didn't wish for Galba's death—that I was unable to prevent it. And you'll understand that I have grieved for him too." And although I knew Galba's murder had always been part of his plan—for how could it have succeeded otherwise?—I somehow found it possible to smile at his lies.

"Don't blame me," he murmured, as if it mattered, and I saw he didn't blame himself. In his view, if Galba had adopted him instead of Piso then they would both have been alive today. He'd have let Galba live out his span, there'd have been no need for murder, and since Galba had lacked the sense to see that, then the whole thing had been his own fault. It was a kind of one-sided logic I recognised, having met it in my brother and Corellia and a great many other people who could never admit they were to blame for anything. But the same fault in Otho took on the colour of his charm and I forgave him.

"I owe you a great deal," he said. "Yes—yes, indeed I do. On one of the bitterest days of my life, a day when you yourself had much to celebrate, you were the only person to speak a warm word to me. I've thought of it often. I tried to warn you, on the day of my coup—I was concerned for your safety and glad—very glad—when I heard you were unharmed. Antonia—you had a glorious future within your grasp. You would have been an empress. And if you can forgive me for Galba and Piso—can you forgive me for taking that away from you?"

He grinned ruefully, quite sure I could forgive him for anything, holding the lives of two men very cheaply beside my thwarted ambitions.

"So," he said, "I am in your debt there, too. I owe you a husband—and watching you tonight, catching a glimpse of you with your lovely pearls and your very special, very elegant head, I made up my mind to attend to it right away. What do you think of that?"

"Isn't it—a little soon—?" I said haltingly, meaning 'Piso's ashes are barely cold', but his smile flashed out and he shook his head.

"No, no. These things can never be done too quickly. You are not just anybody, dear Antonia—not just a pretty girl to please the eye. Now that you are free offers will come pouring in, and in your father's absence, I shall take it upon myself—and how sweet that will be, playing father to someone I could so easily—but, putting that from our minds, I ask myself which man to choose? I looked around the room at dinner and paired you with this one and that one—creating a few delicate situations, I can tell you, since not all my choices were free to marry. But you must have ideas of your own. Even someone so carefully brought up as yourself must have preferences—longings? Will you be wicked—just for a moment—and tell me what they are?"

"Yes," I said crisply, for here at least there was only one correct answer. "I shall prefer—at once—anyone you choose for me."

And since he had already chosen, he smiled and brushed my cheek with the back of his smooth hand.

"Well then—since your mother can't be with us—let us consider it, you and I together—and perhaps it's just as well she can't be here because I have it in my mind to do something rather unusual, and I'd like your reaction before I approach her."

Glancing behind me he made a gesture, an imperial flick of the fingers that brought the soldiers stiffly to attention and sent one of them hurrying away, to fetch the man Otho had warned to be ready. Once again I was going to meet my future husband and although it had happened before—and, at twenty years old, it was high time they got me settled—I still felt that stirring of protest, a tiny voice which murmured, 'How dare they dispose of me behind my back?' My mother had told me that marriages were built painstakingly, brick by brick, implying that for a clever woman the husband was no more than a tool in her building processes, but she had married my father, who was gentle and handsome, and I couldn't believe she had ever been troubled by the brutal prospect of getting into bed naked with a stranger. Since all men were equally gross and objectionable to her, any husband would have done just as well, or fared just as badly. But some men had always charmed me—like Otho—and others chilled me—like Piso—and it only added to my confusion to know that my judgment was unsound. Piso had certainly been the better man, but Otho—like Corellia and Fannia—had a far better chance of touching my heart.

"Your mother will not at first understand the choice I have made," he said, drawing me deeper into the alcove. "But it may please you—it should please you. I could have obeyed the conventions and promised you to a man whose fortune almost matched yours—giving him more of what he already had and transferring you simply from one successful magnate to another—yes, that would have been the obvious thing to do, but I have an absolute dread of being obvious—it makes me feel unshaven, and is there a worse feeling than that, I ask you? And so, I thought why not a man with his way still to make, a man of good family, naturally, but someone who would owe everything to your house, who would come to you with no more than his good breeding, excellent education, and the highest—really, the very highest—hopes for the future. Yes, Antonia, someone close to me, one of the few I am grooming for high office—and you must know how expensive high office can be. Naturally, one makes a profit in the end but every rung on that official ladder costs money, a great deal of money. The entertaining, the presents, simply maintaining a way of life in keeping with one's expectations—my dear girl, I know what I'm talking about. And just think how grateful such a man would be to the woman who smoothed his path—who made the waiting seem sweet—and how happy she would be, later, when all the plum appointments came rolling in. I could give you to a man who has already built a successful career without you—with other women at his side—and no doubt he'd value you. But how much better to be your husband's partner right from the start—to be the making of him. That's something, eh?"

It was indeed, but before I had time to weigh it in my mind—for it had its bad side too—someone entered the alcove behind me and when I saw it was Camerinus I thought he was just another messenger, come to remind Otho that his time was precious and he had already given me more than my share. For a moment no one spoke and then Otho, suddenly very emotional, quite carried away by his own generosity—for he could easily have found a way to keep my property for himself—threw an arm around Camerinus' shoulder and hugged him in an embrace that had 'congratulation' written all over it. "Dear fellow," he said, easy tears filling his eyes, "I made you no firm promise this afternoon, and I make none now. I am simply stating a wish—letting you see what you can win for yourself, perhaps quite soon, if you continue to please me. Antonia, come, give me your hand—do you remember the last time we three stood together in this house? Yes, you remember it as well as I do— the day ruin stared me in the face and you were kind to me. I asked you then if you'd be willing to take a graceless young scamp like this and save him from himself, and now I am asking you again. The first time it was a pleasantry, an impossibility —beyond his dreams and beyond my powers of giving. But now I ask you as your emperor, who wishes to make your future and his my special care. He has done nothing of note in the world up to now, but with my favour and with you beside him— Come, let me put your hand into his—what pleasure this gives me, so much better than if he'd been old and ugly, eh, Antonia?— The formal betrothal, naturally, must await your mother's pleasure, but let this be the real betrothal, just the three of us standing together as we did before. Hold this evening in your hearts, and love each other well."

And taking my hand and Camerinus' hand he pressed them together, held them a moment, and then swept out of the alcove —an actor returning to his eager public—leaving us in a silence that stabbed me to the heart and turned my eyes blind.

7

I COULDN'T LOOK at him. I would never look at him—never. This was the worst thing that had ever happened to me, far worse than Metellus or Piso or a life-time chained to my mother's side. This was an indecency I couldn't face and I understood, for the first time, why men will sometimes die for a cause. I knew that, whatever it cost me, I wouldn't bring this man into our house to laugh at my brother and go on making love to Corellia behind his back. And if that was the only cause I'd found to believe in then it was better than none at all.

But I still couldn't look at him.

"Well," he said easily. "What can I say? When he sent me to talk to you this morning I thought he wanted you for himself. I was sure of it—we all were—so you can imagine my surprise this afternoon when he took me on one side and told me he'd got something really special in mind for me, if I behaved myself. It really is the most fantastic piece of luck. I can still hardly believe it—although it's like him—and won't it stir them all up when the news gets out. You don't mind, do you? I'm really quite nice when you get to know me—my mother thinks the world of me—and I expect you'll be able to keep me in order, even if you have to do it by brute force, like this morning. Physical violence doesn't agree with me, it brings me out in cuts and bruises, but perhaps I can learn to love it. You don't mind—really—do you? And you are going to back me up when I come to see your mother, aren't you? Because she absolutely terrifies me. Old ladies usually want to pat me on the head and call me a naughty boy, but yours just looks at me as if I hadn't shaved—and that's very upsetting."

He was still holding my hand and I removed it gently, for to snatch it away would have implied emotion of some kind, and I didn't want him to think I cared one way or the other. Anger, perhaps, steadied me for in the whole of his airy, silly speech he hadn't shown one grain of feeling for anything beyond his own grasshopper satisfactions, had said nothing—as he could have done, since words came so easily to him—to suggest regret for Corellia or that he knew how awkward the situation must be for us all.

"Perhaps Otho will see my mother for you," I said coldly,

ignoring his smile which invited me to relax and be friendly—to make the best of it—and that if I wanted a kiss and a cuddle to mark the occasion he had lots to spare.

"Well, let's hope so. But I shall be dreadfully, dreadfully worried about it until it's over. You can't imagine how things like that get under my skin. I'm sure you can cope with anything, and be absolutely splendid about it—but I bleed so easily. Shall we join the others?"

And here, at last, I caught a whisper of anxiety in his tone, for Corellia was in the other room, waiting for him, and with her passions at fever-heat wasn't there a ghastly possibility that she might lose her head and make a scene in public? And, since Otho had warned him to behave himself, he couldn't afford that. Cruelty stirred in me, the desire to humiliate him, to go back to the party leaning on his arm and let Corellia do her worst. But in the end I couldn't use her like that and I said, "I think not. If you could find my servants and have them bring my litter I'd like to go home. My head aches." He sprang forward, instantly alert, for this was the kind of thing he was trained to do, and as he escorted me through the glowing corridors—having first assembled my litter-bearers and torch-bearers and a maid with my cloak—his relief was unmistakable. He looked like a schoolboy who'd just got himself out of a scrape and could now start getting up to mischief all over again. He offered to see me home, gambling I'd refuse, and then, bowing over my hand, wondering whether I wanted him to kiss me, he said, "Don't worry about a thing—there's really no need." But at that moment it was as if the strength of Corellia's passion suddenly struck him a blow, warning him that a few whispered words of regret would not suffice, and as he watched them settle me down among my cushions and carry me carefully away, his dazzling Othonian smile faded and he became a worried man.

I went home with no thought of sleep, every nerve in me listening for Corellia's arrival, not wanting to think how it would be, and because I was afraid of her bitterness and her hurt, I kept my maids with me a long time, having them make and remake my bed and fuss around me with rose-water for my forehead and the chilled juice of citrus fruits for me to drink, until there were no more tasks left for me to invent.

I dozed, seeing impossible dream combinations of Clarus and Corellia, myself and Camerinus, limbs tangled obscenely together, faces grinning foolishly, so that I awoke sickened and full of aches and pains, to hear a step outside my room and the rattling of an outraged hand on my door. Perhaps for a moment she couldn't see me, but my eyes were accustomed to the dark and it seemed to me she stood there like a ghost, a murdered ghost so pale that there could have been a dagger in her side, blood staining her chest. And then she walked forward stiffly, breathing hard, staring, so that I sat up and drew my arms across my body to ward her off, for her empty eyes were not seeing me at all, but simply the woman who'd stolen her man. "Corellia," I said sharply, trying to cut through her nightmare, and she sat down on my bed as if her legs had given way, her hands clenched tight and her body shaking. I didn't think she could speak and, seizing on these moments of shock, before she came back to herself and started screaming abuse at me, I said, "What choice did I have? What could I do? I don't want to marry him. He doesn't want to marry me, any more than you wanted to marry Clarus. What could any of us do? And it may never happen. I've been engaged before. Don't blame me. You are more important to me than any of the men I've known. Reason it out, Corellia."

"Reason," she said, as if she were choking, and I saw there were flecks of blood and raw patches on her lips where she'd bitten them. "No—that's for people like you. I'm not reasonable. If I had any sense I'd be pregnant now with your brother's child, waiting for him to come home—playing the loyal little wife so that not even your mother would have anything to use against me. That's reason. But I'm going mad. You're driving me mad, all of you. I've lost my reason so I'm not responsible for what I do. I can't help it."

She was still shivering, still biting those raw lips, her hands twisting together, fighting each other perhaps to keep her fingers away from my eyes.

"I'm sorry for myself," she said. "Yes—I am. But I'm sorry for you too. You wouldn't have Metellus because he was in love with his lute-player. But what is it going to feel like with Camerinus, knowing he's in love with me? Because he is in love with me. You do know that, don't you?"

"It doesn't matter what I know. I could refuse Metellus because he was my father's choice. But this time I'm up against an emperor, not a father, and you know there's nothing I can do."

"I didn't ask you that." Her fighting hands separated and one of them fell across my wrist and held it down. "I asked you if you know he's in love with me. Tell me."

"Yes," I said, although I wasn't any too sure. "He's in love with you." And my admission relaxed something inside her, cooling her eyes with tears and softening her grip on my arm.

"I won't survive it," she said. "Don't worry. You'll be all right. I won't bother you for long. How can I survive it? I can't go on living here, as Clarus' wife, and watch him with you. And I can't really sleep with him behind your back, can I? I thought I could—he told me that's what we'd do—but I've had them carry me round and round the streets for hours, thinking about it, and I know it wouldn't work because I won't be able to hate you long enough. When I calmed down—after he told me—I hated you all right, you and Clarus and your mother, and I thought 'yes, he only wants her for her money and I'll make sure she knows it. I'll pay her back. I'll have Clarus and his money and position and the man I love both at the same time, under the same roof. After all, that's what Camerinus intends to do so why shouldn't I go along with it? I wanted to do it. I still want to do it—make no mistake about it—and at this moment I hate you like hell just because I can't hate you—not enough anyway—not like I'd have to. Do you see? And I'm going mad with it. I just wanted a little fun while Clarus was away, so I'd be able to settle down when he came back and put up with him in bed and have his boring kids. But I can't do that now. I'm finished. I can't live with him again. I can't let anyone else touch me again, and I can't live with Fannia—so what else is there?"

She started to cry again, her chest and shoulder heaving, and I had no power to help her.

"Don't," I murmured inadequately, but she tossed her head and began patting her cheeks dry with the palms of her hands, shrugging off my concern with a sudden nonchalance that reminded me, for an instant, of her mother.

"Well then—before I die of it—this is what I'm going to do. We should stop seeing each other, but we can't. It's as simple as that. We can't. He may have to go away. There's a war coming with Vitellius—so—whichever comes first, war or marriage, that's when we'll stop. But until then I'll see him every moment of every day and night I can get to him. No one will stop me. Not you, not your mother, not Clarus, not Otho. No one. And afterwards, I don't care. Afterwards he's yours, what's left of him—but not now. This is all the time I have—you'll help me, won't you? You won't make a fuss?"

And, feeling her heartbreak and knowing it as a far greater, far more overwhelming experience than anything I could feel, I nodded and lay down on my bed, bone-weary, blood-weary, wanting nothing but the darkness—the silence—wanting simply not to think about it any more.

The next morning my mother received a visit from an imperial freedman—a highly-paid professional negotiator of delicate matters—and when he'd gone, and she didn't send for me, I went once again to her door without an appointment and pushed her secretary, and her maid, and the steward of our Campanian properties, aside. She was sitting, straight-backed, on an ivory stool, reading something, far too busy for any nonsense of mine—as she'd been all my life—but I went up to her and said bluntly, "Is there any possibility—any way at all—of avoiding this marriage?"

She put down her work carefully, unhurriedly, and although she dismissed her entourage she didn't send them far—just into the next room because this little matter wouldn't take long and she'd need them again.

"Well, dear," she said, "if there is a way I'm afraid it eludes me." And her manner suggested that I should be satisfied with that and take my leave.

"You can't possibly approve of it," I told her, knowing she didn't, and furious with her for refusing me the comfort of admitting it, "He's wellborn but there's no money, no prestige—and he's positively good-for-nothing. You called him a gigolo yourself, when he called to invite us to the palace, and that about sums him up. How can you take it so calmly. You refused to see him the other day, and now you're not even prepared to put up a fight."

I was losing control, my voice growing shrill as my mind flooded once again with those images of Camerinus and my brother, and she raised one long, narrow hand and sighed.

"Antonia, it seems to me that we have had this conversation before—several times before, in fact—and it saddens me that you are still not sufficiently adult to understand your situation. An invitation to dinner is one thing—and one can afford to be capricious about it now and then—but marriage is another matter entirely and must always be treated seriously. The young man may well be completely worthless, but what has that got to do with it? Marriages are not about personalities, they are about property and politics. Must we really go through it all over again? Your marriage is a contract entered into by your family as a whole. You are merely our agent, if you like, and as long as the contract exists—because you are our representative—you will be expected to honour it. If your behaviour as a wife should be less than impeccable then the disgrace is ours, as well as your own, but should the union cease to be to our advantage then it would, of course, be dissolved and you would return home with both your dowry and your reputation intact. That is the kind of marriage I have brought you up to expect, and it worries me that you feel the need to make such a fuss every time a husband is proposed to you. Camerinus, or someone like him, is necessary to us at the moment. Our close connection with Galba makes us vulnerable—you yourself, only yesterday, took the liberty of pointing that out to me—and we must view this marriage as an indication of his peaceful intentions towards us. Having heard nothing to the contrary, I believe your father and brother are still alive, but Vespasian is still an unknown quantity, and if he chooses to declare war on Otho and your father joins him, then our situation could become desperate—so desperate that we would need your marriage to a good Othonian in order to survive at all. And whatever Vespasian does, we still have enormous interests at stake, and if you refused this man it would give Otho a perfect excuse to help himself to everything we have. I'm sure you wouldn't wish your father to return home to find his estates confiscated and strangers living in his home—all because you didn't feel up to marrying a man you don't like?"

She paused enquiringly, knowing there could be no answer, and then said crisply, "You must pray for war with Vitellius. Camerinus will certainly be involved—and these dashing young men often take foolhardy risks. He may not come back. And if he does then you'll just have to console yourself by considering what a blow this marriage must be to Corellia."

Taken off guard I gasped, "So you know about that?", and amusement—disdain—came briefly into her face. "Doesn't everyone know about it? And if that is the reason for your alarm then be at ease. You misjudge me if you think I would allow such a three-cornered situation to exist in my house. If this marriage takes place Corellia will have to go off somewhere, to our house at Praeneste or down to Tarracina if she wishes, and I doubt if we will ever see her again. Clarus will return her dowry—and if the foolish boy wishes to give her a present to help her along I won't stop him—and I imagine he'll marry again within the year. Does that cheer you up a little?"

"No. It saddens me more than ever. I'm fond of Corellia, you know that."

"Oh yes, I know it. And this is yet another conversation we've had before, your faults are so predictable, child. I sometimes wish you could show more imagination. Corellia has no one but herself to blame. She understood her marriage contract—just as you understand yours—but she chose to break the rules. She knew there was a price to pay for her folly and she'd do well, now, to pay it with a good grace. Fannia, at least, has always carried these matters off with a certain style, and we must hope —for Clarus' sake—that Corellia does the same. I must ask you to stop wasting your sympathy. Her problems are no more acute than those of hundreds of other women I could name who did not choose their own husbands—but who manage, nevertheless, to live in harmony and good faith because they recognise the value—to themselves and to their families—of these unions. Many of us are called upon to sacrifice ourselves in this way—and I feel sure you have never heard any decent woman complain."

But I had, for she was talking now about herself and my father, and I wondered just how wide a gulf there really was between her and Corellia and if this was the reason for their open enmity. Could she be so cruel to Corellia because, having come to terms with a loveless marriage herself, she couldn't bear to see another, younger, woman getting away with it? And why was her marriage so barren of any true feeling? Naturally my grandparents—a pair of proud, impecunious aristocrats—had chosen my father for her but I couldn't understand why she hadn't grown to be at least fond of him. He was kind and attractive, and so very much in love with her, yet it seemed to me that when she looked at him she saw no more than the man who had salvaged her father's estate at Luceria and restored the family mansion here in Rome—the man who should consider himself amply rewarded by the connection she gave him with the Sulpicii. And it was incredible. There was something not right about it, some false note I couldn't trace. Had she once, in some impossible springtime, loved someone else? Did she still love someone else? And because even thinking about it made me feel that I had committed sacrilege, I said hurriedly, "If there is a war, will Otho lose?"

She shrugged, disdainful but rather pleased, just the same, that I had something in my head beyond my unbecoming squeamishness at the idea of marriage.

"Oh, I think not. Otho may be far from satisfactory, but at the moment he is popular and with Rome so firmly in his grasp I doubt if anyone will challenge him. Vitellius? Yes—he may make angry noises from Germany, but really, darling, I have some acquaintance with him—years ago now, of course, but he can't have changed so very much—and what amazes me is that he ever consented to let his officers proclaim him emperor in the first place. I can only conclude they had all been dining too well, and that in the cold light of day he was just as appalled as the rest of us. No—the German question will settle itself without any need for war. Otho will offer to buy Vitellius off—in fact he must be negotiating with him already—and Vitellius will be only too glad to accept. He's not the stuff emperors are made of, that much I do remember about him. And perhaps Vespasian will be quiet too. If Vitellius sells the Northern provinces to Otho it may be rather too much for Vespasian to take on alone, so he may content himself with fighting the Jewish war, as Nero asked him to do, and get Otho to adopt one of his sons. Otho has no children and both Vespasian's boys are charming—Domitian is rather young but very clever, and Titus is already a brilliant soldier in his own right. It would be an ideal solution—Otho now and either Titus or Domitian later. I'm sure Vespasian would be satisfied with that."

She smiled, having arranged matters to her liking, seeing the empire—the whole of civilisation—as an extended family not very much larger than her own which could be governed by the same rules—marriages, adoptions, good-taste, personal restraint—and I left hurriedly, knowing she had nothing more to say. If I had been religious I would have gone to pray, to ask the gods of my father's hearth to strengthen me and remind me of my duty, or I would have gone out to find some mysterious Eastern cult which would promise me an after-life and a reward for my sufferings. But, unlike Fannia, who sometimes fasted and attended strange rites which transported her briefly to a paradise she could never afterwards remember, I found no consolation in such things and I went instead to the atrium to see what the day had to offer. But the first person I saw was Corellia, in bridal orange once again with gold in her ears and around her wrists, waving goodbye as she skipped out of the house to meet her lover and warning me, with that brave gesture, that the last thing she wanted from me was my pity.

8

I PLACED CAMERINUS' betrothal ring on my finger a few days later, at a dinner-party attended by Otho and my mother and a beautiful, very languid lady who seemed to be Camerinus' aunt. We ate oysters and purple asparagus and a sweet dish the colour of a bridal veil topped with artificial orange blossom, created specially for us by the imperial chefs, while in the background, Greek singers, robed alternately in orange and white, sang love-songs which no one but myself seemed to think out of place. Camerinus, beautifully dressed in white lawn, his glossy hair curled and his chin as smooth as his idle hands, scattered smiles at everything and nothing, putting his handsome body on display because he had nothing else to offer, while I, stiff with embarrassment, seemed so very cold and severe that his lovely aunt seemed quite sorry for him.

Otho, sentimental with wine, explained to us at great length that the third finger of the left hand had been chosen to wear the betrothal ring because of a nerve supposedly connecting it with the heart, and, on taking his leave, he kissed Camerinus on both cheeks and held me for a long moment, whispering, "He'll be good for you. Relax. You'll be delightful together. And we shall meet so often at court." And when he'd gone there seemed no reason for anyone else to stay. Camerinus held my hand for a moment and swallowed hard, glancing swiftly over my shoulder as if he thought Corellia might be lurking in the dark with a knife, and after that things returned so very much to normal that I often needed the weight of his ring on my hand to remind me that the engagement had taken place.

The news from Germany was again giving cause for alarm and, although my mother, barricading herself behind her domestic concerns, continued to scoff at Vitellius—"My dear child, he'll never get started. And if he did arrive he'd be too drunk to remember what he'd come for"—other people were beginning to take him seriously, and as whole provinces began to go over to him, I found her attitude hard to understand. "I know him," she said, "Surely you must have seen him somewhere?

Not in this house, certainly, but hanging around the circus on race-days gambling with other people's money, or out on Mars Field driving racing-chariots, pretending to be nineteen years old and fooling no one but himself. That's Vitellius. My dear, he's quite ridiculous—he was such a keen supporter of the 'Blue' faction at one time that he actually groomed their horses for them—or perhaps he just needed the money. Hardly the kind of man to lay down one's life for." And yet the city, on his account, was beginning slowly to prepare itself for war.

Fannia knew him too—better, I assumed, than my mother—but when I asked her what kind of a man he was she gave me her slow, sleepy smile and very little reassurance. "Oh, he's all kinds of a man, darling. But an emperor—never, in a thousand years. He's too simple and too easily pleased. And he doesn't like hard work. He's the kind of man who hunts all day, eats half the night and makes love the other half—and he's quite straightforward about it. None of your subtle spices and sauces, just good roast meat and plenty of it. And in bed—well—he's quite a pet but he only knows one way of going about it, and one needs stamina, not imagination where he's concerned. If he's let them make him emperor then he must have been drunk at the time—or they had a knife at his throat. He can't possibly want to take on all that responsibility. He's not made that way."

And perhaps that made him more dangerous than ever, for the man who had held that knife to his throat, or had kept on pouring the wine and whispering to him about imperial glory, was an unknown quantity to us all.

"Is Vitellius badly in debt?" I asked, and Fannia flung her arms wide.

"Well, darling—aren't we all? I imagine he must be. He's a gambler—and I seem to remember hearing he'd been forced to let his town house and move his wife into a flat somewhere—not very nice, actually—before he went to Germany. Yes, he's in debt all right. Near bankrupt, I'd say." And that, at least, made it easier to understand.

Galba had sent Vitellius to Germany instead of my father, because he'd judged him safe and stupid, a big, beefy man who'd appeal to the soldiers and not have the brains to do any harm. But now, suddenly, the Northern provinces were going over to him with sickening speed—Germany, Britain, Aquitania, Gaul—and were sending their armies, packed tight with uncouth, native auxiliaries, wild Britons and long-haired Germans, painted tribesmen in trousers to add weight to his claim. And then Spain, which had been Othonian, remembered that it was Otho who had murdered Galba, and declared for Vitellius too.

"Oh dear," Fannia said. "Poor Otho," But that night the palace and its landscaped, manicured acres shone with laughter and good conversation, while Otho, moving among his guests, had a witty remark for every man, an enraptured sigh for every woman, and a serene smile for all. We knew from Flavius Sabinus, my mother's friend and Vespasian's brother, who was urban prefect just then, that Otho had written to Vitellius offering to buy him off, and had very likely sent assassins on ahead too, in case the offer was refused, but he was far too accustomed to living on a knife-edge to let his anxieties show and nothing seemed closer to his heart that night than restoring a little gracious living to a city coarsened by the depravities of Nero's last years and Galba's shoddy economies. There may be trouble in the North but here in Rome Galba's auctioneers had taken their hammers away, the streets were no longer hideous with the plight of the evicted, the Praetorians had their bounty, Fannia and others like her had their pearls and their peace of mind, and if serious people still found Otho too light, too easy, at least he was better than Laco and Vinius, or a pack of wild barbarians. As the property market recovered he was gaining more support from the senatorial and merchant classes, along with the solid backing of the Praetorians, and the declared loyalty of Africa, Syria, the Balkans, the whole world to the South and East, and when the news finally came through that Vespasian and the army in Judaea had sworn allegiance to him as well, the threat from the North began to lose its bite.

There were people who rejoiced openly and gave dinner-parties to celebrate Vespasian's good sense, others who muttered together in secret and wondered what on earth he was playing at, but for us the news was of special significance, forcing us to admit the possibility that my father and brother were dead.

"It is a thing which must be faced," my mother said calmly. "I have spoken to Sabinus who is in direct communication with his brother Vespasian in Judaea, and he has been unable to obtain any information whatsoever about either of them. When your father heard the news of Galba's murder his journey could only have been half completed—and I think a return to Rome, to Galba's killers, would have seemed unwise. He may have decided to stay where he was and wait until things settled down, but he may have pressed on, preferring Vespasian, who has done no injury to our house, to Otho who has dashed some of our fondest hopes. So—let us consider the possibilities. He may be safe and well in some provincial town, although if that is the case I find it hard to understand why he hasn't written to tell us so. But he may have met with some accident on his way or, arriving safely in Judaea as a committed Galban, Vespasian—on declaring for Otho—may be holding him in custody, or may even have put him to death as a gesture of loyalty to his new master. Sabinus, naturally, denies this, but it must be faced. One must, in any situation, consider the very worst that can happen, however painful. All we can do now is hope and pray."

"He may be lost," I said hotly, "or held up by storms—a hundred things—"

And she nodded. "We must hope so. And more than ever now we must show loyalty to Otho. If your father is being held prisoner our behaviour—your marriage—could be the means of saving his life. And wherever he is, I know he could not possibly wish us to associate ourselves with a creature like Vitellius. That wish at least we can respect."

But it was her wish, not his, and although her animosity to Vitellius puzzled me, I wasn't ready to dwell on it just then. For the rest of the day I saw servants weeping at their tasks, mourning a kind master but also worrying about their own fate, for bereaved households often break up and if my mother married again or retired to the country, they had no way of knowing who would be sold and who would be kept on, who would be given to Corellia or to me. Their gloom, added to my own, set me prowling restlessly, needing someone to talk to, someone who would listen when I insisted my father was alive, but my mother had retired again behind her household accounts, rather as Galba used to do, and I was afraid of approaching Corellia because if she was wishing my brother dead I didn't want to know about it.

His death would make a tremendous difference to her. If he came home her fate was sealed, but, as his widow, what could my mother really do to her? She'd have her place in society, money to spend, freedom to be with Camerinus or anyone else she chose, and because I loved my brother and at the same time couldn't blame her for not loving him, I thought it best to keep out of her way. Not that it would have been easy to pin her down. Her threat to see Camerinus whenever she could had not been idle and, having nothing more to lose, she came and went very much as she pleased. She never dined at home, returning noisily in the middle of the night or not at all, and when she did sleep in her own bed she never left it until noon, spending the rest of the day, heavy-eyed and ill-tempered, in her bath, being massaged and repaired and brought alive again for the evening.

"She's burning herself out," Fannia said sadly. "Did I ever do that? Did I ever love anybody so much? No—I must admit I haven't got it in me. I suppose it's splendid and all that kind of thing, but it's killing her—and Antonia, I'm so sorry—for her, for Clarus and for you—dear children, I hate to see you suffering. I'd like to take her in my arms and comfort her but whenever I try we end up screaming at each other and it only makes things worse. I'm sure he's very charming, and he's a positive delight to the eye, but he doesn't understand her, you know. He's taken her into a world where she's a complete stranger—a lamb to the slaughter—and what plagues me is that he thinks she's as sophisticated as she looks, that she can cope with it—like he can, like I can—and it's not so. She's not like that at all. She looks like me, but she feels things—she's straightforward and simple and not at all easy-going—and this golden dream of hers is going to turn into a nightmare. Believe me, she couldn't have survived a day at Nero's court, and Otho is a perfect pet, but really, he's just the same, you know. He only sees the surface of things, and it just doesn't occur to him that people who look like Corellia can be so vulnerable—can actually die of their wounds."

And it was true that Otho's world—Camerinus' world—had puzzled Corellia and that she'd bruised herself more than once on its elegant but needle-sharp corners. Otho had behaved very well since coming to power but he'd been brought up in a licentious atmosphere where it had been fashionable always to be slightly in debt and in disgrace, always in bed with somebody's wife, and although he was making an effort these days to display the more responsible side of his nature, he was basically very cynical, very light-weight, and the young men of his suite were exactly like him—images of himself as he'd been ten years ago, in Nero's day, when a man could be dissolute and unreliable so long as he was never boring.

These young men created a court within a court, an inner circle where places could not be bought but had to be won by wit or charm, rarely by beauty alone. Life, to them, was one long entertainment, and they took themselves seriously. They were always putting on plays by obscure authors, composing music, writing poems, or playing complicated intellectual games which crucified the unwary. They spent hours selecting the right perfume to suit every mood, the right combination of fabric and colour to suit every occasion, they invented fashions and catch-phrases, turned gossip into an art, and made everyone who didn't belong to their charmed circle feel clumsy and dull-witted.

Love, of course, took up a great deal of their time. It was the only strenuous game they played yet, because 'enthusiasm' was frowned upon—labelled 'childish' and 'unsophisticated'—they made love lightly, imaginatively, and talked about it afterwards. Originality was what they required, not the sweaty antics of a brothel but some subtle blending of physical and spiritual joy which was difficult to achieve and sparked off enormous discussions and a great deal of wit. Corellia and Camerinus made love in every conceivable way and in every conceivable place, and when he began to write letters to her about it and she realised he expected her not only to do the same but to tell all his friends what it had felt like and how she thought it could be improved, she'd been horrified. Her vocabulary had always been blunt and limited, conversation had never been required of her before, but she was a mirror for the things she loved and gradually she became very like Camerinus in manner. She'd always been prickly, very ready to take everything the wrong way, but now she struck languid poses, spoke in the clever, silly jargon of the Othonian elite—whether she understood it or not—and insisted, as they did, that everything, from birth to death and all stages inbetween, rated no more than a certain mild amusement.

She was no intellectual and couldn't always follow what the others were talking about, but she was beautiful and her imitation of their die-away airs and graces became flawless. She managed, somehow, to make her silences seem mysterious rather than vacant, her slight air of boredom—and she was very often bored to tears—marking her as a woman who had seen it all before, rather than a girl who'd never bothered to learn her lessons because she'd been too busy swimming and riding and flirting with her tutors, and couldn't even remember the names of the Greek dramatists, let alone quote them. Camerinus, it seemed, knew whole chunks of Euripides by heart and wrote elegant little verses himself, but when Fannia—who wasn't averse to a little honest sweat and found Camerinus, who shaved his chin and his armpits three times a day, far too soft for her taste—raised pained eyebrows over one of these effusions and said, surely, hadn't she heard it somewhere before, Corellia returned to her old self and shrieked, "I suppose you'd rather have me settle for an oaf like Vitellius?"

"Would I?" Fannia drawled, "Well, darling, I don't think you're in a position to settle for anybody—not until you've had a few words with your husband, at any rate. But, since you ask me—oafs like Vitellius do, at least, take some things seriously. Is anything serious for Camerinus?—except being in the fashion? You may interest him now because you're a new face, but that won't last. There'll be another one along soon, and its simply not fashionable to be faithful to one woman for very long—never has been. Believe me. I know about these things, and so does your Camerinus. And really, darling,—really—you won't like it you know, when they've all got used to you—when they start thinking of you as their common property. You may think you can cope with that kind of life, because of me—but it's not so. You're really not like me at all."

"Well then, I must be like my father," Corellia said bitterly. "If you can remember who he was."

Fannia cried a little after that but tears came easily to her and they did no good.

"Why worry about it," Corellia said callously, "I'm a ruined woman already. As soon as Clarus comes home they'll throw us both out in the street—you and me, mother—so let's enjoy ourselves while we can. But you'll come out of it all right, whatever happens to me. Antonia won't desert you. She'll have her own money and she'll look after you—won't you, Antonia? You and Camerinus?" And she went stamping off, hurt by her own cruelty yet unable, when she was in such pain, to be kind.

I saw Camerinus infrequently, officially, for although my dowry dazzled him, he wasn't physically excited by it and when he touched me it was only because he thought he should. He was polite, escorting me here and there, a delightful, informative companion full of undemanding chatter, reclining beside me at dinner and making sure I had what I required, always on hand with my fan and my cloak like the good courtier he was, smiling through all my ill-tempered remarks and my painful silences. I made none of it easy for him. I had been educated to treat servants and dependants with care, but something in Camerinus aroused a streak of cruelty in me I'd never suspected and with him I became a tyrant. The wine he brought me was always sour, when he handed me my fan I dropped it again, usually under a couch, and forced him to his knees to pick it up, I kept him waiting in uncomfortable places, sent him on pointless errands, and when he invited me to dinner at his aunt's house, offering me a meal which had cost more than he could afford, I declared myself slightly unwell that evening and ate nothing, praised nothing, was irritable and bored and, in the end, slightly ashamed. I didn't like myself this way and I didn't like him for putting up with it, but he went on smiling that brilliant Othonian smile, pouring out all his professional charm, and that in itself goaded me on. I tried to push him to his limits, to a point where he'd stand up and say, "That's enough. Go to hell." But if he had any thoughts of revenge perhaps he was saving them until after marriage, when my body at least would be in his hands, even if I retained control of the bulk of my estate. Perhaps then he'd strike out, but I doubted it. My marriage contract, already under preparation, would bind him hand and foot, giving him little more than an allowance and anything else he could wheedle out of me, and although my money would be used to finance his official career, make him a consul and give him a province to govern, I'd always be able to limit his spending-money, and he'd always have to be grateful. Otho could order me to marry him but, so long as I paid his official bills, he couldn't compel me to treat him well, couldn't, with his own dazzling smile, dissolve my new-found cruely, my desire to humiliate Camerinus because I couldn't escape him. He couldn't make me come to terms with this cold, capricious woman I was fast becoming, couldn't make me smile when I saw my own face in the mirror. There were times when I could almost hear Camerinus' sigh of relief as he put me into my litter and watched my bearers carry me away, and at such times I pitied him too, along with the rest of us, knowing he couldn't be different. His problems were the same as Corellia's. They'd both been born beautiful and poor, forced to sell themselves to survive, and that alone had been enough to draw them together.

Her love for him was a real, devouring fever. His love seemed to me less certain, but there were times—when he'd spent his days running Otho's errands and his evenings running mine—when fatigue dulled his effervescent gaiety and made him far more human. There was a night when he tried to tell me about his childhood in Toscana, and I cut him short, not wishing to see him as a real person, an afternoon when he mentioned his mother and a sister he was fond of, and I looked away and began talking about something else, refusing to allow him his feelings.

And there was a moment at the palace, during one of Otho's vast receptions, when I lost my way and, straying down unfamiliar corridors, caught a glimpse of Camerinus and Corellia, who should not have been there, standing close together, not touching but alive, happy, his face wiped clean of the artificial charm, hers full of absolute wonder. And I left a message for him with a servant and went home, setting him free for the rest of the night, because if he cared for her too then my judgment of him was faulty and I liked myself even less. She'd said to me, "How is it going to feel with Camerinus, knowing he's in love with me?", and I'd put it aside, not believing it. But now I came near to believing it and that made it all more unbearable than ever.

I lay, struggling with sleep, listening to the rain beating on the tiles above my head, the driving rain that had started in that cold, Galban December and lashed its way through January and February, washing the Forum clean of Piso's blood, turning the alleyways to fast-flowing streams, dampening even our gay, Othonian world from time to time with its chilly gusts. The rain that seeped into my dreams and came creeping through the house, its level rising, covering me and washing away all my anxieties so that, in the end, all that mattered was to stay alive.

9

"He won't negotiate," Corellia cried, meaning Vitellius, her voice tinged with hysteria, "The murderous oaf won't negotiate. He says he's coming to Rome—and the biggest laugh of all—yes, the real laugh—he says he's coming to avenge Galba. That's his excuse—poor old Galba—digging him up just so Vitellius can call Otho a murderer—just so he can feel right about trying to murder Otho, unless Otho gets him first. He calls himself our emperor—Vitellius—and he's disgusting. I know him. He used to borrow money from Fannia in the old days—from Fannia—and she used to borrow from someone else so she could lend it to him, or go and earn it for him, spending the night with some filthy old man, or one of her ex-husbands. That's Vitellius. They say he's never stopped eating since he made his proclamation—he's trying to cram as much of the empire as he can into his gut before they take it away from him. Why doesn't he burst out of his skin, or choke on his vomit? If he was here and I had a knife I'd stick him—and I'd laugh."

But Corellia's fear was purely personal, for if Otho went to war Camerinus would go too, and when Fannia, in her well-bred drawl said, "Don't worry, dear—no one will expect him to lift a sword. We all know how sensitive he is and how much care he takes of his hands. They'll just put him in the background and get him to write a poem about it," they almost came to blows.

I separated them, calmed them down, sent for the heavy, sweet wine Fannia insisted was good for her nerves but Corellia's eyes remained bright with tears and suddenly, just as Fannia was reviving, she almost shouted at me, "Don't you see the nightmare I'm in. I can only have Camerinus if Clarus is dead. So I keep wishing Clarus dead and what does that make me?—he's never done me any harm, he's a better person than I am—the only reason I can't bear him is because he's so much in love with me. So I wish him dead and hate myself for it. And Camerinus—he's going to war too—and how do I know how I'll feel if he gets killed? Perhaps it would be easier to bear—his death—than to see him come back and marry you. How do I know? You're stronger than him, you could dominate him and have him eating out of your hand—like your mother and father. And I couldn't stand that. I'd want to kill him. I told you the other night—I'm going mad."

She ran off, upsetting a stool, bumping into a flustered servant who looked hastily to see if there was any damage, a chipped mosaic, a splinter of wood, something my mother would be sure to notice, and Fannia shook her head.

"Yes, I think she is going mad. This is the kind of thing the poets write about—going mad for love—and it sounds so well in verse, especially after a good dinner when some devastating young Greek walks into the centre of the room and starts to recite and all the women think he's doing it just for them, and one's husband gets terribly annoyed because the man one is sharing a couch with can't keep his hands to himself. Yes, I've listened to it a hundred times and I never knew how sad. It's not a fit subject for a poem at all. There's nothing beautiful about it. Thank God it never happened to me."

She went on drinking her wine, growing drowsy, her gown slipping off one shoulder and wisps of her fine hair shaking loose in a disarray that suited her. She sat, dreaming, perfectly content with her body's ease until my mother, who never drank wine during the day and whose black hair seemed sculpted to her head, joined us, glanced pointedly at Fannia's bare shoulder and told us that in her view Vitellius would never get to Rome. "No, no dear. Such a fuss. And all about nothing. Vitellius is merely coming a few steps nearer to ask for more money. Even he—with his limited understanding—must realise he can't win. And if it came to war—how amusing—just think about it. What a pair. Otho would be sure to faint at the sight of blood and while Vitellius wouldn't do that, he'd probably stop the fighting every hour or so while he had his dinner."

Her laughter—a rarity in our lives—tinkled out, thin perhaps from disuse, and since she so rarely made jokes I listened respectfully, leaving Fannia to ask, "But Sulpicia, how do you know Vitellius?"

Her pointed face sharpened. "Is there any reason why I shouldn't know him? He's perfectly well-born—and his father was a man of considerable ability, three times a consul and held in very high esteem. Unfortunately none of his talents were passed on to his sons."

She paused primly, letting her scorn take root in our minds, and then, as if compelled to say more. "If you must know the details—although I feel no obligation at all to give them—one of their estates bordered my parents' property at Luceria. The father dined occasionally at our house, but as for Vitellius himself—well—he was the kind of young man no one would have dreamed of inviting to a house where there were young girls. His reputation was always bad. They were wealthy enough in those days, of course—before their father died—but it was always very apparent that neither Vitellius nor his brother were fit to handle their own affairs. Their mother was extremely indulgent with them, well-meaning I'm sure, but silly. I believe their father tried to exercise some control but whenever they were in trouble all they had to do was go to their mother and she'd move heaven and earth for them. She had money of her own but they soon went through that and then she went into debt to pay their debts, concealing it from her husband as long as she could—anything to make those boys happy. A completely chaotic family—their values quite upside down—and dangerous, because none of them, except the father, had any scruples about anything. Poor man, he would have done better to have divorced his wife and removed his sons from her custody when he first realised how unstable she was. He must have known, very early, how frivolous—how unfit—she was turning out to be, and if he'd acted sensibly we might have been spared some of this nonsense they tell me threatens us from Germany. However—I was warned against Vitellius as soon as my mother judged me old enough to interest him. Not that I needed a warning because I had eyes—and a certain amount of judgment even then—and I needed no one to tell me he was coarse. Yes—coarse—that's the only word to describe him."

"Oh, I don't know." Fannia, who considered herself an expert on men and my mother hardly a beginner, looked amused and was perhaps too full of wine to see her danger. "Not the only word, Sulpicia. He can be coarse—but so can a great many other men, dear. Some of them would really surprise you—but there are other things about him. He has a gigantic appetite for life, he laughs from the heart and he can cry too—great big tears—over the most unlikely things. His life has been in a mess more than once, but he's always human. When he falls down he hurts himself, but he gets up again."

I saw something in my mother's face I didn't understand, but when she spoke her level voice was no more unfriendly than I'd expected. "Well, Fannia, we all know your kind heart, and obviously you have more tolerance—more understanding of the grosser side of life than I have. I often feel handicapped by a certain fastidiousness—I really can't master it—and because of it I absolutely can't put up with sloppy morals and criminal behaviour of any kind. I do admire you for being able to meet these people at their own level, but I can't—I really can't. I find them so offensive that it makes me ill. Otho may belong in a boudoir, which is bad enough, but Vitellius belongs in the stable-yard and—do you know, if he ever got to Rome, which he won't, I would really have to go away. I will not—cannot—exist in such an atmosphere—I'd never feel clean again—and how dare he?—how dare he set himself up as my uncle's avenger?—how dare he come here and say he's doing it for Galba, it's insulting and preposterous, I absolutely will not—" Suddenly very angry she almost jumped to her feet and I saw, with amazement, that it cost her an effort to walk away at her usual stately pace, summoning secretaries and stewards in her wake and drawing them around her like a barricade, so that there could be no more questions.

"Why?" I asked, when she was out of sight, and Fannia shrugged her rosy, lazy shoulders.

"Some trouble between the families, I expect. Perhaps your grandfather fancied Vitellius' feckless mother—which would have been a change from your grandmother, who was so prim and proper that going to bed with her must have seemed like indecent assault. But it wouldn't be anything so serious as that—nor so interesting. The Sulpicii are easily offended, and they bear grudges too. You are entirely your father's child and I love you—but the Sulpicii are a prickly bunch. Just think about old Galba, and your grandfather was very much like him. He probably took a dislike to Vitellius' entire family because he once saw the mother in the street without her head covered, and after that none of them could do anything right. And the Vitelli may have retaliated by making fun—and being laughed at would crucify your grandfather—and your mother too, for that matter. Obviously whatever happened is still rankling with your mother, but Vitellius won't remember the first thing about it. So if he does get to Rome, don't worry that he's going to come here sword in hand looking for revenge. He's never mentioned your mother to me, and I still saw him occasionally at the time of Corellia's wedding, which would surely have reminded him—if there's been anything to remember. Don't worry. He's a perfect pet. But Otho's a perfect pet too. And no one seems to realise how painful it will be for me if I ever have to choose between them."

I re-filled her goblet and, wrapping myself in a dark wool cloak, I went out to walk a little under a sky that was still pregnant with rain, my litter-bearers trudging sullenly behind, splashing through the puddles and, no doubt, cursing me for a fool. I still couldn't pass the spot in the Forum, near the Basin of Curtius, where Galba had died, couldn't look at the steps of the Temple of Vesta—where they had butchered Piso, and one of them had inexplicably saved my life—without a shudder. And I felt, lately, that other people were beginning to shudder with me. Otho did very well in times of peace, a shrewd diplomat, an adornment to the civilised world, but there was still something very light-weight about him and people were beginning to ask themselves if he was really man enough to go out and fight Vitellius, or anyone else who threw down a challenge. And if he let Vitellius get away with it there'd be others—plenty of them—ambitious army officers who may only want to tear themselves off a small piece of the empire to make a quick profit, but who would cause a great deal of trouble just the same. No one wanted a future plagued by local wars and, as I walked through the rainswept streets that day, it seemed the whole city was watching Otho, waiting for him to change his elegant synthesis for a general's field uniform, and go and settle the matter once and for all.

I went home, soaked to the skin, to be scolded by Fannia who poured hot, spiced wine into me and a milky concoction so thick with honey that it almost choked me. The next morning my head burned and my bones ached and my body's discomfort seemed somehow to confirm my belief that war was coming. The city began to prepare itself uneasily, and, just as before, when men had cheered Galba in public and Otho in private, now they took oaths of allegiance to Otho and wondered, not so much about Vitellius as about who was behind him. Certain names had already been mentioned—Fabius Valens and Alienus Caecina—the legionary commanders who had murdered their governor, Vitellius' predecessor, at Galba's command. But now it seemed that the assassination had taken place long before Galba's instructions had reached them and it looked very much as if, instead of bringing the province over to Galba, they'd really intended to grab it for themselves. They were coming towards Rome now, at the head of the British Legions, at the head of the German Legions and heaven alone knew how many half-savage auxiliaries, and according to Otho's spies, they were treating the peaceful Gallic provinces like enemy territory, taking what they wanted, raping and burning and looting, while Vitellius followed on somewhere behind them, stupefied with food, and drunk every day at noon. And what they had done to the gentle cities of Gaul they'd do to us, here in Rome, unless we went out and did it to them first.

Otho's agents were everywhere now, in the taverns and the barber-shops, mingling with the crowds, pretending to be refugees from Gaul and whispering about the Vitellian atrocities, about what it felt like to see one's property go up in smoke, or a daughter and a mother gang-raped by tattooed barbarians. "Their officers can't control them," I heard as I walked in the streets, and then, when ordinary brutalities began to seem commonplace, "They sacrifice children to their mistletoe god. They worship standing stones and butcher human beings on their altars—and eat them." And after that the whole city mob was fervently Othonian.

At least Otho was his own man. No one propped him on his throne as Laco and Vinius had propped Galba, as Valens and Caecina propped Vitellius. And who were Valens and Caecina? Vitellius, if nothing else, was a gentleman, but these other two were just soldiers of fortune, ready to tear the empire apart to feather their own nests. Valens and Caecina—Romans, or at any rate Italians, but certainly not gentlemen. A pair of adventurers who had gone too far to draw back and who, having nothing to lose, would stop at nothing. Few educated people really believed the tales of human sacrifice. We knew that Vitellius' auxiliaries—disciplined by Roman officers—would have to behave better than that, but we also knew that the systematic greed of civilised men could be far worse than the haphazard grabbing of barbarians, and my mother, in common with a great many other people, shook off some of her complacency, and began sending jewellery, a piece at a time, to one of our estates in Campania where there was a hide-away specially constructed for a time like this.

"Merely as a precaution," she said airily, "Nothing more." But beneath her rigid calm she was nervous, and Corellia, sensing it too and having good reasons for wanting us both out of the way, said "Why don't you go to the country yourselves—you and Antonia? Miserable just now, I agree, with all this rain. But spring can't be far away. Baiae in April is a positive dream." But dreadful things could happen to women in lonely places in troubled times and because of that—and because there could still be a message from father—we stayed in town.

Corellia went every day now to Mars Field to watch the drilling and the parades as Otho gathered his forces together, not only the polished Praetorians but the crack troops from the Balkans who were coming in to join him, not only the dazzling prestige of the famous Fourteenth Legion—not yet arrived—which had put down Boadicea's rebellion in Britain, but a great many young men who had never seen action before and, alongside them, bands of gladiators who were being given a chance to win their freedom. "Superb specimens," Fannia murmured, looking the gladiators over with an expert eye. "None of them will ever come back, you know. Otho will be a gentlemen and keep them in reserve—which is only right—but some hothead is sure to want to take them on a suicide mission, and the ones who survive will just run away. One can't blame them—but it's a pity just the same." And because I'd heard the rumours that, during one scandalous period of her life when even my father had forbidden her our door, Fannia had been involved with a gladiator, I looked keenly at the rows of foreign faces—liquid eyes of the East, blue-jowled, thick-set Spaniards, Northerners with skins that peeled in the heat, men from the islands of Greece and wild places beyond Troy—and, although I was shocked, I couldn't help wondering what Fannia's gladiator had looked like and how he had died.

"Scum of the earth," Corellia said harshly, glaring at her mother as if she remembered only too well how Fannia had lost what little reputation she had following her lover from arena to arena. "I can't stand the sight of them—all scars and muscle and stink—"

But Fannia only smiled and, taking no notice of anyone else, began making arrangements, through one of our freedmen, to send decent wine to the gladiators that night at her expense.

Camerinus was on parade too, riding a dark bay horse, very splendid in his crested helmet and his swirling military cloak. He sat his horse well and cut quite a dash, but when he stopped to greet me his main preoccupation seemed to be with the new hairstyle he'd invented to accommodate his helmet, and his big fear that he might somehow lose his barber in the fighting.

"I expect you'll be able to borrow one," I said coldly, and he nodded his plumed head.

"Yes, I daresay I shall. Otho is taking all the Senate with him, you know, and they'll come well attended. I'll be able to beg a shave from one of them, I shouldn't wonder. I just hope it stops raining for them—they're not looking forward to it at all but we can't very well leave them behind, can we? You never know, one of them might take it into his head to proclaim himself emperor while we're away and refuse to open the gates when we come home. And that wouldn't do. We've got two emperors already. We don't want three."

He rode off through the puddles, turning the dank water into a flying spray, soaking the gladiators as he passed. But no one in their silent ranks moved a muscle.

"What a gallant gentleman he is—this Camerinus," Fannia said softly. "One would think he was setting off on a pleasure trip to the coast. Such courage—unless, of course, he hasn't quite understood—" And anticipating Corellia's reply she retired behind the curtains of her litter and ordered her bearers to take her home.

All day, all night, the rain continued to fall, drenching the soldiers on parade, hammering on the roof tiles of that great, golden house people still called Nero's, so that Otho's guests arrived damp and out of sorts, and these fabulous mosaics were stained with mud once again, just as in Galba's time. The rain got inside my litter as they brought me home, followed me across the threshold, and, even as I huddled beneath the weight of extra quilts, there was no escaping it. It was there, searching around the house for a crack, a weak spot, hurling itself against the walls with a force borrowed from the wind, and it was easy—cowering there in the dark—to hear spirit voices in the storm, warning us of our peril, reminding us how very small we were.

10

THE PILE BRIDGE gave way that night, carried off by the swollen, angry river and by morning all the low-lying parts of the city were awash. High up on the Esquiline we were safe enough—although we knew the garden of our riverside villa must be underwater and valuable plants and statues and summerhouses probably lost—but one of the worst affected areas, the tangle of alleys that criss-cross their way between Tamarisk Street and Myrtle Street, contained a great deal of our property. We owned apartment-houses there packed full of tenants who would be cut off this morning from heat and food, and since many of them were personal clients of my father's, owing service to our house, they were entitled to our help in times of crisis. We had set a freedman of ours up in a bakery on the corner of Tamarisk Street, there was a fuller three blocks away, and then, on the ground-floor of our biggest tenement, a leather-goods shop, another baker and a carver of ivory figurines, all of them freed slaves of ours, running businesses my father had financed. And since he took a share of their profits—however small—their plight could not be ignored.

All day our cooks stirred enormous pots of gruel which we sent, with warm clothing and hot wine and anything else that seemed useful, to the stricken area. And although the food would arrive cold and unpalatable and the blankets damp from the still falling rain, it was a token, if nothing else, of our concern. I ran errands for my mother, made suggestions which somehow she had already put into operation, and then, in the late afternoon, when the weather cleared and the floodwater had receded sufficiently for our doctors to risk themselves abroad, I went with them.

"Darling, is it wise," Fannia murmured, "Is it even necessary? Such a mess—not just river water, but the gutters, the sewers—rats. Darling, must you really—?"

But my mother for once agreed with me when I insisted that what we asked our servants to do we should be willing to do our selves, and merely warned me to keep a look-out for falling masonry, since the storm must surely have loosened tiles and damaged balconies.

"Just keep your eyes open," she said "and try to make an accurate assessment of what is needed. The servants panic—or they exaggerate so we'll give too much and they can sell the surplus. Bring me back a clear picture. Don't ask people what they need because very few of them ever know. Use your own judgment. And remember, our charity is only for our own people. Please don't take pity on strangers. If their plight upsets you then look in another direction."

I got into an old litter—the one our upper servants used for running errands—and set off under a thin, grey sky that held a distant threat of more rain to come. Halfway down the hill drizzle brushed against my face like a fine veil but it cleared almost at once and even as we reached Tamarisk Street the water was no more than ankle deep. Walking beside my litter Lucipor, one of our senior stewards who looked after our city properties, dragged his feet through the mess and said quietly, "It's gone down too soon. Mark my words, it's gone into the foundations of these old buildings and it's going to bring some of them down before we're much older. Best stay where you are madam. No point in getting wet just for the sake of it."

But I had come out fully prepared to get wet and although I knew my mother had sent Lucipor to look after me and that he would make all the real decisions, I told them to set me down and stepped out into that dank, grey world, concealing my disgust as my feet went into that foul water.

I expected chaos, people running amok, searching for their possessions and their families, but the time for that had passed and there was nothing now but a damp, aching misery rising in odd steams and vapours from the sodden pavements, and dropping in silence from the heavy air. This was a battlefield with the fighting over, cheering and wailing alike stilled in the smoke of burned out fires, leaving only the debris, the litter of human suffering—a grey woman stooping in a dark doorway, grey water lapping around her feet, covering the mess of squashed fruit and vegetables that had been her trade; a grey man rooted in an unspeakable puddle of oil and water—our tenant, the fuller—his arms full of steaming cloth, his living too, ruined beyond any hope of repair. And what would he say when his customers came for the togas they'd given him to clean? Rough chaps, some of them, from the tenements up the alley, who only had one toga apiece. And when they needed it—for a funeral or a lawsuit, to get a seat at the circus or to scrounge a few coppers from a patron—they'd say he should have taken better care, try to make him pay. And they'd come asking for payment with knives. It wasn't fair. It was cruel, but he could see their point of view. "You can't leave a man without a toga to be buried in," he said, his jaw trembling, but here at least was a heartbreak that could be mended and I told him to make a list and that Lucipor would see what could be done.

The bakery, lower down the street, was even worse. The shop front had disappeared entirely, wrenched off by a mighty gust of wind that had sent a life-time's store of earthenware dishes flying and splintering around the shop like a shower of hail. The water had got into the ovens and the grain-store, into the mattresses on the floor of the back-room, splitting the covers so that handfuls of dirty straw were spilling out, and lay with all the half-baked bread, rotting among the puddles. Two children crouched on one of the mattresses shivering, holding a wild-eyed dog in their arms, and a woman—the baker's wife—lay close by them, so bloodless that I thought she had drowned until one of our doctors whispered to me that she had just miscarried a child which, he suggested, in her reduced circumstances, she'd hardly consider much of a loss. I left him to do what he could, giving orders that the children should be fed and clothed, the mattresses replaced. "Decent mattresses," I said to Lucipor, "filled with something better than straw." And I understood, from the smile he tried to conceal, that he thought me very young, very green.

The baker, standing in the place where his doorway had been, murmured a word of thanks but he seemed less concerned with mattresses and new ovens than with the five over-crowded floors of the tenement above his head. "The water's gone away too fast," he muttered. "But it's there somewhere—under our feet—down in the foundations. And if the building comes down what chance have we got, down here, on the ground-floor? I thought I was drowning this morning, but I'd rather drown in water than in brick. Best go home, miss. If it starts to fall it won't ask any questions. You'll be crushed with the rest of us. Best go on home."

And he turned away, convinced, like Lucipor, that I couldn't really understand. If I lost one house I could choose from twenty others, if I had no bread I could still my hunger with dates from Africa and caviare from the Black Sea, and if the building collapsed it would be no real loss to me for I could get a good price for the site, or I could build another, sounder structure and increase my rents accordingly.

"Send your children to our house on the Esquiline," I said roughly, for sympathy always sharpened my tongue. "We will care for them until your wife is better—and they'll be safe."

Next door the small, yellow man who carved ivory was prowling around his shop like a caged beast, muttering to himself. His stock had neither melted nor broken, but thieves, he said—'thieves', his yellow eyes snapping, his yellow hands dancing with fury—thieves, calling themselves helpers, had come running to save him, they'd said—a poor, old yellow man all alone—and how could he tell now what was missing? How long would it take to re-assemble all those chess-pieces, all those carved flowers, all those miniatures of Isis and Osiris? How long? But instead of making a start he went on pacing, twirling, hugging himself in his thin arms, and when I tried to calm him he cried out, "What does it matter—just a few scraps of ivory—when tomorrow we'll all be buried under the rubble. Go home—go home to your father, lady. He'll look after you. I can't take the responsibility. If you die here they'll have to blame somebody—somebody will have to pay—so go home now, lady, before the rain comes again."

I left him an amphora of wine and then, because they all wanted me to go away, I had Lucipor help me up the waterlogged steps leading to the main building and went inside, offended, as I always was, by the mean, narrow staircase, the dirty walls covered with vulgar drawings and ill-spelled obscenities, and by the litter which had not all been left by the flood.

"Are there any of our people here?" I asked and he wrinkled his nose fastidiously.

"God knows. They let and sub-let and sub-let again—it's a rabbit warren—I don't know who lives here and who doesn't. The principal tenants pay their rent on time—that much I do know—but what they do with their spare rooms, how many people they cram into them—I really couldn't say. And what does it matter? These people can look after themselves. I know them, madam. Perhaps you could leave them to me?"

Lucipor had done well in our service. My father trusted him and I suppose I trusted him too, but his manner irritated me and instead of getting back into my litter, as he clearly wanted me to do, I walked in the opposite direction, down the narrow corridor behind the stairs, leading to rooms at the back of the building which were barely above the level of the shops and must have suffered damage too.

The corridor had been cleared but there was a foulness about it, the smells of over-crowding and stale food, the smells vermin leave behind them, that I recognised instinctively, and I would have gone away, ashamed of my own curiosity and Lucipor's scorn, if a door hadn't opened and Camerinus appeared, blocking my path.

We stood in comic amazement, gaping, and I thought at first I had caught him visiting a woman—a whore—but the room behind him full of sodden garments and fragments of what looked like books or letters, had no woman in it. It was just a small, windowless square, the floor covered with a sea-weed tangle of objects no one could now identify, and Camerinus, in the uniform he had worn for yesterday's parade, looked grim rather than ashamed.

"I live here," he said, anticipating my question and I shook my head, unable for a moment to take it in.

"I thought—I assumed—you lived at the palace."

"Well—yes—when I'm on duty I sleep there sometimes. But it gets overcrowded—Otho has a lot of friends—and we're expected to make our own arrangements. This is mine."

I had never thought about it. He'd seemed part of the palace, part of Otho, inseparable from those silken couches, the flowers and the music, and the gracious living, yet all the time he'd been coming home to this hole in the wall, to a straw pallet no better than the baker's, to a room without a window, without lights, where summer must be a choking agony and winter a fight for survival. And the reality of his poverty overwhelmed me. I'd always known he was poor but I hadn't realised he lived like this. Perhaps I hadn't realised anyone lived like this, but Corellia would know, Corellia wouldn't stand here, shocked and speechless, she'd remember the feel and the smell of this place from her own childhood when Fannia's debts, or her indiscretions, had driven them both into hiding. She'd know what to say to him, how to laugh it away, she'd even manage to colour it over with her own vivacity so that it became bearable. And it struck me once again how natural it was for them to be together—how right they were.

"You've lost all your beautiful clothes," I said sadly, knowing what they meant to him, and he shrugged and gave me one of his brilliant, Othonian smiles.

"Well—perhaps I won't need them in Gaul. And when I come back you'll buy me some more for a wedding present, won't you?"

He'd never spoken to me quite like that before and I would

have given him a sharp retort—told him to mind his manners—but something, in the wreck of the room behind him, had mattered more than clothes and toiletries and guessing, rather than seeing, the tears in his eyes, I asked, "Did you lose anything else?"

"No—no. Nothing of value. Just little scraps of parchment with words on them—letter, actually. But what can they be worth?"

"From a girl?"

"Why yes—yes, of course," he smiled again, very brightly. "My sister—she died last year, having a baby. I told you about her once, don't you remember? Or perhaps you had a headache that night— She wrote poetry—just sentimental, flowery little things, the kind of stuff young girls write—because she was very young. Well—I liked them, her poems, and now they're gone. And if I write them down myself while I can still remember them, I don't think it will be quite the same. Her handwriting was different, and she drew funny little pictures in the margins, whereas I can't draw at all—well, so much for that."

"I'm sorry," I said firmly, knowing he wouldn't forgive himself if he broke down, and by no means sure I could cope with him if he did. "I'm really sorry. And I'm sorry I can't help you. But no one can."

He swallowed, blinked, and then it was over.

"Of course not—sweet of you to think of it—however, there's no cause for alarm—no fuss. But my dear Antonia—I must ask you this—what are you doing here? I'm sure there is a very proper explanation, something quite logical and ladylike, but this isn't the kind of district I think of when I think of you. Do tell me—curiosity is absolutely one of my chief delights."

"We own the building," I said and he threw back his head and laughed.

"Yes, of course. That would be it. What else?"

I felt myself stiffen with annoyance, for how dare he ridicule me for being rich when he couldn't wait to get his hands on my money, when he was willing to sell himself and sacrifice the woman who loved him, willing to fetch and carry for me and play the fool in the hope I'd be generous? How dare he? And yet, how terrible to live in this airless, sunless kennel, to be the tenant of a tenant of mine. How terrible. And how could I—who owned the building and most of the street as well—ever understand his needs or what drove him on? In his place—or Corellia's—or the baker's—would I be different? And how could I expect any of them, seeing me with all my luxuries, to believe that I could be unhappy too?

I looked down, suddenly conscious of the chill in my bones and of the hem of my dress, heavy with water, flapping around my ankles, conscious that there were rat droppings among the debris on Camerinus' floor, and that I had really been of little use to anyone. I shivered and when Camerinus said, "You must go home," I had no protest to make.

That night a giant, female warrior was seen in the midnight streets, clashing her shield and wailing—for Otho? for Vitellius? perhaps even for Galba?—and the next morning there were rumours of statues shedding tears, of strange animals with too many heads or no head at all, born in out-of-the way places, and every street corner had its orator and its soothsayer, ready to tell us that all these things—the rain, the monstrous births, the weeping marble—had been sent to warn us of our doom.

Our houses in Tamarisk Street suffered no further damage. The little yellow man recovered his ivory and his nerve, the baker installed new ovens and impregnated his wife all over again, the fuller's customers were dealt with by Lucipor who stood no nonsense from any of them, but in older parts of the city, buildings weakened by age or perhaps never intended to last very long in the first place, buckled at the knees, sagged and tottered and, in a few cases, came tumbling down, filling the narrow alleyways with destruction. The rain stopped, the sky lightening from grey to a thin, washed-out blue, but the city was still malodorous and uneasy, full of stinking vapours and sudden, harrowing discoveries as the rubble was cleared away and death exposed as the mouldering, maiming thing it is. And all this too was a sign of heavenly displeasure, a warning that there would be a price to pay.

I had expected my wedding to take place before the Othonian forces left Rome but neither Camerinus nor I pressed the matter and when Otho continued to be gracious and encouraging but named no definite day, I began to breathe more freely. Camerinus was still in high favour, our betrothal still rich with imperial approval, but no one could guarantee his survival in the coming war and perhaps Otho, with his great sense of the artistic, thought it better to wait and see, preferring, if Camerinus should die, to be able to offer me to the next man he wished to honour, not as a wealthy widow but as a virgin bride.

There was a tremendous banquet at the palace, an evening of sheer enchantment, something never to be forgotten, and the next morning Otho marched out of Rome under a clean, blue March sky, taking with him practically everybody of rank or influence, and the devotion of those he left behind. Rome was passionately, hysterically Othonian and now that the sun was shining again—now that the Flaminian Way, the road to Gaul, had been re-opened after the flood and all the damage hidden from view—it was easy to forget the omens and the storm, easy to cheer the soldiers on their way and call out to them to hurry home.

Otho's young men were riding off to war freshly shaved and curled, light-hearted and debonair as the coming spring, and taking his place among them Camerinus showed no further sign of the humanity I'd glimpsed in him the day of the flood. Lounging beside me at Otho's farewell banquet he did nothing to remind me of the man who'd mourned his sister's letters. He was flippant, shallow, mercenary—stupid, even, since he seemed to have no appreciation of his own danger—and when Corellia, waiting indiscreetly in an alcove, threw herself into his arms and burst into tears, he said nothing to indicate any true feeling.

"Dear girl," he murmured, hoping I couldn't hear and wasn't looking. "Such a fuss about nothing. Vitellius has nothing but a rabble of ignorant provincials—wild men from Britain and Germany in animal skins—real fair-skinned savages like the ones they used to frighten us with when we were children. All they can do is yell and scream—and the climate will finish them off if we don't get to them first. They can't stand the heat, you know. Haven't got the sense to take off their furs—they only strip when they're going into battle, which hardly seems the right time, and the summer will be here before we know it. So we're really going out on a mission of mercy to stop them melting in the sun. Two or three weeks—that's all its going to take—and then—darling—darling—"

He whispered the rest into her neck and, as she pressed wildly against him, his eyes met mine over her head and, although he was embarrassed and attempted to laugh it off, I saw he didn't really expect me to make a fuss. Otho wouldn't cancel our engagement for a little indiscretion like this, and as for Camerinus, he had no intention of getting himself killed. He'd be coming back very soon, covered with as much glory as he could grab, and when he did he saw no real reason why he couldn't have us both.

11

THERE WAS STILL no news from father—no certain news from anywhere—and when the Festival of Ceres began in April there seemed no reason to stay away from the games. "It indicates a certain lack of respect," my mother murmured, but she didn't try to stop me and it was a relief to get out of the house. My mother had changed since Otho went away. She'd always been busy, immersing herself in domestic trivia which could have been left to others, but now she'd become almost vague, spending hours staring at nothing, and I found her behaviour unnerving. "She's fretting for your father," Fannia said consolingly, but we both knew that couldn't be true and it did nothing to explain her strangeness.

Corellia was strange too. I had expected her to miss Camerinus noisily, but instead of the sighs and the tantrums I could have coped with, a quality of intense brooding settled on her, something quite sinister which I couldn't penetrate. She went entire days without speaking a word, so motionless, so very withdrawn, that I feared she might harm herself and hoped the games would, at least, distract her.

"Come," I said busily, "Let's get dressed up and go out," and her sombre eyes told me that I was a bore, a fidget and a nuisance.

There were very few gladiators this season, Otho having taken most of them to pad out his armies, but there were still enough charioteers left to make a reasonable display, and only the empty seats at the Circus Maximus, and the absence of able-bodied men in the sparse crowd, made it all seem so strange. We sat forlornly in our silks and our embroideries, surrounded by other women, and had nothing to compete for but the easy attentions of old men and young boys who ogled us so stupidly that my temper frayed and I longed to box someone's ears. But Corellia looked straight through them, heavy with her odd, smouldering humour, as unapproachable now as my mother.

Otho had been gone for less than a month and although I couldn't forget him, I found that his charm faded somehow, like perfume on the breeze, when he wasn't there to renew it. But he'd return, I was sure of it, for with the troops at his disposal and the support of the Senate and the Roman people, I didn't see how it could be otherwise. Vitellius would die, which would make my mother happy if nothing else, and if Camerinus survived we would have to play out the tragedy and the farce Otho was writing for us. That was the way it would be, and as I thought about it, dreaded it, Corellia turned her sullen face towards me and said bitterly, "He'll lose. That's the way my luck goes. Otho will lose and Clarus will come home. He's not dead, your brother, you can be sure of it, so don't worry about him. And he'll forgive me. Your mother won't let him get across the threshold before she tells him what a slut I am. And there'll be scenes and tears—I can hear them already—but in the end he'll forgive me, and then I'll be under an obligation to him for life. I'll have to be grateful—and that won't do any of us any good—I can tell you. I'll hate him for making me grateful and I'll hate myself for letting him do it. It all sounded very splendid, didn't it, talking about dying for love. And I believed it too. But I cheated myself with that just as I've cheated myself all along the line. I won't die. I'll live. And I'll live damned well."

"Why?" I said carefully and she gave her new, hard laugh.

"Don't you think I can get away with it?"

"Oh yes. It's not that. I think Clarus could forgive you. I think he may even break with us, on your account, and take you off somewhere, just the two of you. He has his own money. But would it be right? Is that what you really want? If he won't divorce you, then you can get a divorce yourself. No one will try to prevent it, except Clarus, and you can deal with him.

"Oh yes," she laughed again, nastily. "I can deal with him. Your mother has a surprise coming. She thinks I don't stand a chance against her, but what she doesn't realise—because she has ice-water in her veins—is how badly her son wants to go to bed with me. And she has no idea how one can dominate a man with that—no idea at all. I've had time to think—since Otho left—and that's all I've done. I've stripped myself bare inside my head to see what I really am, and I tell you this, there'll be no divorce. I'm no grand romantic when it comes down to it. I need to know where my next million is coming from, and Clarus can always tell me that. I suppose you think he'd get over me—if I divorced him—and marry some decent, affectionate little girl. And you're quite right. He would. He'd suffer for a day or two, a month or two, but he'd soon find life a lot more comfortable without me. Don't think I don't know that. And your mother certainly has someone in mind for him. I think she only let him marry me as a kind of treat—the way other women let their sons take a mistress and don't make a fuss because it's good for the boys to get it out of their system. She never intended it to last. But what about me? She thought she could dismiss me, like a slave, when I'd served my purpose, but she'll see—she'll see. I told you—I'll hate myself for asking his pardon—but I'll do it because I haven't the guts to do otherwise. Divorce? Like my mother? And what then? Living somewhere in a rented flat with Fannia, letting the landlord stroke my backside because we're late with the rent and he doesn't want to stroke hers anymore? Watching people use her like a whore when they've an hour to spare? And then letting them use me the same way when she gets too old? She told me the other day I'm not like her, and she's right. She's a fool. Any decent-looking man who breathes down her neck and tickles her ear can have the rings from her fingers—her last penny—she'll go into debt for him and hang around like a little dog until he can spare the time to say thank you. And that disgusts me. Do you think I'm going to live like that? Oh no. So, when Clarus comes home I'll go running to meet him with my hair hanging loose the way he likes, I'll throw myself at his feet and get him into bed with me before your mother has time to say a word.

"And Camerinus?"

She bit her lip and then said dully, "Can Camerinus protect me from the things I can't face—poverty and having to be beholden to people, and all that? Would he even try to protect me? He understands about poverty, but he only knows one way to cure it. He'll make you a good husband. He'll behave himself because—like me—he'll be terrified of losing his meal ticket. And if you won't have him he'll get somebody else. And if she's ugly he'll just have to make sure she has some pretty slave girls. Don't think I didn't love him, because I did. But I've been away from him for a few weeks now and it's not the same. I couldn't think clearly when I was seeing him every day. He made poverty sound like a lot of fun but it's not—it's dirty and disgusting and I won't have it. He can talk about the 'power of love' but all he has is what Otho gives him and I couldn't bear the uncertainty of it. I'd be a nervous wreck within months, and then we'd see how powerful love really is. I've thought it all out, and when he comes back, if he ever does, he'll be damned glad that I've made my decision—that I'm not going to make scenes or try to stop him from settling down with you, or anyone else. He talked a lot just before he went away, said a lot of foolish things and made some promises he'll want to forget now—and he'll be grateful to me for not reminding him. I've made up my mind and I know exactly what I'm going to do. I don't know how long I've got before Clarus gets back, but I can't afford to waste any of it. I want memories—as many as I can get together—experiences, fun—the things I won't be able to have later on when the gratitude and the fidelity starts. I may never see Camerinus again. Vitellius won't have anything to give him. So—unless Otho wins—it's goodbye Camerinus. And who knows how many interesting people Vitellius will be bringing with him? All those half-naked savages, darling—just think—they may be something to remember all right."

She nudged me and winked, copying Fannia's gestures and her rich laughter, but there was no mirth in her. She was hard, tense, cheated, resentful, and I couldn't bring myself to judge her. No one had ever laid a predatory hand on me, there'd never been a rent I couldn't pay, no one who could force me to beg, and so I looked away and began to talk about the races and the weather.

Otho won a battle at Placentia and pushed the Vitellian general, Caecina, back across the Po. We heard that Caecina was bolting towards Cremona in some disarray to wait for Fabius Valens and the rest of the unruly Vitellian troops and that Otho, on the right side of the river now, was bringing up his own reinforcements—the glorious Fourteenth and the legions from Moesia, all those crack regiments who wouldn't let him down. It seemed we could expect him home any day now. His statues were garlanded every morning and evening with fresh flowers, his portraits were on sale everywhere one looked, and the city seemed to breathe easier again. Otho would do as well as anyone else, and, when it came down to it what did it really matter so long as there was peace?

On the nineteenth of April, in the tender, pink and green spring weather, Corellia and I went to the theatre and had hardly taken our places before we realised that something was happening. The actors, playing out some dreary, domestic Italian farce, seemed false and distracted, the audience inattentive, and then suddenly there was a man on the stage—an actor or a senator escaped from Otho's custody I couldn't tell—who announced that a battle had been fought at Bedriacum, some miles from Cremona, that the Othonian forces had been completely crushed and that Otho—the traitor, the murderer, the biter of the hand that fed him—was dead. There was a silence—a great, terrible stillness—and then, all at once, that entire assembly of loyal Othonians rose to its feet, laughing and applauding, and rushed outside to find pictures of Vitellius and Galba and parade them around the streets. The garlands were stripped from Otho's statues and piled up in the Forum at the place where Galba had died—to remind us that Vitellius had not acted from ambition but simply to avenge his former master—and everybody shouted, "Long live Vitellius—our saviour—down with the murderous Otho and all his cronies."

"What did I tell you?" Corellia said loudly. "The pigs. The way my luck runs I knew it would come to this." And because her face had turned to stone, and there were sure to be Vitellian spies among the crowd, I took her home.

Our house was quiet, for my mother didn't allow the vulgar triumphs of emperors to invade her privacy, but, although she was nowhere in sight, a man came striding across the atrium, someone I knew vaguely, and then saw to be Sabinus, Vespasian's elderly brother, who had sworn allegiance to Otho at the same time as Vespasian and may well be in trouble now that Otho was dead. But he didn't look troubled. He was beaming all over his smooth patrician face and, clasping my hand and Corellia's, he said almost emotionally, "My dear young ladies—marvellous news—I have received letters from Judaea, from my brother, and I am delighted—honoured—to be the first to tell you that your father, your brother, your husband—they are alive and well and send their warmest greetings."

"How splendid," Corellia said oddly, jerkily, but my father's life was important to me and I collapsed against Sabinus' shoulder in a flood of uncharacteristic tears. "There, there," he said, a man of the world who had comforted weeping women many a time before. "Your mother was quite overcome too. She's resting and asked me to say she couldn't be disturbed. Your father, of course, won't be coming home just yet. He intends staying with my brother—much the best place for him until things calm down—and although he gave no instructions, your mother seems to feel that Rome under Vitellius will be no fit place for any of you. Quite determined to get away, as fast as she could, when I was talking to her just now. Very sensible—although perhaps there's no need to go very far. You have a villa at Ostia and another at Praeneste, as I remember? Yes—well then—I should take your mother there, both of you, and enjoy the country air until the city is fit to live in again. She's full of fears and anxieties—your mother—and I must say that Rome, certainly, could be—tricky—these next few months. Praeneste, that's the place—always liked it myself—mountain air and country food. Do you all the world of good."

"I won't go," Corellia snarled, her whole body shaking, and, digging her fingers into my arm she shouted, "Do you hear me—I won't go. Tell her—fix it for me, Antonia—or I'll make trouble we'll all be sorry for." And she ran out of the room, her feet spelling out their frenzy on the marble floor.

Mother dined alone, and when she joined us later, in the garden-court where we had gone to bask in the lovely spring evening, there was an urgency struggling to break through her composure that I'd never seen before. She intended to leave Rome immediately—next morning—and Praeneste, it seemed, was not far enough. Vitellius would turn the city into one enormous pig-sty and she wouldn't wallow in his reek. We must all get away, put as much distance between him and ourselves as we could. Our estates in Narbonese Gaul were out of the question since Vitellius' drink-sodden barbarians would be prowling all over them by now, but we had a property in Calabria—no, she'd never been there, but it was far to the south and Vitellius was approaching from the north. We'd leave at first light and have our things sent on after us.

"But Sulpicia," Fannia drawled, "he's not exactly at the city gates. He's still in Gaul, or Northern Italy at the nearest—and he won't rush, believe me. Every town he passes through will want to wine him and dine him and he won't refuse. He'll linger and enjoy himself. Really, Sulpicia, so much emotion for a man like Vitellius. He'd be flattered—because he's not dangerous, you know. He's a perfect pet."

My mother spun round on her heel and for an instant she wasn't my mother at all but a much younger woman, capable of spitting venom and pulling hair and making an idiot of herself like the rest of us. But the enormity of what she'd almost done—or said—shocked her back into decorum. "My husband is with Vespasian," she said, immensely dignified now. "And consequently my position is delicate. Vespasian swore allegiance to Otho and may not support Vitellius—Otho's murderer. And it is no more than prudent to anticipate danger."

But Fannia, who had lived with politicians all her life, merely shook her elegant head. "Oh no dear, you can't get away with it so easily as that. Vitellius may be Otho's murderer, but you're not supposed to be an Othonian. Have you forgotten that Otho murdered Galba and that Galba was your uncle? You're a Galban dear, and whether you like it or not, Vitellius is a Galban too—or so he says. You're both on the same side and it would look odd if you went scuttling away like a fugitive—so odd that I really think he'd have to bring you back. People would talk, dear—they wouldn't understand it. In fact, I don't understand it myself. He's avenged your uncle's murder, dear, and it's only common decency to thank him. And if Vespasian makes trouble and your husband joins him, you still won't be able to get away because Vitellius will need you as a hostage. Do stay at home, dear—gossip can be so destructive, and has such a wild imagination."

My mother's eyes were slits of fury, her mouth a tight, cruel line, hating Fannia, hating all warm, easy women who could laugh their way through life, but a servant came into the room bringing her some routine, domestic problem—something she could solve—and our departure was not discussed again.

April melted into a fragrant May and, as the refugees and the Vitellian agents came limping home, news came in with them too. Otho, we heard, had died by his own hand, not from cowardice but because he'd been sickened at the sight of so much destruction and had judged his suicide the only way to stop it. "Romantic nonsense," my mother said. "The man probably died from fright." But Otho, after the defeat at Bedriacum, had had troops enough to fight another engagement, fit men who hadn't yet seen action. But he hadn't used them. Instead of sending them out to be slaughtered, or to slaughter their fellow-countrymen, he'd chosen to die himself. And although Corellia muttered, "Silly fool," I knew she'd wept for him, and so had I.

Rome was now wholeheartedly Vitellian and, as we waited for our new master, life went on much as usual. I took Camerinus' betrothal ring off my finger and put it away with all the others, but I knew my dowry would be just as attractive to Vitellius, and that I wasn't free. Vitellius would have his own favourites, all expecting their rewards, and even coarse-grained fighting men from the North would know the advantages of marriage to someone like me. Did Valens and Caecina, the Vitellian generals have wives? I felt sure they did, but they'd discard them soon enough at the first whiff of my dowry, and I might well learn to regret Piso—and even Camerinus—with all my heart.

My mother became very busy, Corellia oiled her body and had her hair done ten times a day, Fannia sighed, mourning Otho yet very excited by the prospect of meeting her old flame Vitellius again. We waited. And perhaps the stirring and whispering of the spring was a torment to us all.

One night in the middle of May, I went out to dinner—a self-satisfied, self-conscious gathering of the Sulpicii—and, returning home, I was too bored and too cross to feel any great alarm when a shadow moved to the side of my litter and said, "Spare a penny for an old soldier, lady." It wasn't the first time I'd heard that plea, for the soldiers were coming back into the city now, leaderless and troublesome, but this voice was wrong for the part and I suppose I knew, even before my eyes penetrated the rags and the ten day's growth of beard, and the unmistakable, sweaty odour of distress, that it was Camerinus.

"I told you I'd lose my barber, didn't I?" he said, grinning beneath his whiskers when he saw I'd recognised him, and I asked instinctively, knowing the answer, "Are you in danger?"

"Only if they catch me."

"And you're looking for Corellia?"

He grinned again, ruefully, and as he gave a sketch of an Othonian shrug, I saw how thin he was, how sunken and yellow, like a man recovering—perhaps not too quickly—from fever.

"Well—no—I'm not looking for Corellia. I already found her and—let's say she's the kind of girl who sees no point in covering the same ground twice. Quite understandable. Don't think I blame her. I'm not exactly fashionable at the moment. I quite understand that."

"Then why are you hanging around?"

Suddenly the street seemed full of eyes, although I don't think there was anyone there. And the house was quiet too, everyone asleep, except Corellia who would be weeping and biting her pillow, and my mother, for whom sleep, like sex, was a vulgarity she seemed able to do without.

"Well," he said, "I can't think of anywhere else to go. And I was hoping—just hoping, mind—that you could help."

I was, for a moment, incredulous, and then I wanted, irrationally, to laugh, to hurt him again.

"And why should I do that? Because we were engaged? We didn't do that for love, did we? We did it for politics and money, and now you're not a good investment. Look—I don't wear your ring anymore. I didn't love you—but Corellia did. And if she won't help you, then why should I? Why should I take a chance for you? Would you take a chance for me?"

But, in a quick shaft of moonlight, I saw the black stains under his eyes, the unsteadiness of his bearing, and knew that unless someone helped him he wouldn't get far. He needed food and rest and his wounds— because he certainly had some somewhere— needed attention. Perhaps he wasn't really in danger now, but he'd have to be strong enough to get away before Vitellius and his wild cohorts arrived and the mopping up process began. And of course he needed money too. But why me? I hesitated, wanting to refuse, but, swaying towards me and then regaining his balance with an effort, he said, "I know one shouldn't remind a lady of these things— but I do think you owe me something."

"Oh no," I said. "Nothing— I owe you nothing. Go away."

And seeing my anger he made a shaky gesture of surrender.

"So you really didn't recognise me that day? I've often wondered, but I wasn't sure. Well, darling, you must admit that if I hadn't shoved you inside the Temple while they were butchering Piso, they'd have carved you up nicely too. Do you remember now?"

I did, a young man, an officer, throwing me to the ground inside the Temple of Vesta, staying just long enough, until the fiends outside had moved on.

I still couldn't remember his face, had never really seen it, but if Camerinus knew about it then it must have been him, and I nodded.

"Yes— what do you need?"

"Food— a warm corner— and there's a gash in my shoulder, nothing much to look at, but its burning and throbbing— do you know much about things like that? You look the kind of girl who would. I've got to join up with Vespasian, somehow. It's my only chance. He'll need men if he's planning a coup. And if he isn't then I'll just have to go back to smiling at old ladies again— or put a knife between my ribs."

"Yes," I said unkindly, "it could come to that. But while you're making up your mind you can stay at our house across the Tiber— in fact I'll take you there now, so get in the litter— quickly, before you pass out. The house is empty and you'll have to wait until morning before I can get you something to eat. I can't go prowling around my mother's kitchen in the middle of the night. But I expect you'll last that long."

I had no intention of being kind to him. I was paying a debt, no more, and there was no one in whom I could confide. I took him to our riverside villa, left him to his own devices, and came home with no fear of being questioned, for I had never done anything unusual in my life before and no one suspected me. My litter-bearers and my own personal maid would, of course, have to be silenced, for the servants' whispers always reached my mother's ears, but they were easily bribed and, in any case, if they betrayed me I'd sell them and they knew where they were well off. The next morning I sent my maid to the market for bread and oil, cheese and fruit, some decent wine, a cold roast bird, and, standing over Camerinus, I made him eat slowly, for I could see he hadn't eaten for days and would certainly be sick. But he struggled manfully to keep it down, knowing he had to get his strength back somehow, and when he'd swallowed as much as I thought wise, I dressed his wound—not too gently—and dared him to be sick again. I'd brought towels and the things he needed for shaving—the toilet articles that meant more to him, even now, than food—and when I returned that evening with some of Clarus' old clothes, he looked ill but clean.

"What fun," he said weakly. "Is this an adventure? When they come for me with daggers drawn will you bar the door? Or will you just raise your eyebrows and turn them to stone for me?"

But conversation was not a part of what I owed him. "Eat," I said coldly, "and sleep as much as you can. It's a long way to Judaea and the sooner you get started the better."

I dressed his wound again, told him how to make his bed and where to make it, told him how much to eat at his next meal and what to leave for morning, and I gave him money too, rather a lot of it, because something could happen—to me or to the city—to stop me from coming again, and if he had money at least he could try to look after himself. "Yes," he said. "Money, that's the thing. Buy me a sound arm, Antonia, and a safe passage to Judaea. Buy me a good night's sleep." And because he was still feverish I chose to ignore him.

I didn't really know where Vespasian was, but his brother, Sabinus, thought he was still in Judaea and so I gathered as much information as I could on the routes Camerinus could take and what he'd need on the way. I gave him a list and he smiled. "Is there anything you can't do?" he asked me sleepily, saucily, but without his silks and his sexual athletics and his clever remarks, he was just a young man like any other, not too different from Clarus. And now that no one was trying to make me marry him he didn't bother me.

Corellia still loved him. Everything in her sullen, angry renunciation told me so, and I wasn't sure why she had refused to help him, nor, indeed, how she could have turned anyone away in that sorry state. Since Otho's defeat she hadn't once spoken his name. Her talk had all been of Vitellius and his blond, Northern giants, of his generals, Valens and Caecina, who had bad reputations and unlimited money to spend, of parties and new clothes, and how her fair hair was going to be all the rage when the Germans arrived. Yet all the time she knew Camerinus was somewhere not far away, sick and possibly dying for lack of the help she could easily have given, and watching her nervous, painful gaiety, I wondered if she had deliberately set out to destroy him in the hope that her love would die too. There were one or two moments when the agony behind her smile was so intense that I almost told her he was safe and offered to take her to him, but she was too wild and strange to be trusted, and my words of comfort died unspoken.

"Are they all well at home?" Camerinus enquired once or twice, "Your mother? And that scandalous aunt—that delightful lady?" But Corellia's name was never mentioned and if she'd disappointed him—hurt him—he didn't let it show.

"I'm a ruined man," he said lightly. "Doesn't the thought of it pierce your heart? It pierces mine. If it wasn't for the drama of it all I don't think I could survive. I shall just disappear into the morning mist—or the twilight, depending on the weather—with my pack on my back and pain in my shoulder—and you'll always remember me, won't you?—wounded and weary—I think I could shed tears over it myself." And because I was dressing his shoulder and the wound had festered again, I told him to be still.

The villa was perfectly secure. The gardens, sweeping straight down to the river, were surrounded by a thick hedge and a fringe of ancient trees, and the house itself could be seen neither from the river nor the road. Camerinus was safe, but he wasn't built for solitude and although I brought him copies of Greek plays and any new books I could find, he was an actor not a spectator, and couldn't read alone.

"Stay a little longer," he pleaded now, every morning, every evening, and sometimes it was easier to stay with him than to go home to Corellia and my mother.

"I don't suppose you thought much of Otho, did you?" he said suddenly, one rose-pink May evening, as we sat watching the river disappear in the failing light.

"Why? Because he murdered my mother's uncle? Galba would have murdered him, I suppose, without thinking too much about it. That doesn't make what Otho did right—but I liked him. Yes, I really did. I think he was every one of the bad things people said—but I liked him."

"Do you know how he died?"

"Not really. Only what they're saying around town."

He swallowed painfully, emotionally, and once again, in the twilight, although I'd thought he was getting stronger, he looked thin and drawn and grey.

"It was madness," he said wearily, "madness. We thought we were heroes, all of us, but there was only one hero, and that was Otho. Believe me—whatever they say around town—the only blood he spilled with his own hands was his own blood. He was a hero. I can never forget him." I thought he was going to cry, but he steadied himself, sighed, and went on like a man shouldering a too heavy load. "I saw some action out East with Vespasian—not much—just six months, and then I went on to Lusitania. That's where I met Otho—fell in love with him, if you like, because it was love. I'd have done anything for him, not just as my commanding officer, but for him—just for Otho. But this campaign—if it hadn't been such a tragedy I could have died laughing. Half the fellows on the Vitellian side had brothers or best friends on ours, and in between the fighting they kept slipping across the lines to see if everybody was all right, and if they got caught they just made out they were deserters come to join us, until they got the chance to slip away again. Everybody knew what everybody else was doing—if you saw it at the theatre you wouldn't believe it. But we beat them at Placentia. We pushed them back across the Po and into Cremona—we were winning—I swear it. We had it all our way. We'd got fresh troops South of the river, we'd got the Moesians and the overrated, bloody Fourteenth, and the Vitellians were a rabble. All we needed to do was leave them alone and they'd have clawed each other to death. They hated each other worse than they hated us—Caecina's lot and Valens' lot. All right, maybe they had their crazy Germans, but everybody knows Germans melt in the heat, and all we had to do was wait. It was a conspiracy—it damn well had to be. Our generals did a deal with Vitellius—the bastards—nobody trusted them from the start, and when they talked Otho into withdrawing to Brixellium, everybody knew what they were up to. Packed him off with his suite and a few crack cohorts, told him his person was too precious to risk on a battlefield—but we all knew it was just so they could have it their own way. I could have gone with him, but I stayed at Bedriacum. I wanted to do something clever—something brave—to impress him, I suppose, or maybe even to impress your sister-in-law. But after he'd gone there was no sense to any of it. Nobody knew what was happening any more. First we were advancing, then we were staying put, then we were advancing again—the bastards, the swine, they did it to confuse us, make us lose heart—my God, the bastards. Anyway, there we were at last, advancing again, although I wouldn't like to say where, and even in that weather, with all the rain, they managed things so that we were short of water. And none of us could control the men after that—we didn't trust the generals, the men didn't trust us—but we kept slogging on with our baggage wagons and every damned encumbrance they could devise—on that damp ground. We were up to our eyes in mud half the time, wagons getting stuck and horses coming down in the slime and men underneath them. It wasn't so bad on the road, but most of us strayed off the road into the vineyards, and we didn't know what the hell we were doing, any of us—and there's something about mud—don't ask me what it is. Heat, and cold, thirst, pain, there's dignity in that, of a kind—but mud. And we didn't even believe we were going into battle. Who goes into battle with all the gear we were carrying? And then the Vitellians were at us—God knows where they came from, I don't—but our bloody generals, Celsus and Paulinus and Proculus—they knew all right, I swear it. They sold us. They got away, didn't they? Every one of them. And where are they now? With Vitellius somewhere, drawing their blood money—may they rot. Anyway, anyway, there were still a few of my lads left alive and we tried to get back to Bedriacum—sixteen miles, eighteen miles, I don't know—but the roads were blocked solid with corpses—things—my God—I'll never forget it—wading through them, slipping and falling on pieces of what used to be alive. And there was still the mud and the stench. Some of us got to Bedriacum and some didn't. There was no skill in it—just chance. And then I went down to Brixellium, to Otho. I needed him. We all did. I got there just a few hours before he died—and whatever they say now, whatever tales the Vitellians are spreading about—I tell you this. He died because it was the only way to stop the fighting. He had a new army ready to put into the field. He could have gone on—he could even have won—but it wasn't worth it to him any more. He wouldn't let us die for him. Instead he died for us. And if only that old fool Galba had done what he ought to have done then none of it need ever have happened. He said goodbye to us all, one by one, thanked us, knew our names and our circumstances, smiled, advised us, told some of us to make peace with Vitellius, and told some of us to make a run for it. The only thing he asked us to do for him was to burn him straight away because he didn't want the Vitellians to get their hands on his body. He didn't want them to cut his head off and make him ugly. And then he went into his tent, alone, and put a knife in his chest. Some of us made up our minds to die with him. Two good friends of mine killed themselves at his funeral. But I—I didn't die—but I'll never forget him. My God—I'll never forget him."

And Camerinus—frivolous, shallow sophisticate that he was—turned his face away from me and wept.

12

It was time for him to go. Vitellius was only days away now and I wanted him gone. But, just the same, hiding him, healing him, had given me something to do and I would miss—not him—but the pleasure of being needed, and of being in control. I had saved him and so, in some crazy, possibly dangerous way, he was my property. And he was doing well. He had gained weight, his wound was healing cleanly, he'd started shaving his armpits again, doing his nails, and his requests now were not for books but for curling tongs and something to put the gloss back into his hair.

Frivolous, flighty, but stronger, and I was pleased with him. "I'm not a prize pig. Stop trying to guess how much I weigh," he told me one evening, and because he had finally made up his mind to leave in the morning, and we probably wouldn't meet again, I managed not to scold him.

"You're sure you know where you're going?" I asked and he smiled.

"Yes, yes—and I have everything packed just as you told me, and the money and the knife and my sword hidden away like you said—so stop bullying me and come and sit down here, in the summerhouse. I may never get the chance to watch the sunset with a pretty girl again—and such things matter to an old Othonian like me."

I sat down beside him and, as the pink glow of evening faded and warm shadows closed around us, the moment came when I knew I should get up, wish him luck, and go away. But I didn't. The strangeness that was in Corellia and my mother had infected me too and I wanted to do something out of character, something rash. I wanted, just for once, to act on impulse, to be a giddy girl and think about the consequences later. And so, when his hand brushed mine, hesitated, and then raised it to his lips—because what else could one expect of an old Othonian in the moonlight?—I still didn't move. He waited, giving me time, because a kiss on the hand can easily be explained away, but when he turned my hand over and kissed the palm and then the wrist, lingering, worrying—because, after all, I was a difficult, prickly girl and he didn't want another smack in the eye—I didn't pull away.

"Antonia?" he said, asking a question, and then, still not really believing it, "Oh, Antonia—I do so want to make love to you."

"Yes—well—perhaps it would be a good idea. In fact I think you should." He swallowed, very much taken aback, and then rallied because no gentleman could turn down an offer like that.

"Yes—yes, I will. I intend to—really—I've had it in my mind ever since I got here—but I didn't expect—I didn't think you'd want—I thought you'd laugh at me and turn me down."

"Well, in normal circumstances perhaps I would. And in normal circumstances you probably wouldn't ask me anyway. But in these unsettled times—with Vitellius' army coming at us from the North and Vespasian's army very likely to arrive from the East—there is bound to be trouble and the chances of getting raped seem—well—fairly high. And if that has to happen to me then I think I'd rather give myself to someone first—someone I know. It would make the other easier to bear."

He swallowed again and his fingers closed briefly around my hand, crushing it and then pressing it against his cheek.

"My dear sweet girl," he said, Otho's words but in a truer tone than Otho, "Yes—I understand—I really do—and I'm so—so pleased that you can confide in me, actually tell me about a thing like that. Antonia, you're beautiful—" And although it wasn't true I knew what he meant and I felt no fear, no disgust, as his mouth brushed mine, lingering in an instant of pure friendship, before his tongue parted my lips and his arms came, still a little enquiringly, around me.

"Please don't do anything very unusual," I told him, remembering the tales Corellia had told me, "I wouldn't appreciate it—or understand it." And he laughed.

"Don't be afraid—I'll be gentle with you—I'll cherish you. I'll even carry you to my couch like a bride."

"Your bad arm," I snapped. "Be careful." But he swung me off my feet and carried me into the house, to the bed I'd shown him how to make. My house, not his, and my bed, but I'd always known that was the way it would be.

"No summerhouses for you," he said. "Not the first time, anyway. A proper bed for my proper darling—and I won't do anything to hurt you or shock you. Trust me."

I hadn't thought it out, hadn't planned it, and I certainly didn't trust him, but it seemed logical in its way—it seemed good sense. My virginity was a definite liability in times like these and this was no more than a necessary precaution, something that needed doing, something that would lessen the physical pain and moral outrage of being forced by strangers. But I couldn't deny that his gentle, stroking hands were pleasant against my skin and that the smooth slenderness of his body, the almost delicate feel of him, was pleasant too. It had worried me that he would make silly speeches and say he loved me, but he didn't. Instead he took me in silence as far as he could into the world of sensation—his world, totally strange to me—and he lingered with unexpected kindness, waiting until I was ready to take each unfamiliar step, careful not to hurry or offend me, asking nothing from me but the things I could spontaneously give. And his consideration so moved me that my caresses became less awkward, and even when he came inside me and put me in some slight degree of pain, I had no thought of pushing him away. I held him until he judged his weight to be a burden and then I lay in his arms, surprised and not a little grateful, and wondering very much what my mother would say if she could see me now.

"I've never touched a virgin before," he said suddenly, making a confession, "I wasn't sure—I didn't want to hurt you."

"You didn't."

He sighed. "No? I'm glad. But it's not really enough. I'd like to give you pleasure—and there isn't time. I'd like you to have pleasure—from me—"

"Yes. But, as you say, there isn't time."

I got dressed thinking 'I'm not a virgin' and wondering how I'd feel about it tomorrow, and he said slowly, as if something puzzled him.

"Antonia—if I live and if I ever get back to Rome—I don't suppose your father, or your brother, would let me marry you now, would they?"

"I shouldn't think so. You were very close to Otho, and you haven't any money. No, I don't think so. Not unless Vespasian takes a fancy to you and gives you a command. And then, of course, he'd have to win, wouldn't he?"

"Yes," he said. "Oh damnation," and, looking at each other, we laughed ruefully and if there'd been time I would have crossed the space between us and gone into his arms again.

"I have to go," I told him.

"Yes. So do I. Antonia—what can I say?—if you should be pregnant—? My God, why didn't I think of that earlier? We did nothing to stop it—or don't you know about things like that? But of course you don't. How could you? What a dreadful thing I've done to you."

"Don't fuss," I said, "Don't fuss. If I'm pregnant I'll just have to say I got raped after all, won't I. Don't worry about it. You'll have enough to do worrying about yourself."

He got up and came towards me, wanting to touch me again, and I resisted the emotion in him just as I resisted my own, for it seemed wasteful, hurtful, when nothing could ever come of it.

"You're not—not at all—the girl I thought you were," he said unsteadily. "You seemed so aloof and difficult. Antonia—I actually disliked you. I lay awake wondering how I was going to cope. I once dreamed I'd killed you and woke up in a sweat. Why didn't you let me see you as you really are? Why did you pretend?"

He was far more emotional, far less in control than I was and I said quickly.

"Well—you're not the cold-blooded sophisticate you pretend to be either—otherwise you wouldn't care a scrap about hurting me or getting me pregnant—or anything."

Had he cared whether Corellia was pregnant? But I couldn't ask him that and I wasn't sure I wanted to know the answer.

We stood for a moment looking at each other, neither of us in complete control, and then we both began to speak at once.

"I'll get that command from Vespasian," he said and I answered, "Don't forget—you have to clean and treat your wound every day, otherwise it's bound to fester again and then you won't have the slightest idea what to do." And then I kissed him, rather roughly, and hurried away.

I slept late the next morning and on waking—in my own room, my own bed, my own maid hovering with towels and rose-water and hair-pins—it took me a moment to remember what had changed. Virginity—pregnancy—weighty matters, but they didn't oppress me. I'd spent half my life guarding one, and I didn't relish the other, but Camerinus had entered me so lightly that I couldn't believe the result would be pain and blood and a child I'd find hard to explain. I experimented with words—'shame' but I didn't feel ashamed, 'fear' but I knew I'd manage one way or another, 'passion' and here I hesitated because it had hardly been that. Passion was Corellia. Antonia was something much calmer and, with an Othonian shrug, I got dressed and turned my mind to the business of the day.

Vitellius entered Rome five days later, crossing the Milvian

Bridge in full dress uniform, bringing with him his gleaming legions, his shaggy Germans, his Batavians and his Britons, and more harlots and entertainers and hangers-on than the city could hope to hold. His progress through Northern Italy had been one long dinner-party and now half the city mob and a great many leaders of fashion, Fannia and Corellia among them, rode out to meet him. Corellia, in a shimmering gold dress, her eyes hard and greedy, and Fannia, meltingly eager to renew old acquaintances, had asked me to go too, but for once I was glad to stay with my mother. Camerinus had had five days start but was it enough? And why did I care? Standing in my father's riverside garden, wearing my brother's clothes, he'd seemed a different man, but give him back his silk tunic and his hairdresser and he'd soon be vain and shallow again—the man who'd wanted me for money and Corellia for love. My father wouldn't like him. And, in any event, he'd never get to Vespasian. He'd get lost, or get sick again, and he wouldn't remember to dress his wound or put on dry clothes. Yet, even so, I found it necessary to remind myself that he'd been grateful, that last night, not loving, and that the sparks of decency—and sweetness—I'd glimpsed in him would never be enough to compensate for his frivolity, his downright silliness, his weak, impossible, extremely lovable self.

Vespasian's brother, Sabinus, called to see my mother that evening and she withdrew into a quiet corner of the garden with him, leaving me to entertain his nephew Domitian, Vespasian's younger son, a pest of a boy of about eighteen, who insisted on stroking my thighs and trying to get his hand down the front of my dress. And when I stopped him he said huffily, "I suppose you'll be going to crawl to Vitellius like everybody else?"

"Since he's emperor I won't have any choice. And neither will you."

"Oh yes I will." Domitian was clever and sharp and usually had his wits about him, but he was at the age when he needed to impress and he muttered indiscreetly. "Vitellius won't last, believe me. My father'll soon make short work of him—if he hasn't started already. How do you know my father hasn't proclaimed himself emperor too? He could, you know—he's got the soldiers and he's got good friends. And there are plenty of people who'd like him to do just that."

"Yes, I daresay—and if you don't watch your tongue somebody is going to come along and cut it out."

His odd, narrow eyes flashed, anger exploding suddenly in him, and he hissed at me, "Take that back. Don't dare talk to me like that again. You'll see—my father will make fools of them all. He may have taken an oath of allegiance to Otho, but what does that mean. Who was Otho anyway? He hadn't the right to ask allegiance from anybody. But my father gave it—and then he sat back and let Otho and Vitellius fight it out. There was no reason for him to take them both on. He let Vitellius take care of Otho, and now he can come along and take care of Vitellius. And he has a perfectly valid excuse. Vitellius came to avenge Galba's murder and my father will come to avenge Otho. So you'd better be nice to me, because my father's an old man and my brother Titus hasn't any children—and he won't have any, either, because he only fancies old, married women. So I could be emperor after them. And in any case they're bound to be thinking of a rich marriage for me now, and it could be you. An honour for you—so come on, Antonia—stop sulking—I like older girls too—just let me put my hand there—just for a minute—nobody's looking—"

I pushed him away, but his uncle, bland and smiling beneath his anxiety, took him away soon after and I went to sit with my mother again, feeling uneasy, unhappy.

"Well," she said briskly, "I think we can ignore this new reign, Antonia. Midsummer-madness, that's all. We'll close our eyes and when we open them it won't be here anymore."

"Has Vespasian made a proclamation?"

"It would appear so—at least, his staff-officers and the governors of his neighbouring provinces, and, I hope and trust, your father, are all urging him to do so. That is what Sabinus tells me, and I am telling you because, in spite of all our differences, I can rely on your discretion. And perhaps it will ease your mind about your father."

But she was telling me, not because of father, but because her hatred of Vitellius was so intense and her joy in his expected downfall so great, that she couldn't keep it to herself. She wanted Vitellius dead and since Vespasian seemed willing to do the deed she was a happy woman. I didn't recognise her like this. I'd known her to be unfriendly, unkind, but never deliberately cruel, never seeking to do harm for harm's sake, and I wondered again what Vitellius had done to her, or what his father had done to her father, to create such a mighty grudge.

"Yes," she said, "we'll ignore Vitellius. He'll be dead soon. And then I suppose your father will come home." And here, at least, we were on familiar ground, for although she bore father no grudge, she would have no very warm welcome for him either.

13

THE EMPEROR INVITED us to dine and none of us were prepared for my mother's reaction. As the invitation was delivered—a few imperial words on a scroll of parchment—she took it in her hand, turned chalk-white, and went crashing to the ground in a dead faint. But when we had picked her up and carried her to her bed there was nothing for Fannia and Corellia and myself to do but dress in our best and make our way once again to the Palatine.

The trees in the park were green with early summer, all the fountains were playing, and the golden house once again was ablaze with lights, but this time it was the noise that struck me first, the noise—although I'd never heard it before—of drunken soldiers in general's uniforms, and the harsh cackling of soldiers' women. Vitellius had been haphazard in his choice of guests and the vast, jewelled rooms were as crowded, as frenzied, as on the day Galba died. The cultured, dainty Othonians had all gone and this was an untidy throng, loud and befuddled with wine, and, mingling with the crumpled senators and their bewildered wives, and all the old reprobates and shady, sporting characters who'd answered Vitellius' call, I caught my first glimpse of those legendary men of the North, Italians mainly who'd seen long service abroad and were at great pains now to make themselves look as foreign as possible. They wore their hair too long and their tunics too short, exposing thighs full of muscles and twisted veins and old scars. They were tough and noisy and nervous, and there was even a beard or two among them, but the strangest of all was a tall, fair man who was actually wearing trousers and I was deeply shocked when Fannia told me this was the Vitellian general, Caecina. "He's an original," she said. "Absolutely unique. But don't stare, darling. He has a jealous wife. They say she carries a knife and that she used it all the way through Gaul." And, glancing at the woman beside him, a lean, restless blonde in an outlandish, multi-coloured robe, I could believe it.

We stood for a long time waiting, drinking, feeling sick as the wine hit our empty stomachs and I began to wonder if we had misunderstood the invitation and there was to be no dinner. Conversation rose and fell, men made jokes that belonged in a mess-hall, women shrieked with mirthless laughter, there was some flirting, some sulking, a great deal of jostling and groping, and then abruptly, what looked like a cohort of Praetorians shouldered their way in and looked us over, rock-hard, hawk-eyed, to make sure there were no assassins among us.

The new Imperial family came into the room and such reverence was shown to Vitellius by that crowd of ex-Galbans, ex-Othonians, it was as if they all thought he'd been born to the purple. No one, it seemed, could remember him when he'd been just an ordinary senator, six months ago, and had left Rome just one step ahead of his creditors. And as he began his royal progress, a word here, a word there, a hearty slap on the shoulder for the favoured few, men who wouldn't have lent him a sesterce when he'd been frantically borrowing before leaving for Germany, were willing to give him their wives and daughters tonight, just for a smile. I was burning with curiosity but I didn't expect him to have much time for me. His life had been far more eventful than my mother's and, whatever it was she was brooding about, must seem very small to him. But he came up to Fannia, giving her a familiar pat on the neck, and then, turning to me, the smile froze on his lips and became a grimace that chilled me to the bone. He stared, stooping a little from his great height to see better, as if there was something in me he couldn't quite believe, and then, giving a visible shudder, he looked away with shock in his face.

"My niece, sir," Fannia said, pronouncing 'sir' as if she was really saying 'darling', and he nodded and walked away without speaking a word.

"Have I offended him?" I gasped, my mouth dry with fear, and Fannia shrugged her naked, opulent shoulders.

"I don't see how. I expect he's drunk." And I could only hope she was right.

He was a large man in every way, his big bones heavily padded with flesh, his face flushed and wet and over-crowded. He had a wide mouth, a great many teeth, a gigantic beak of a nose, and although he'd once been an athlete of considerable prowess, he was flabby now, his physique ruined by years of self-indulgence. His family stayed close around him—his wife, a plain, pleasant woman no one seemed afraid of, his brother,

Lucius, very much like him but a little smaller in every way, and Lucius' wife, Triaria, pushing Lucius forward as much as she could and behaving as if Vitellius' wife—the empress—wasn't there at all. The other Vitellian general, Fabius Valens, came in with them, correctly dressed for the evening in a white synthesis with nothing more barbaric than a few gold chains around his neck, but although he looked like a gentleman I didn't suppose for a moment that he really was. He and Caecina greeted each other cordially enough but it struck me as odd that Valens had arrived with the emperor while Caecina had been kept waiting with the rest of us. And I wondered if the trousered Caecina thought it odd too.

We went in to dine and as the dishes were brought in all other anxieties faded before the problem of how to cope with this mountain of food, and with the slaves who set cup after cup of wine before me and seemed deaf when I asked them to stop. This was not Otho's food, full of voluptuous nuances to stimulate the palate and leave room for other things. This was food for food's sake, hefty joints of beef and pork smothered in spices, red mullet and pike, lobsters and lampreys and pigeons, and then more complicated dishes, pies and pâtés and sows' wombs stuffed with chicken livers and oddities I couldn't identify. I didn't touch the wine but there was so much of it in the sauces that after an hour my head was reeling and I went on eating only because the slaves refused to take anything away and I was embarrassed by the food piling up before me. I lay on the couch feeling like some dreadful, bloated snake, but Vitellius had a giant's frame and a stomach stretched by years of over-eating, and his front-line officers and the majority of the senate seemed determined to keep pace with him. Their chins and hands and chests were covered with grease, their faces were flushed, their eyes helpless and silly as they drowned their senses in wine and suffocated themselves in food, yet no one would be the first to call a halt. Galba had demanded economy and sobriety, Otho had required them to be witty and rather refined, but if Vitellius wanted gluttony and drunkenness they could supply that too. Voices grew louder, conversation coarser, men of good family I'd met at my mother's house, began to call out obscenities so as not to be out-done by the Vitellian officers who were re-fighting their campaigns and crowing their sexual exploits out loud like a gathering of barn-yard cocks. Galba had neglected Nero's lovely house, Otho had adorned it, but Vitellius, in the space of a few days, had turned it into a barracks and I was glad, suddenly, that my mother had stayed away.

The room was hot and despite the perfume that flooded out of the trick ceiling, and the bowls of rose-water handed round by wilting slaves, I knew I was sweating. I could smell my body and the bodies of everyone near me and, as I watched the steam rise, a woman close by twisted abruptly side-ways and was sick all over herself and the person beside her. The odour of vomit threaded itself through the wine and perfume and body heat, and, knowing I was going to be sick too, I looked hastily for Corellia, and saw that she was quite drunk and that a man—a soldier, no one I'd ever seen before,—was unfastening the shoulder of her dress. I called her name and she gave me an insolent stare—not quite so drunk as she seemed—and stretching out a bare, dimpled arm, started to tickle the man at the nape of his neck and then slid lower down on the couch to make it all that much easier for him. Fannia was nowhere in sight. I hadn't seen her leave but people were wandering all over the place now, couples going off together undressing as they went, or just people too drunk to sit still, prowling dangerously. In his place of honour Vitellius was burning up with a red, roaring delight, drunk only because he'd been drinking for days and had reached the stage of being in love with the whole world. His brother, Lucius, appeared to be unconscious, but one of his generals, the well-dressed Valens, had his hand up somebody's skirt, while Caecina, displaying yet again his ignorance of high-society manners, was doing much the same thing to his own wife.

Entertainers came and went, nude acrobats, erotic dancers, a woman who balanced knives on the tips of her breasts, another who juggled with fire, crude burlesque acts Otho would never have tolerated. They were jeered, applauded, dragged on to the couches, and I couldn't even claim to be sober myself for, besides the lethal sauces, the air was so laden with wine fumes that every breath I drew made me dizzier and stirred my outraged stomach to nausea.

I thought it would never end. I would be marooned here, on this couch, in the middle of this mindless debauch, for the rest of my life. I would die here and they'd never notice. They'd just go on eating and drinking and pawing each other, too drunk even to make love, just fumbling and giggling, and Vitellius sitting at the head of it all, crowned with laurel, until the heat of his enormous body burst into flame and consumed us all. My head began to swim and, opening my eyes to stop myself from flying away, I peered through the murk to find Corellia again, wondering how she could bear it. She'd called it love with Camerinus, but this sordid abandonment of herself, on a supper couch, to strangers, had no love in it. For an instant she disgusted me but then I saw the hardness under her glittering gaiety and realised, with shock, that she was hating it too. She was lying in one man's arms thinking of someone else—of Camerinus? of Clarus? or of someone she hadn't yet met?—or was she thinking of herself, trying to fill up the empty spaces in her life with noise, any noise, so long as it was loud enough to dull her brain and stop her from caring too much about the future? Her mouth was smiling seductively, but her eyes told the man leaning over her that he was a greedy fool, and that if she took his money, cheated him and lied to him, he had only himself to blame.

But every ordeal can be endured and comes to an end, and eventually Fannia returned from her meanderings and came with me to find my people. I was sick in the corridor, sick again in the enormous reception hall, but others had been sick before me and no one had bothered to clear it away. The marble floor was strewn with debris, garlands of crushed flowers, a few odd sandals, someone's palla draped around a bust of Nero, but the servants were lounging around in groups, some of them drunk too, all of them listless and very much inclined to pretend I wasn't there. But I clapped my hands and stamped my feet, scattering them, so that eventually they found my litter and my bearers and I could go home.

Mother was waiting, pacing the garden-court, and her agitated step and her quick, nervous breathing, seemed so out of tune that, despite the sourness in my mouth and the pain in my head, I went to join her.

"So," she said, "you dined with the emperor. And is he as disgusting as people say? No—no—don't answer—it's not necessary. I can well imagine—a bloated mountain of flesh turning mouldy before one's eyes—a ruin—a mess—isn't that what he's like?—yes, of course it is. What else?"

Her violence once again amazed me, upset me, and I said, "He's not too bad to look at—overweight and coarse-grained, but not precisely green-mouldy. He's a big man and it takes a lot to fill him. And he doesn't seem to make any rules. But perhaps he doesn't mean any harm either."

"Sloppy," she said bitterly. "Wild, no good to anyone—anyone at all." And as she sat down beside me, keeping her distance, I realised she was trembling. It was almost daybreak. Already the sky was a pale, empty grey, waiting for its first glimpse of the new sun, and the waiting spread its hush over the city. But the night was not yet over. Suddenly there was an army at our door, battering it down with the force of their drunken noise, and, too quickly for fear, the house was full of military boots, swirling cloaks, insolence and outrage. We stood side by side, my mother and I, with straight backs, for we were patrician women who had been taught how to die, but then the noise fragmented, receded, and just one man came through into the garden-court, a giant swaying on huge, drunken feet, moving towards us in a cloud of wine fumes and scorching breath.

"Sulpicia," he said thickly, and as my mother took a step forward I shrank back into the shadows, for he had come as a man, not an emperor, and it was a private matter.

He was very drunk, but his body was used to that and it held him upright, pointed him, generally, in the direction he wanted to go.

"You wouldn't dine with me—Sulpicia. My own mother wouldn't dine with me either—and you—" His words came clumsily, as if there was a weight on his tongue, or his mouth was full of sand, but before she could answer there was a sudden flash of excitement in his face and he said, more eagerly—

"I saw your child tonight. I couldn't look at her. She hurt my eyes because I was looking at you. I'm a wreck—like you said I'd be—but you—Sulpicia—you're the same."

"Vitellius," she said, "Go away." And it wasn't her voice. I didn't know the voice and I didn't know the woman who spoke.

"The years haven't touched you," he said, tears mingling with the sweat on his broad face, the emotion in him pathetic—ridiculous—because it was a young man's emotion and already his middle-aged chest was beginning to wheeze, his eyes to glaze. "You're just the same. Have you been locked away in ice? How is it—after all this time—Sulpicia—I'm the same man—and even now, if you'd let me—if you'd take me—"

And as she turned and ran it was the first time I had ever seen her cry.

14

I HAD TO know and although her door was guarded I thrust her maid aside and went it. She was curled up on her couch like a child in the womb, shuddering and sobbing, and it seemed, in truth, that she had been locked away in ice and that now, as it cracked, it was tearing her body apart with it. "Don't," I said, trying to put an arm around her, but there had never been any tenderness between us and it was too late now. She had excluded me from her real life and now she'd have to fight her heartbreak alone.

I could get nothing out of her but the next day her door was bolted, her doctor in attendance. And I perfectly understood how necessary it was for her to fall ill, for in her place I couldn't have faced me either.

An imperial freedman arrived in the mid-morning, and my blood ran cold for I knew she'd refuse to go with him and they'd have to bind her and carry her out. But his message was for me and it was almost a relief to put on a palla, call my litter, and escape the tortured air of the house. They took me, not to the golden reception halls, but to a small room set off a shady courtyard where an elderly patrician woman—familiar to me because I knew hundreds like her—put down her needlework and got up to greet me.

"How kind of you to come," she said, giving me a plain, honest smile. "I am Sextilia, the mother of Aulus and Lucius Vitellius. And this lady is the wife of my eldest son, Vitellius. But she is going to leave us alone for a while because I have something to say to you that is very private and important." And immediately the empress of Rome gathered up her bits and pieces and took her leave, like a good daughter-in-law should.

Sextilia patted the place beside her, settled me down, and smiled again. "My son was very keen on giving me the title 'Augusta'," she said comfortably. "But what do I want with that sort of thing? And what's in a title anyway? It's what you do and what you are that counts, not what people choose to call you. That's what I've always told my boys. And I told my husband the same thing too. He was consul three times, you know, my husband—and censor—a very distinguished career. He was a clever man. I always thought it would be difficult for the boys to follow him—and so it proved. My husband was a sound man financially too, but neither of my boys have ever been able to handle money. Spend it, yes, but invest it, make it grow, just be sensible with it—no—they've never been able to do that. Nero, of course, wasn't a good influence. He was a strange boy, an odd little thing, really, and he grew into a most peculiar man. I was not pleased when my boys took up with him. He led them into bad habits—some people have a talent for bringing out the worst in their friends—but I can't blame him entirely because if the wildness hadn't been there to start with— And one must resist temptation, that's what it's there for, after all, to be resisted. I've told them that often enough. But I still worry, you see. One never stops worrying, even when they're grown men. I suppose your mother worries about you too."

I was fascinated and amazed, but apprehensive too because I didn't think she was quite so guileless as she seemed. Sitting beside me, plump and rosy, just a little too brightly dressed for her age, she reminded me of my old nurse who still called Clarus a naughty boy and told endless tales of our childhood, refusing to believe that it was over. But my mother had spoken of the Lady Sextilia as a flighty woman who had spoiled her sons, borrowed money to pay their debts, condoned and concealed their criminal behaviour, and in that case she was no helpless, lovable old grannie but a society-woman with the skill and ruthlessness to get her own way.

"Well," she said, "don't lose your tongue. Does your mother worry about you?"

"I don't know. Possibly—but she doesn't show it."

Sextilia beamed. "Well of course she doesn't show it. She believes, as many of us still do, that emotion must be controlled—as a simple matter of good taste. Emotions can be messy things, dear, very messy. And your mother had beautiful manners. She wouldn't disgrace you—as some mothers do—by a display of excessive feeling. She's always been like that—just like her own mother before her."

"Then—you know my mother well?"

"But of course I do. Didn't you know that? I haven't set eyes on her for over twenty years but my son tells me she hasn't changed, and I wouldn't have expected her to change. Her kind of beauty had a timeless quality. Women like that are never precisely girlish but they never really grow old either. And you are her very image. That's why I wanted to meet you. Your grandmother and I were close friends at one time, neighbours at Luceria, and I saw your mother grow up. She was always sweet and affectionate, but high-spirited too—strong-willed—and we liked that, my husband and I. We thought it was just the quality she needed to cope with— However, I'm delighted to see you and I hope you weren't too upset by that dreadful party last night. Thank goodness your mother had the good sense to stay away. I warned my son against asking her but there was no moving him. I said he should invite her to a family dinner, something I'd be prepared to attend myself, but he insisted it would be best to meet her again for the first time at a really big reception. Silly boy. Naturally, although he'd die before admitting it, he needed a crowd because he was scared. Yes—he's not comfortable in this palace and neither am I. I told him not to come here. Our house on the Aventine is the place for the Vitelli—not here—but his brother Lucius, and Lucius' wife, talked him round. And all those odd-looking men he's brought home with him seemed to expect it. What a collection of oddities. You must have seen them last night. The best of them are only middle-class adventurers and the others—well—one can't address a civilised word to them. But they wanted him to come here—to this palace of Nero's—and so here he is. But I feel sure it's not for the best. He was very much in love with your mother."

She was prattling artlessly, rambling on as old people do from one thing to another, passing herself off as a sweet little lady who doesn't quite understand what her children are getting up to. But her old eyes were shrewd and clear and her mouth shut tight after those last few words, giving me time to realise the shattering implications of what she'd said.

"But you knew that dear," she murmured at last. "You saw him, last night, when he came bursting so disgracefully into your house. Will she ever forgive him?"

I opened my mouth to say 'I don't know' but even those words wouldn't come for I was still stupid with disbelief. I'd seen him ready to fall at her feet, I'd seen her tears, I understood, with the thinking part of me, why she'd made such a show of hating him, but I still couldn't grasp what there was in her to appeal to a lusty, sexy man like Vitellius. Fannia possibly. Corellia certainly. But my mind refused absolutely to think of my mother in terms of passion. She belonged in her spotless flirtation with Piso, her cold manipulation of my father, she belonged in her shrine at the centre of our house, not in the arms of this coarse-grained, warm-hearted, heavy-handed giant. I was bewildered and uneasy and very close to tears, for if my mother was not what she seemed then there was no certainty anywhere in the world.

"Do you want me to tell you about it?" Sextilia asked and when I nodded she beamed again and patted my head.

"Good, good. That's exactly why I asked you to come—to tell you about your mother and my son. It was one of the greatest disappointments of my life. I was fond of your grandmother. A marriage between our children, in normal circumstances, would have been both delightful and obvious. Even though my son was wild—very wild—it should not have mattered. Men are like that and sensible women understand—. However, he was older than your mother, a grown man, and he was away from home a good deal. But that particular year, when you mother was perhaps seventeen, we persuaded him to spend the summer with us at Luceria. Persuaded him, I must add, by settling his more pressing debts and clearing up some other trouble—a misunderstanding—which could well have been his ruin. He was not in the best of health either. His dissipations were beginning to show, but that, of course, can be very attractive in a man and he knew how to make the most of it. Your mother was very pretty, but she'd been very strictly brought up, too strictly—in fact your grandmother was always something of a prude—and no one ever imagined she was the kind of girl who'd appeal to a man like my son and agree to slip away and meet him in lonely places. But that's just what she did. They were so much in love. That's what gave them away. They couldn't conceal it. It poured out of Sulpicia like sunshine and although my son was, naturally, more devious, having had more experience, he was a changed man—gentler, warmer, just as he'd been as a child. My husband and I were delighted. We pressed the match. Our family is just as distinguished as yours. We had nothing to be ashamed of. We thought it would be the making of our son—and I'm still of that opinion. But your grandparents—well—there were other men circling around, other offers—and, as I've already said, your grandmother was a good woman, but she was assuredly a prude. My son promised to reform. He made great efforts. But his idea of virtue was not the same as your grandmother's, and once she'd made up her mind there was no moving her. They would have refused us straight out, your grandparents, if your mother hadn't been so heartbroken. Well—it's done now—neither of your grandparents were particularly rich, and Sulpicia's marriage was of great financial importance to them—there were mortgages, you know, and your grandmother was very keen on keeping her summer villa at Baiae. Your grandfather was a clever man but money was always a problem to him, and my son was spendthrift, I admit it. He hasn't changed. But she loved him, and rather than have her lose her looks or her wits over him, their plan was to convince her that by marrying him she'd be letting her family down, putting herself before her great name—and of course, the Sulpicii make a positive religion of their past. It took them a long time—a cruel time—I saw her waste away to a shadow, the poor child—but in the end she did her patrician duty and, when they'd managed to get some of the bloom back into her cheeks, she married your father. I'm sure she's been an excellent wife to him."

I nodded, too astounded, too hurt to speak, and she went on, "Yes, I felt sure she'd be a good wife. And my son, of course, has been married too, several times. His present wife is a good enough little girl—an improvement on his last one. She's fertile and docile, but she's not quick enough. She hasn't the strength to have any real influence over him. They were wrong, you know, your grandparents, when they told your mother my son would deceive her and drag her down with him. They were wrong. And there are times when I blame them most bitterly for what they did. He is basically a good man, a decent man. Weak, yes, and easily led, but he would have been led by Sulpicia. And she wouldn't have brought him to this terrible place. Tell me, when do you expect your father back from Judaea?"

"Oh no," I said. "Please—she wouldn't leave my father—" But Sextilia's dry old hand came down on mine, squeezing it, and I saw the determination, and the fear, in her eyes. It was Vitellius, not my father, who mattered and she would sacrifice anyone who had to be sacrificed, for his sake. "My son is riding on the back of a wild beast" she said harshly, all her old woman's vagaries gone. "Fabius Valens and that other one—the wild-eyed young man in trousers—Caecina?—they raised him to the purple for their own benefit, and he doesn't know how to get down. He doesn't always know that he wants to get down. But your mother would give him the strength and the confidence—would give him a reason, a purpose to his life, other than this. He has never rooted her out of his heart. Obviously he hasn't spent all these years pining exclusively for her, because men are not made that way, but he never forgot her and now that he has seen her again his feelings have come to the surface. And I know she could save him. You must help me. I didn't want to be called 'Augusta' but since I am I'll make use of it and command you. Talk to her. And when you've done that let me know what she says and I'll talk to her myself. She wanted my son, all those years ago, just as badly as he wanted her and if she had shown more determination, more courage, she could have won through. She failed him then and I have no intention of allowing her to fail him again. She owes me this."

Her hand was still on mine and even as I tugged it away the double doors flew open and the Emperor of Rome stood there, his face yellow from the night's debauch, his eyelids puffy, but remarkably wide-awake for all that. "Ah, there you are," his mother said easily. "You look quite worn out and I don't wonder at it. All that silliness last night—and I expect you were quite drunk. And if the pork didn't agree with you then you have only yourself to blame. It always did upset you. I've just been having a nice little chat with this charming girl, but she's going home now so perhaps you could ask some of those soldiers of yours to see her to her litter. They don't seem to have anything else to do."

The emperor kissed his mother, laughing affectionately, and then turned to me, not quite meeting my eyes, but managing to smile, and now that he was sober and in control of his feelings, there was nothing very terrifying about him. He was a big, jovial old uncle, the kind who always has bags of nuts and sweets and a few sesterces for a pretty child and who likes to do a little harmless stroking and pinching when the child gets older. And he seemed no more capable of sustaining a grand passion than my mother.

"Now then, Vitellius, stop ogling the poor girl," his mother told him. "I agree, she's quite delightful, and you could give some thought to finding her a husband. She's been decidedly unlucky so far in that direction and I'd like you to put matters right. You must have plenty of men about you who'd jump at the chance—although I shall insist on interviewing anyone you have in mind myself before allowing you to propose him to the family. Her father's still abroad, but her mother can be consulted, so I advise you to get on with it at once. Sulpicia has always been very brave, very well-organised, but she needs support in these troubled times—it can't be easy for her, alone with an unmarried daughter on her hands, and I really think you should stir yourself and do something about it.

I bade the Lady Sextilia goodbye and went out into the corridor in a daze, and Vitellius came with me, his bulk hemming me in against the wall. His eyes said it to me, 'You are so like your mother—too like her—but there's something of your father in you too and I can't bear to see it'. But his thick lips smiled and his hands hovered, not touching me, but wanting to touch, wanting to remember the feel of another body like mine, long ago. And I thought I was going to be sick.

The men with him—for an emperor is never alone—stiffened to attention and, his eyes flickering over and away from me, he beckoned to one of them.

"Valens, dear fellow, I'm going to do you another honour. I'm getting so much into the habit of pinning medals on your chest that I don't seem able to stop. But this honour—well—perhaps even you don't deserve it. I'm going to introduce you to this young lady—she's beautiful, she's of the highest nobility, she's exceedingly wealthy and although I only met her yesterday, I know—and don't ask me how I know—that she's intelligent, honest, spotless, a damn sight too good for a dog like you—or a dog like me, for that matter. And I'm going to allow you to escort her—and do it gently—to her litter, and pick out a couple of good men to see her home. Don't go with her yourself, we have something to do here that you already know about, but see you choose some reliable lads. The city is crawling with those mad Germans of yours and every hair of this child's head is precious. Antonia, this is my general, Fabius Valens. Give him a smile, it's all he's worth, but he'll look after you."

He was stocky and very dark, his black hair growing in tight, vigorous curls down the nape of his neck. He was a regular soldier, tanned and fit, with a hard barrel of a chest and insolent eyes that went through the fabric of my dress. A few months ago he'd been no more than the commander of the First Legion at Bonn, a gambler in debt to half the province, but he seemed perfectly at ease here in Nero's palace, and there was nothing in his brown face to show that he'd been drunk last night too and had probably had no sleep at all.

The advantage should have been mine. His rank was brand new. I had been born to privilege. I knew the palace and the city intimately. He had spent years in the middle of nowhere. He was an adventurer, who may or may not last, I was a patrician who would be here for ever. But as I walked with him through those interminable, painted rooms, his assurance irritated me and, somehow weakened my own. Soldiers stiffened to attention as we passed. Lazy, uppity palace servants scuttled for cover or tried to look busy. And although he seemed not to notice it, he liked it well enough and I thought that, for their own sakes, they'd do well to keep it up.

He had them bring my litter, chose not two soldiers but four, and cut my protest short by telling me, astoundingly, that he'd noticed me last night and thought I looked even better in the daylight—and one couldn't say that of all women. I didn't believe him. I'd seen him last night too, in his expensive evening clothes, far too busy on his couch with one of the ballerinas to notice much else. But that was not the point. He was speaking to me in the familiar manner men used with Fannia, or with the giddy girls who allow themselves to be picked up at the circus, and I found it offensive. Admittedly, he couldn't know that Vitellius, at his mother's devious suggestion, had decided to find a husband for me, but most men—especially men like Valens—are alway angling for a rich wife, and if he thought his army manners would excite me, he had made a mistake.

I smiled frostily, letting him know I wasn't impressed, but as I got into my litter he leaned across me, much too close, and said "Will I see you at the races tomorrow?"

"I really couldn't say."

"You'll enjoy it. The emperor's a keen racing man—knows all the angles, backs all the winners. I was just trying to make up my mind who I'd most like to see in the Imperial Box tomorrow—and it's been no effort at all. I'll send an escort for you."

"Please don't trouble. I have engagements all day."

"Yes," he said. "So you do. All day—because after the races—which are my contribution—my friend Caecina is giving a dinner-party, and he's a very sensitive fellow. If you come to my races you'll have to go to his dinner, or you'll upset him. Did Vitellius forget to tell you? Amazing, isn't it? That's why he came looking for you, to invite you for tomorrow. You know, he's really very lucky to have me to do these things for him."

And with that, having converted what was certainly his own personal fancy into an imperial command, he gave me a mock imperial salute and sent me, fuming, on my way.

15

THE CITY WAS swarming with soldiers, not the suave Praetorians or the dashing young officers on leave we were all used to, but battle-scarred veterans who hadn't been in the city for a long time, and the auxiliaries, those shaggy men of the North, who'd never been in a city at all. Even Rome couldn't hold them, and they were everywhere, camping out in the parks or in any shady corner they could find, milling about aimlessly, with their long hair and their trousers and their animal pelts, sweating in the heat, always half-drunk and half-wild, and totally bewildered because there was no one to tell them what to do. Vitellius, Valens and Caecina—the names they knew—were too busy dipping their hands into the treasury to bother about the auxiliaries, and, in the less reputable areas of the city, the prostitutes and the con-men were having a field day. It seemed that when the Germans were drunk they would believe anything, buy anything—public statues, other people's houses, other men's wives—and we soon learned that to frustrate them meant blood and broken bones and sometimes death. There was trouble—over the cheating, the drinking, over women, since the soldiers couldn't always tell who was willing and who was not—but my imperial escort saved me from any annoyance that day, clearing the rabble from my path so that I was home almost too soon.

I didn't want to see my mother. I didn't know how on earth I was going to look her in the eye, knowing she'd once gone skipping off to make love to an unsuitable young man under a tree, and keep myself from laughing. There was no mirth in me, but harsh, hysterical laughter was very near and try as I would to think of my father and the terrifying web Sextilia was spinning, all I could see was beefy, boozy Vitellius and my immaculate mother twisted together in an embrace that shocked me as much as the gross couplings of ill-matched circus animals. I felt soiled and scared, and yet I had to keep biting my lips to hold back those peals of sick, unforgivable laughter.

But she sent for me and, since disobedience was unthinkable, I went to her room and saw at once that she was really ailing.

But she rallied bravely and made a last attempt to get back into the character she'd been playing all these years.

"You will oblige me by disregarding what you saw last night," she said. "The man was —drunk—and doubtless had mistaken me for someone else."

But I shook my head. "I can't disregard it. I've just been with the lady Sextilia. And she told me—quite a lot of things."

She half-turned her head so I couldn't see her eyes and stood, rock-still, rock-hard, silence spreading out from her in ripples that swamped the room and seemed to drown me. And then she said, "Did she indeed. Well, she does nothing without a reason. She was always a calculating woman—always scheming and re-arranging things to suit herself. So you'd better tell me why."

"Because Vitellius is in trouble, and she's his mother. And she's worried about him. She thinks you can help him. And she pulled rank on me and ordered me to tell you so."

"Tell me what? What does she want me to do?"

Her lips had gone white, disappearing into the pallor of her cheeks, and I said, quite roughly, "I imagine she wants you to leave my father and offer yourself to Vitellius, on condition he steps down and gives the empire to Vespasian, or whoever wants it next. She wants you to take him back to Luceria. And she thinks you owe it to her because if you'd married him in the first place none of this would have happened. That's what she wants. I'm simply conveying a message, not offering advice. And in any case, if he wants you that much he'll just come and take you."

"No," my mother said. "No, he won't." And the warm flood of her tears shocked me profoundly. I had resented her coldness, but I'd grown used to it, and now that it had melted away my security had gone with it.

I let her cry and when it was done she took a few nervous steps up and down the room and, as the brilliant afternoon came flooding in through her windows, I thought she looked old.

"So," she said. "I seem to be rather at a loss for words—which is rare in me, you'll agree. I'm sorry if this has offended you. It must be distasteful to you, at your age, to think of me—at my age—"

She paused, afraid of becoming incoherent, and waited, taking deep breaths, until she'd put her thoughts in better order.

"I don't blame you for being harsh, Antonia. These revelations of my past—which should not have been made to you—I can never forgive Sextilia for that—at any rate, your attitude is understandable, right. Naturally, your loyalty is to your father

—as it should be—as I've taught you—" And I watched with horror as tears began to pour down her exhausted face.

"I was loyal to my father too," she said, as if she couldn't hold back any longer, "and he did a terrible thing to me—a shocking thing."

"By forbidding you to marry Vitellius?"

"Oh no." Her eyes looked bright now, her mouth hard, and her voice seemed to hold the bitterness of twenty years. She had brought me up to revere her father, had told me he was everything that a patrician gentleman should be, and I understood now that even while she'd been teaching me to sing his praises, she'd hated him.

"He didn't forbid me. I could have borne that. Vitellius could have borne it. It was what we expected. He didn't forbid me. He destroyed me. He left me free to choose and that choosing murdered me—I died. He made me stand before him, hours and hours every day, until I believed it all—the debt and the disgrace, the breach of family loyalty, my mother's heartbreak, my degradation. I believed I couldn't choose otherwise. And when I'd made my decision I had to go and tell Vitellius myself. My father called it 'freedom'. And having chosen to do my duty I did it to the best of my ability. Your father has never had cause to complain of me. Oh yes, Antonia, I know very well you don't agree with me there. You love him and it has always troubled you that I do not. But he has received from me everything to which our marriage contract entitled him. And if I haven't loved him, at least I haven't loved anyone else."

"Vitellius?"

"No, no. Don't you see? I knew the only way I could live was to stop thinking about him—to forget him entirely. It was easy enough to avoid him. The circles I frequent could never attract him. And he had promised never to seek me out. At the beginning there were times when I despaired. When Clarus was born I made up my mind I was going to die, and when you were born I almost succeeded. But things don't happen so neatly. Life goes on, and one finds pleasure in small things—one establishes a routine. One keeps oneself safe. No one dies for love. And if you imagine I have been pining all these years—no, and neither has he—but a moment came when I was obliged to think of Vitellius again, when he was too much in the public eye to be ignored, and I found it easier to despise him— Self-discipline, determination, I have those things—and I won't throw away twenty-five years of effort. How can I go back now on a decision that cost me so much agony? To do so would be to admit I was wrong, to say that I needn't have suffered, that he needn't have suffered. It's like saying we could have been together—happy—and the only thing that stopped us was that I was a fool. My father would have had to sell his estate at Luceria if I hadn't made a rich marriage—but he'd have survived. My mother could have managed without her villa in Campania, without those emeralds she couldn't bear to be separated from. And I could have coped with Vitellius—because I loved him—and I did love him. Do you expect me to say that? Does Sextilia expect me to say that? Do you want me to drive myself mad? Leave me. Run to Fannia. She doesn't have scruples, or a conscience, or a sense of duty. He was her lover—my God—she doesn't know what the word means—I can't look at her—get her out of my house—and you don't know what it means either. But don't worry. Your precious father won't suffer, just as mine didn't. He'll keep what he paid for. I won't go back on anything—I won't. I won't crucify myself a second time."

Her doctor came swiftly, hearing her scream, and I staggered away completely overwhelmed by her emotion and by my own useless, impertinent pity. I went into the garden-court and sat in the fragrant air, watching the water-lilies in their alabaster basin, listening to the fountain, looking at these familiar things I was used to seeing every day and wondering if any of them were real. I sat for a long time, feeling that my life had abandoned me, until Corellia, who had just got out of bed, came yawning and stretching, to join me.

"Well, well," she said, trailing her hands through the water, disturbing the lilies. "It seems I'm not the only woman in this family who isn't praying for her husband to hurry home. Who would have thought it?"

"Oh—you've been talking to the maids again, have you?" I said coolly, and she smiled, smug as a cat with an unexpected dish of cream.

"Don't underestimate the maids. I'm sure you and your mother thought nobody was peeping last night—because, after all, how dare they disturb a patrician lady when she's having her high-jinks?—but everybody knows about it, darling. Vitellius had a whole crowd with him, and they say he wept all the way back to the Palatine—so come on, Antonia, give me the details. I couldn't be more interested."

"Why? So you can whisper them all over town, to those disgusting people who were taking your clothes off last night?"

"My, my," she said, laughing. "We are sharp this morning. What is it dear, a surfeit of virginity? They say it can do the strangest things if it's allowed to go on too long."

But my mother's pain—too real, too amazing to be ignored—made me unwilling to quarrel.

"Leave it, Corellia. It's too serious. They were really in love but she married my father—and now they've met again and find they still want each other. And what do we really know about love, either of us? She hadn't the courage to take him on in the first place and she hasn't the courage now. And it's killing her. She's trying to hide herself in what she calls her 'duty', like she's been doing all these years, but the walls are getting thin. You should pity her—you know something about what she's going through."

But Corellia's face had gone hard again. "On the day she pities me," she said. "That's when I'll pity her."

"She's really suffering, Corellia."

"Oh yes, so my maid tells me—and when she starts to feel a little better I'm sure she'll be glad to have us all suffer with her. I can perfectly understand it. It helps, you know, when you're suffering, to make everybody around you bleed a little too."

We sat in silence for a while and then I said, "Corellia, I think you should leave Clarus. I really do. Listen—don't interrupt—I know you hate being poor and you're ashamed of Fannia—but you're free, don't you understand. And that's something I'll never have. I shall have to marry as my mother did, go where the money goes, but no one will stop you from leaving Clarus. You'd have enough to live on—I'd help you—and you may meet someone you could care for. Darling—otherwise—what is there, really?—Corellia—you'll end up a raddled old woman buying yourself pretty boys with Clarus' money. And there's more to you than that."

She laughed, a rich, insolent sound, and her hands, sparkling with Clarus' rings, travelled slowly down her silk-clad body, and then passed on to the silver frame of the couch and the priceless gold and ivory statuette on the table beside her.

"Oh no," she said, 'no one is ever going to separate me from this. You can afford to be romantic, Antonia, I can't. There's never going to be a morning when I don't wake up swathed in silk with a maid to help me out of bed and a maid to do my hair and another to paint my face and another to bring my jewellery box, and someone else to hold my mirror. I want clothes and jewels and houses and city merchants bowing when they see me in the distance, and holidays whenever I want to go, and I don't even want to ask how much anything costs. That means nothing to you—you may think me vulgar because it matters to me—but try living without it for a while, Antonia—just give it a try. There was a moment when someone very beautiful came and said he needed me—and that's when I really made my decision, just like your mother made hers. She sacrificed love for duty. I'm sacrificing it for your brother's money. I turned away the man I loved, told him to go to hell, because I knew if I didn't—if I let him touch me again—I'd go off with him somewhere—to some stupid, mean kind of life. And I couldn't do it. And if you have any thought of telling tales to Clarus, don't risk it. Because if you do I'll just have to have a word with your father about Vitellius, and it won't please him to think the only way his wife can bear him to touch her is to pretend he's that big, drunken oaf of an emperor of ours. So unless you want him to know that, keep your mouth shut. Your mother won't say anything now—how can she? So I'm safe. Love's a trap—nothing else—just a trap, and I won't fall into it again. I don't know where Camerinus is now—whether he made it or not—and, just like your mother, I don't allow myself to care. So don't ask me to feel sorry for her. She's not doing anything I haven't done—she's just older."

And she flounced off, yelling at every servant she passed to fetch her this, carry her that, and when she'd gone I found that I, usually so very busy, could think of nothing in the world that really had to be done. Nothing at all—except to wonder, absurdly, whether Camerinus was alive or dead.

16

I UNDERSTOOD AS soon as I arrived at the circus next day that Vitellius had let it be known that my marriage was in his gift, and that Fabius Valens was staking his claim.

I had never been in the Imperial Box before, but neither had anyone else, and so I made my entrance coolly enough, determined to be no more than polite. Vitellius—who had raced chariots in the arenas himself in Nero's day—had made a recent attempt to give the sport back to the professionals by forbidding noblemen to participate, but racing was in his blood and, as I arrived, he was telling everyone, loudly and with no fear of contradiction, what the drivers were doing wrong, and how, in their place, he'd have turned in closer to the posts, taken a chance, cut more of a dash. Valens and Caecina stood, one on either side of him, just as Laco and Vinius used to stand beside Galba, whispering to him and watching one another. Caecina was younger, his thin face and body rippling with nervous energy, but his eyes reminded me of a horse I'd once owned, swift and beautiful and perfectly reasonable, except for now and again when, for the space of a moment or two, she was totally mad. Caecina had that same uncomfortable fascination, and Vitellius seemed more at ease with Valens, whose vices were just straightforward greed and promiscuity—things Vitellius could readily understand.

Caecina frowned at me, seeing me as a prize unlikely to come his way, but Valens' black eyes kept on searching me out and exploring me in a way I found embarrassing and unnecessary. I didn't need my mother, this time, to remind me that it was my duty to marry a Vitellian, for—setting aside the rapacity of Valens and Caecina, who had already made themselves millionaires by the simple process of taking whatever they fancied—Vespasian had still not declared for Vitellius, and unless he did so very soon the confiscation of his estates, and ours along with them, would be the only possible result. And if that happened, even if Vitellius was defeated and Vespasian entered Rome as our new master, we had no guarantee of ever getting them back again. Victory is expensive and if Vespasian needed our money he'd find good reasons for hanging on to it. But if Vitellius gave me to one of his cronies a sizeable chunk of our property would go with me and then, whatever happened, we wouldn't come out of it empty-handed. Yet Valens—if it was going to be Valens—was the strangest husband they'd ever offered me. All the others, even Camerinus, had been noblemen, but this middle-class adventurer, this legionary commander turned king-maker, was an unknown quantity. And when he stared at me again I stared back quite rudely, for he was my social inferior and I was determined to let him know it.

Beside me, Caecina's eccentric wife, Salonina—another social inferior—stirred restlessly. She was expensively dressed today in green silk beneath a flame-coloured palla, and had a strand of some poor Othonian lady's very decent emeralds in her sandy hair. But she was very carelessly put together, her dress slipping off one shoulder, her draperies badly arranged, as if her maid couldn't quite handle such fine fabrics, and the jewels in her chignon looked as if they had every intention of coming loose. I had nothing to say to her. Soldiers' wives, who dressed badly and couldn't sit still, had no appeal for me and when she gave me a belated and unwilling invitation to her dinner-party that evening, I accepted with no more than a nod. She turned away from me in a huff and spent the rest of the day with her eyes glued to her husband, reading his lips and wincing whenever Vitellius threw back his head and laughed at Valens' jokes or put the heavy, imperial arm around Valens' shoulders and made plans Caecina couldn't hear, and in which he wasn't included.

It was very hot, the dry air full of dust and sand and artificial excitements, for Valens, who knew how fanatically Vitellius supported the 'Blues', had come to an arrangement with the other factions, so that 'Blue' won every time, and even a half-wit could make money. Heat and dust, Salonina's nervous twitchings as she clutched at her emeralds, Valens' bold eyes telling me he'd never had a patrician girl before and that he was curious and—just once—a glance from Vitellius, something wild and hot that warned me he could take me for himself if he chose—if my mother turned him down—and I was glad when the time came for me to go home and get ready for the evening.

I wore pale, rose-coloured silk with an opal at the shoulder, opal earrings, opals and pearls in my hair and around my throat, and I had them paint my eyes and soften the tint of my skin so that no matter how sick I felt in the course of the evening, at least I would look elegant and expensive and a credit to my class. The party was in a riverside garden which, ten days ago, had belonged to an acquaintance of ours, and Salonina was less at home in it than I was. The tables and couches were very prettily set on a paved terrace overlooking rose-beds and ornamental fountains, and the servants, who had come with the house, seemed to know what they were doing, but Salonina herself was so tense that she couldn't leave well alone. She was constantly giving fresh orders, having things moved around, taken away and brought back again, confusing her staff until one man dropped a tray of wine-goblets and someone else bumped into a garden statue—a stone satyr holding a basket of potted plants—and came down in a heap with it, scattering soil and leaves and stone chippings, as they fell.

Salonina was instantly on her feet, hurling abuse, and as her panic, her painful eagerness to do the right thing, spread among us, we too became jittery and a dish of sauce slid from someone's fingers, staining an expensive dress, and everyone began to talk at once, trying desperately to pass it off, because no one really wanted to break Salonina's heart, and we could all see how near to breakingpoint she was.

The Lady Sextilia appeared, bright and beaming, and, because of her, the barrack-room manners I'd been dreading were set aside and decorum prevailed.

"You will stay by me," she told me and, safely under her wing, I watched as Caecina scowled into his wine and Salonina did everything she could to draw the emperor's attention to her husband and away from Valens. Her hatred for Valens was transparent, pathetic, totally deadly. Her eyes shot flames at him, telling him she'd tear him apart with her bare hands if she got half a chance, but he only went on whispering, chuckling, into Vitellius' ear, telling him dirty jokes, making him laugh, while Caecina sulked and Salonina held his hand and smouldered with rage.

"Yes," Sextilia said, reading my thoughts. "He was popular with the soldiers—the one they call Caecina—but the fighting is over now—and he can't understand that what my son really needs is a little peace and quiet. Valens tells him dirty stories, and although I can't approve of ribaldry, it seems to soothe him. Whereas the other one—Caecina—is always nagging him to make laws, make changes—nagging him to govern. It's far too soon for that. There's no point in making new laws until we know where we stand—until we're more settled. Otho offered my son a fortune, you know, to give up his claim to the empire—offered him honourable retirement wherever he chose to settle, and the income to support a very pleasant way of life. And if it hadn't been for those two scoundrels—Valens and Caecina—he'd have accepted it. If I'd only been there with him, they wouldn't have found me so easy to dazzle. But I was here in Rome and he had Caecina on one side of him and Valens on the other, urging him on, filling his head with all this nonsense. However, I don't despair. It may well be that the same kind of offer will be made to him again, from another quarter, and this time I will be by his side to influence him in the right direction. Caecina, of course, is becoming a nuisance. He is beginning to irritate me and he's far too stubborn for anyone's good. But as for Valens—well—he's older. He can be sensible, persuadable, if one has the means to persuade him. He knows the value of property. I think one could purchase his silly ambitions for hard cash and make quite a domestic man of him. No, indeed, I don't despair. I have every reason to hope that my son will decide to retire—with the right companion—and leave all this pomp and circumstance to others."

She smiled in perfect content for she had made her plans in detail and saw no reason why they shouldn't succeed. Caecina would be disposed of somehow. Valens would be bought off by my share, and probably Clarus' share as well, of my family property. And Vitellius would then be free to return to Luceria with my mother, who would make sure he stayed there. What Sextilia had in mind for my father and Vitellius' plain, honest wife, I couldn't say but her sole aim was to save Vitellius' life and she'd know how to make short work of anyone standing in her way. And I wondered if Vespasian too was in her toils, if even now—perhaps through his brother, Sabinus—she was making him offers that Vitellius knew nothing about?

"Did you speak to your mother, as I told you?" she said briskly.

"Yes—and she was upset—frightened even."

"Why, of course she was. It's only to be expected. We must give her time to get used to the idea. And before you condemn me utterly, dear child, please bear in mind that my son will never use force where she is concerned. It would be so easy. He is, after all, the emperor. All he has to do is send for her, as Nero used to send for the women he desired. I confess—I wish he would do just that, because once in his power she'd soon discover she liked it. But he will not be moved. All those years ago, when they were young, he could have had her if he'd pressed just a little harder. You will certainly be shocked, but I advised him at the time to seduce her and get her pregnant, and that would have put an end to everybody's objections. But he wouldn't do it. Sulpicia was sacred and must not be touched. And now, unless she says the word, she's safe from him. You may tell her that. Tell her that he won't disturb a hair of her head unless she wants it. She will appreciate that. It may even do some good."

The emperor, who had gone for a stroll along the river-bank to work up a second appetite, now came ambling back into view.

"Come," his mother said to him. "Walk with me and this young lady a little among the flower-beds." And it seemed to me that she knew, without turning her head to look, that Fabius Valens was following us. She stopped to let him catch us up, smiled straight into his eyes as if sealing a bargain already made between them, and said to me, "Antonia, dear child, you have met my son's—associate and friend—have you not? His general, Fabius Valens? Come, Vitellius, this is your business, not mine. Bestir yourself, and make your wishes known."

"My parents—" I began, intending to say that I could accept no proposal for myself, that my family would have to be applied to first, but, naturally, they knew that very well and I couldn't stop them. Promises had been made to Valens, and he was impatient to have them confirmed. He wanted Vitellius to commit himself, to say tonight, in public, "This girl is yours." And Sextilia, for her own devious reasons, wanted it too. My marriage would provide Vitellius with an excuse to see my mother but, more than that, I was the coin she was using to purchase Valens' services, and he clearly wanted payment in advance.

"Yes—the parents must be applied to first—only common decency—" Vitellius muttered, but then he slowly turned his head and began to stare at me, his eyes full of helpless, drunken pleading, a loss of dignity, that made me ashamed. But his mother felt no shame. This was exactly the reaction she'd set out to produce and, putting a hand on his arm, she said, "Yes, Vitellius, see how pretty she is—how delicate—like something stepped out of a dream—Sulpicia twenty years ago. Her marriage must be our very personal concern. Her father, no doubt, would give her to strangers, but it would give me pleasure to keep her as close to us as we can."

A crowd had gathered, sensing that something was afoot, and he dragged his eyes painfully away from me to his mother and shook his head, wanting to do the decent thing, to behave in a way Sulpicia would approve. But some tender image of my mother must have shot suddenly into his mind, scattering his defences, and as the tears came into his eyes, he reached out blindly for Valens' hand—which shot instantly into his—while Sextilia thrust me forward straight into his hot, trembly embrace. "Yes," he said. "You are right. There's no reason for delay. One hesitates, one obeys the conventions, one remembers integrity, honesty, and one loses everything. Valens, my dear fellow, just once in my life I acted with honour—against the advice of those I most respected—and I've regretted it ever since—regretted it bitterly. But you won't do that. I can trust you, at least, not to be honourable. You'll take her while you can. That's always your policy, isn't it? And why not? Indeed, why not? Come then, let me join your hands together. It is my wish—and the wish of some others—that you marry this man, Antonia. You're not unwilling, are you, child? But of course you're not unwilling? You've been raised to marry as you're bid, that much I do know. And he's no worse than many others. He'll value you, child. Don't be afraid."

He took my hand and pressed it into Valens' square, brown palm, and, as his hard fingers closed over mine, there was a burst of congratulations from all sides, people doing what was expected of them, obeying the rules. Salonina's sharp face flashed hatred at me from the crowd, but Valens himself, although the pressure of his hand was tenacious and painful—the grip of a man who holds on to his own—wasn't looking at me at all. His insolent eyes passed over my head to the Lady Sextilia, old and frail again now that she'd got her way, and his gaze said, "Good for you. That's your part of the bargain and now I'll keep mine."

17

THERE WAS NO reason to suppose that this engagement would last longer than the others—just something to tide us over until father came home. I didn't know how to tell my mother, but Sextilia left nothing to chance and when I got up next morning, my mother had already received a visit from the emperor's sister-in-law, who had taken her up to the palace.

There was an earthquake inside me as I waited for her to return, but I had underestimated her strength. The broken doll of yesterday had become, once again, a lady doing her patrician duty. She looked tired but her moment of weakness was over and in spite of all that Sextilia must have been saying to her, she looked perfectly calm. I had expected her to be indignant about this middle-class alliance, to talk about the insult to our house, but she didn't. In fact she didn't really want to talk about it at all, and it took me some time to realise that, for the first time since I'd known her, she was preoccupied, not with the family as a whole, but with herself. Vitellius and Sulpicia, at this point in time, were more important than Antonia and Valens, Corellia and Clarus, and although I'd hated her for her passionless manipulation of my affairs, I was lonely, and a little afraid, now that I saw she didn't really give a damn.

Valens called to see her that afternoon, and although she made a show of receiving him coldly, he was in full dress uniform with his sword at his side and there was nothing she could do about him. If Vitellius survived Valens would be master of this house, my master and hers, and Clarus' master too, if he came home, and it stunned me to see her so passive, so ready to consider it as inevitable. I wanted her to freeze him, to make him feel like the provincial opportunist he was, but instead, her attention seemed to be wandering and she soon drifted away, giving him the few moments alone with me that were customary, but not essential, at such times.

Embarrassed at this unexpected tête-à-tête, wanting him to speak his piece and be gone, I assumed he was feeling the same, and so I was taken completely off-guard when, instead of talking about respect and money, he grinned and said "Well—so it's done, and since Vitellius himself gave me permission to be dishonourable—will you dine with me tonight?"

I stared blankly, stupid with astonishment. "Dine with you—alone?"

"Why yes—we don't need spectators, do we?" And I still couldn't believe it, because this was the kind of thing that happened to Corellia, not to me.

"Look, Antonia," he said easily, as if I was just a girl he'd picked up at a party, "there are about three ways of going about it. I could deceive you into thinking it was a respectable invitation—even ask your aunt Fannia along and send her away again. Or I could compel you. I have that kind of authority right now, and it has its attractions, no? But instead, I'm going to do you the honour, and myself the pleasure, of saying straight out, 'Antonia, come and dine with me alone tonight.' I'll send an escort."

Once again, this was the light way men talked to Corellia, or to any woman who was desirable rather than just very rich. And although I half-liked it, I mistrusted it too and was determined not to let him make a fool of me. I wanted badly, viciously, to embarrass him, to let him see what people really meant by patrician disdain, but he was an aggressor at all times, and moving in very close to me, he hemmed me in against the wall so that I was almost in his arms.

"You excite me," he said. "Oh yes, don't look so shocked. You're not the obviously sensual type—but it's there, and I want all of it. And time may not stay on my side. Sextilia knew exactly what she was doing when she promised me you. You're the real thing, darling. And I have to make sure of what's mine—I'm like that. So you'll dine with me—yes?"

The tips of his fingers traced the line of my jaw, caressed my neck and shoulders and, fascinated, hypnotised, I didn't make a sound. There was nothing in him that should have pleased me. He had nothing of my gentle, generous father, nothing of my airy, light-weight Camerinus. This was a hard man, who didn't respect a woman's frailty, who wouldn't allow me to be tired or capricious, or weak, and who wouldn't always be kind. But the world had turned upside down lately and perhaps, like Corellia and like Valens himself, I was beginning to feel the need to get what I could while there was still something left to take.

"Yes," he said. "You'll dine with me." And as he brushed his mouth against mine in the promise of a kiss I thought, perversely, about Camerinus—who was surely not thinking of me—and it was one of the saddest moments of my life.

I put on the richest jewels I had, a parure of rubies set in antique gold, not because I liked them but because Valens would appreciate their worth. They had belonged to my father's mother, a stately woman big enough to carry their weight as well as their value, and I had never been easy with them. In fact, I'd never worn the whole set at once before, but now I put on the earrings, the necklace, the diadem, a brooch on both shoulders, bracelets on both arms, even the anklet which my mother, because it came from my father's family, considered vulgar. And although the effect, against a plain white silk robe, was barbaric, it was interesting too. It made me look a little less like my mother and a little more like the kind of girl who was going to dine alone with a man she didn't really know.

Valens' soldiers took me to a villa on the Caelian Hill which he had acquired by the simple process of turning out the owners—no doubt the widow and children of some unfortunate Othonian. He had changed nothing. The furniture, the pictures, the silver plate, the collection of ivory figurines, even—and I admit this shocked me profoundly—the ancestral portrait-busts in the atrium, were just as he'd found them.

"Those statues should not be here," I told him primly and he laughed with total unconcern.

"Why not? I have none of my own, and until you give me yours, I'll have to make do with what comes to hand."

But I shuddered, full of superstitious dread, and hurried past them, feeling their sightless eyes piercing my back, telling me that I was betraying my class.

We ate in the garden, two couches close together under the feathery branches of an old tree, an intimate setting to which he was accustomed and I was not. I had no appetite, no conversation, for what on earth did we have in common? But he hadn't invited me for conversation. He'd asked me to come, quite openly, for sex, to make good his claim to me, because he believed sex made women docile. And I wondered if Sextilia had advised him, too, to get me pregnant so that I'd be less likely to withdraw if the wind changed.

My silence didn't embarrass him. He ate his fill, drank as much as he wanted, and as his strong, white teeth went into the over-spiced pork and his strong, brown fingers curled around the silver stem of his goblet, I could see how much pleasure it all gave him. He'd known luxury before, but always as another man's guest, an attractive young scoundrel, perhaps, in his earlier days, who knew how to sing for his supper, and later, as a legionary commander, there would have been military banquets, invitations from the local nobility, in many ways a luxurious, easy life, but nothing he could call his own. But now the pleasure of ownership was plainly on him and, like Corellia, he loved the fabric of the couch on which he lay, the precious mosaics beneath his feet, every cool, golden drop of wine as it trickled down his throat, and his black, insolent eyes lingered on me with the same canny appreciation. Like the house and the villa he'd taken at Aricia, like the fine lawn garments on his back and the gold chains around his neck, like the chests and boxes he had, locked away somewhere, bursting at their seams with the loot of his passage through Gaul, he knew my exact market value. And I, who had never eaten from an earthenware dish in my life, never given a thought to money because I'd always had too much of it, couldn't bring myself to condemn him.

"Beginning to wish you hadn't come, are you?" he said, and I shrugged as nonchalantly as I could.

"Not really."

"Well—really or not really—you're here and I can't see myself letting you go."

And wiping his hands and his mouth on an embroidered napkin, finishing off one appetite and starting another, he crossed from his couch to mine and kissed me as heartily as if he'd been kissing me for years and saw no reason to make a fuss about it.

Camerinus had hesitated, his first kiss had asked a question, but Valens considered the question already answered—if there'd ever been a doubt in his mind to start with. He had no whimsical, romantic ideas about carrying me to my bridal bed, no ideas at all other than to enjoy me and possess me as he had everything else. His body was harder, heavier, than Camerinus', his hands taking rather than teaching, and there was a moment of protest when I stiffened under him and, quite ridiculously, wanted my mother to come and take me away. But then I rallied. I wouldn't be treated like this, I wouldn't be a spoil of war, a silly, passive female who allowed herself to be used just to give pleasure to someone else. I'd fight him. And as I put my hands into his hair and my nails into his back, as I put my teeth into his tongue and the soft parts of his cheek and the point of his shoulder where I could feel bone, something incredible happened. The Antonia I knew, the cool, reasonable girl I didn't always care for, slid out of my body, leaving me with a panting frenzy that I'd do anything to bring to a conclusion. And as our bodies crushed together, the hot, quivering stream of joy that Camerinus had wanted to give me, flowed over me, touching every nerve, nailing me to this man whose strength burned inside me and then receded, taking my will with it, so that I was as breathless and bewildered, and every bit as docile as he could wish.

"Good girl," he said, patting my thigh. "Good girl. You're going to be important to me—money, beauty, education, and you even like it in bed. You're the best thing I've got."

And, propping himself up on one elbow, he leaned over me, his black eyes dancing with mischief, and said, "Tell me again how rich you are?"

"All of it?"

"All of it."

"Well—estates in Campania, Apulia, Etruria, Lucania, Calabria, Toscana—big estates, lots of farms and vineyards and cattle and horses. Property in Rome, streets of tenements in the Subura, and decent houses on the Aventine and the Quirinal. Warehouses and flats at Ostia, and a villa there too. About half of Praeneste and a lot of Carsulae, Mevania, Tarracina. A lovely old house on the lake at Como, and some farms there too. Villas and farms near Misenum and Minturnae, and a spectacular place at Baiae overlooking the sea. And then my father had very complicated financial interests, and an army of clients, just about all over the place. I only know about the land and the buildings, but I think he could raise its value twice over from other sources."

"You're beautiful," he said.

"Yes—and then there's my uncle, Aulus, my father's brother. He's very nearly as rich as father, and he hasn't any children. So I inherit from him too. I suppose that helps?"

He laughed and got to his feet, stretching himself in the warm, summer air, sleek and self-satisfied, and as I reached for my clothes, he said, "No—no—no. Stay like that for a while. Put your jewels on if you like, but nothing else." And pouring more wine he came back to the couch.

"Yes," he said. "I stole all this. And now I've got you too. You're my legal title to all my loot. You make it right for me. And because of that, and because you appeal to me in other ways, we'll do well together. And I won't even ask you why you weren't a virgin."

"Does that matter?"

"Yes—but I'd be an unreasonable man to start complaining, considering what you're bringing me. And in any case you're the type who'd still look untouched if you were the mother of ten children."

He picked up my grandmother's ruby necklace, weighing it for a moment in his hand, and then clasped it around my neck. The jewels were cold against my skin but as he traced their outline with the tips of his fingers my body began to glow again, something inside me stirring with the eagerness of a young animal. "Yes, we'll do well together," he murmured. "You're not used to this, are you? How many times before, eh? Not more than once or twice, I'll be bound. Some young patrician, I expect, on his way to war. Don't worry. I understand. These things happen. And he won't come near you again, I'll see to that. Does it shock you to find you can want a man like me?"

"I think it shocks me that my body can feel like this at all. But I'm not complaining. And as for a man like you—I don't really know what you're like."

"Greedy," he said, "And I've been greedy a long time. You won't understand, because you've been rich all your life, but ambition in a poor man can hurt—really hurt, like a knife in the gut. In fact it's better to be without it. I was born south of here, at Anagnia—you must know where that is if you have property at Tarracina. And the rest of my family were content to stay there. They've got a decent house, equestrian status, local magistracies. You'd call them poor, and so do I, but they're satisfied. And that's something I've never been—satisfied. I came to Rome as a lad but there was nothing for me here—just hanging around rich men's halls on the off-chance of getting noticed, and seeing girls like you and thinking what I'd do if I could get my hands on one of them. Rome was for rich men's sons, who could buy the future, and the army was the only chance I had. I've seen service all over the damned empire, and army life's not all bad. Not too much responsibility and not too much hard work, if you know how to go about it. I spent years of my life living from one day to the next, from one throw of the dice to the next—because I'm a gambler, and that's something you have to know about me. You'll just have to put up with it. Either you're a gambler or you're not, and if you're not you won't understand it. But it's in me and there's no cure. So—I ended up a legionary commander in a god-forsaken hole like Bonn. And that was good going for a poor lad from Anagnia, a damn sight more than my father ever expected of me, although he wouldn't have been too surprised to learn I was in debt to half the province. And when you're in debt the dice know it, the horses know it, the swordfighters you back lie down and die—and if the governor of your province happens to be Fronteius Capito, you may just as well put a knife in your own heart. Capito didn't allow his commanders to be in debt—it sets a bad example to the men—you can't very well tick them off for doing the things you're doing yourself. So the mutiny was made for men like me. I got rid of Capito all right. And I didn't do it for your uncle Galba, either. I did it for myself, because if I hadn't put him out of the way he'd have had me cashiered. It was a gamble—like everything always is with me. The men didn't know Galba—didn't know what to expect from him—and Caecina came in very handy there because the riff-raff took a shine to him and he was good at going around telling them what a mean old bastard Galba was, and how the work would go up and the pay down—it wasn't difficult. The province was seething long before Nero died and it was easy to bring it back to the boil. I didn't plan it in any great detail. I just wanted to stir up enough trouble to tide me over a bad patch, because as soon as things got back to normal my creditors would be after me again. And then Capito's replacement arrived—Vitellius, no less. I don't know if it was me or Caecina who realised it first, but he was made for us. He didn't want to be an emperor. It hadn't even crossed his mind. He was just grateful to be out of Rome—away from his own debts—and in a job where he had a chance of making a quick profit. But one thing led to another and we decided that if we could bleed Germany white so easily, we may as well have it all. Caecina went on talking to the soldiers, and I went on talking to Vitellius, letting him think Galba was on to him and that he'd got nothing to lose, and that did the trick. He's nobody's idea of a hero, our Vitellius. He's no soldier either. But he had me and Caecina to fight his battles for him, and once we'd pushed him far enough he was too scared to stop. He gambled—like I did—and we won. And if we'd lost—if we'd been beaten at Cremona—at least we'd have had fun on the way down. Thank God Otho hadn't the guts to see it through. They can say what they like about him sacrificing himself to save his men, but the silly sod just lost his nerve. I've seen it happen hundreds of times. And I tell you this, if I'd been with him he wouldn't have put that knife into himself. I'd have bound him hand and foot until we hadn't a man left standing to put into the field. Spineless fool. The gods must have been thinking of me when they made Otho."

"And Vespasian?"

His eyes twinkled down at me. "If he's greedy too then he won't be any problem."

"Will he negotiate?" I began, eager to know, but he laughed, shaking his head, and scooped me into his arms.

"Negotiate? You mean will he do a deal? Will he let himself be bought? How can I know what he'll do? I'm just a legionary commander in a general's uniform—isn't that what you and your mother think of me? What do I know of state secrets? But I know about you—now—oh yes, and I know what you want, although you'd die before admit it. And I want you too—just let me move the lamp so I can see your rubies smiling at me—definitely—you're the best thing I've got."

And once again his hard, soldier's body forced mine to that high peak of joy and left me dizzy and aching. Being with him was like learning to speak all over again in a foreign tongue, but the whole world was so strange to me just then—since my mother had toppled out of her shrine—that I could do no more than take each hour as it came. Tomorrow Vitellius could be dead and Vespasian supreme, or the wild Germans, still prowling in every corner of the city, could go finally berserk and massacre us all in our beds. And compared with that, what did my fall from grace really matter? And, in this crazy world why should it be so impossible to dislike a man and desire him at the same time? He was a brutal aggressor, who stole unashamedly, like a common pirate, who had called Otho a coward, who wasn't Camerinus. Yet, just the same, as he took me to my litter, and leaned over me, admiring the effect of my grandmother's jewels in the moonlight, I said suddenly, "I hope you make it, Valens."

And he laughed, his eyes full of their insolent sparkle, and answered, "Well, either way, it's better than the military prison at Bonn."

18

SUMMER. BRILLIANT BLUE and gold days, airless, restless nights, and a city gone wild with pleasure, caught up in Vitellius' whirlwind, spinning round and round with him into exhaustion as every sultry day threw down its offerings of banquets and picnics, of wild-beast hunts and gladiatorial displays, and charioteers pounding endlessly around their track, promising easy gains and sudden death and the hectic, holiday atmosphere that stops men from thinking about the future.

A frenzied, sun-dappled season, when our household ceased to exist as a unit. The conventions which had held us together, and which we'd thought unbreakable, split apart and we became individuals, living separately under one roof, knowing, as the whole city knew, that nothing was permanent, nothing quite what it seemed. It was a time for fun at any price, parties that went on for days, frantic spending while there was still something to buy, self-indulgence before one's opportunities ran out, and both Fannia, who was at the end of her looks, and Corellia, at the end of her freedom, plunged headlong into the golden flood and seemed certain to drown.

But my mother—that smooth pillar of marble on which we'd all built our lives—withdrew so completely that only her body was left, sitting quietly among us, no longer caring what we were up to. Corellia and I could come and go as we pleased, the maids neglected their work, the stewards were left to make whatever arrangements they liked, so that, gradually, no proper arrangements were made at all, and my mother said not a word. She had spent twenty-five years of her life running this house with matchless efficiency, and now she didn't care what happened to it. She'd gone away, back to some impossible Vitellian springtime, and as far as she was concerned, we could all go away too.

"Is she planning to leave my father?" I asked Fannia, in despair, because how would my father ever cope with a blow like that, and Fannia sighed and shook her head.

"Well, if she is, then you must talk her out of it, because I'm not clever but I do know about men, and I know your mother couldn't live with Vitellius. Not as he is now. She may have some kind of romantic dream of reforming him and healing him, and I'm not saying his intentions are bad. He'd like to be healed and loved—he'd like to be a good man. But, you know, if you think about it, you'll realise that there's only one person who's been stopping him from being a good man all these years, and that's Vitellius himself. The flaw is in him—just as it's in me—and that's how I know. It's all very well to blame life—to say 'I never had a chance and if only they'd let me marry this girl, or if I'd got that appointment, or if my father hadn't lost his money, everything would have been different.' But it's not so. Vitellius thinks all his troubles come from not being able to marry Sulpicia but it would have been just the same whether he'd married her or not. He'd still have been Vitellius, wouldn't he? And he's made that way. Sulpicia could never have changed him. I know it, Sextilia knows it too, if she'd be honest with herself, and your mother knows it in her heart, because that was the reason she turned him down in the first place. But now she wants to convince herself she was wrong, because she wants to try again. And that would be all right if she was the kind of woman who understood the coarser side of a man. But the only man she really knows is your father, and he hasn't a coarse bone in his body. She'd be a lamb to the slaughter. Vitellius would be awfully grateful for a while. He'd hold her hand and talk a lot of sentimental nonsense, but eventually he'd do something to upset her—which you must admit isn't difficult—and imagine how terrible it would be if after cherishing such fond dreams of each other all these years—and after breaking your father's heart—they were to discover that, well, she's a bore and he's a thoroughly dirty old man. Would your mother survive such disillusion? And I must say this to you. Antonia—be very careful with Sextilia. She's a dangerous woman and she's playing your mother at her own game. Your mother used my daughter—don't think I'm not aware of it—to pacify your brother, and she always intended to get rid of her when she'd served her purpose. Well, Sextilia is using your mother in exactly the same way. She needs her now to induce Vitellius to abdicate, but she's a shrewd old bird and she knows they couldn't possibly stay together for long. And she won't care what happens to your mother when it's over—when she's disgraced herself and destroyed her family—she won't even want to know about Sulpicia, just so long as Vitellius is all right."

Fannia, who had hoped to get Vitellius for herself, couldn't quite conceal her pique, but Corellia was overjoyed by my mother's troubles and let everyone know it. She liked to see her in pain, expected it to get much worse before it was mended, and laughed herself silly ten times a day about the pictures such an ill-assorted couple brought to mind. She considered herself perfectly safe now, for if my mother said one word to Clarus, she'd have two to say to my father and—with Clarus, surely, not too far away now if the rumours about Vespasian were to be believed—her behaviour took on the notes of a glorious, desperate swan-song. An indiscriminate host of men passed in and out of her life—an incoherent blond giant from the army of the Rhine, suave old Othonians, hawk-eyed financiers who secretly regretted Galba, a thin, eager man supposed to be in Vespasian's pay, and, just occasionally, Vespasian's vicious, clever son, Domitian.

"I'm non-political," she declared, "and who's going to tell tales on me now, I'd like to know? Not your mother, and not you either, now, eh, now that you know what it feels like. You'll end up getting yourself pregnant, Antonia—nice girls like you always do—so watch yourself or it may be a bit of a nuisance when they throw Vitellius out and Vespasian comes along with another husband for you?"

But pregnancy was her demon, not mine, and every month, as she waited to see if this final disaster had overtaken her, fear twisted her stomach to nausea and frayed her nerves to screaming pitch. In the early days she could have passed it off as my brother's doing, but he'd been away almost five months now and he wouldn't find her desirable—or forgivable—if her body was swollen with another man's child. She swallowed everything Fannia knew about and everything the maids knew about, she visited sinister old women and eloquent Greek doctors in back alleys, and took everything they gave her in double quantities, so that I often feared for her life.

"You'll poison yourself," I told her, but it made no difference.

"What of it. I'd rather be dead than pregnant."

"Well then—you'll get so sick you'll lose your looks. You'll make your hair drop out and you'll get spots—and if you go around stinking of vinegar like that nobody is going to want to get close to you anyway."

"I don't care if I go bald. Clarus won't care. He'll just have to buy me a wig. I can cope with being bald, or dead, but not pregnant, because being pregnant means being poor again, and I can't cope with that. And I haven't much time left. Haven't you heard the rumours? They say all the Eastern provinces are declaring for Vespasian. Nobody's supposed to know—if you get caught talking about it you get your throat cut—but everybody's talking about it just the same. Whisper in your general's ear tonight and see what he can tell you. He must know what's going on, because he'll be the one who has to go out and fight Vespasian—if there's an army left to fight with, that is."

And, indeed, what had happened to those crack troops from the Rhine? Valens and Caecina had promised them loot and glory if they would bring Vitellius to Rome, but now that they'd installed him on the Palatine there seemed no plan any more—nothing for them to do—and the generals had abandoned them to a city-life they couldn't understand and a heat-wave that was doing them no good. There was still a lot of fighting and whoring and thieving, but there was sickness too, and there were areas of the city now into which one didn't go because the Germans were dying there from the fevers that came creeping up the river every year with the summer wind.

"It can't be helped," Valens told me bluntly, "It's always the same. They see action, they get paid, they go whoring, they get sick. But they'll get on their feet again when we need them—if we need them—and if we don't, then the sooner we get them back to where they came from the better."

"Will you need them again?"

"Who knows—who knows?" And he laughed and put his hands on me, his fingers searching through my skin to the bones, the nerves, the pulse-beats, to the sensuality he'd unlocked in me, and which had been no surprise to him at all.

"Do you get your way so easily with all the women you fancy?" I asked, fighting what could only be jealousy, and, suspecting that I was going to question him about his past and tell him he'd have to be faithful to me in the future, he closed my mouth with his own and gave me other things to think about.

I was his prize possession, the untouchable patrician girl who could be touched now whenever he liked, and he wanted me with him wherever he went. Dinners and receptions, long, hot days at the circus, visits to racing-stables which turned into painful drinking bouts, visits to villas and gardens to which he'd taken a fancy and which, soon after, always came into his possession. I waited for him, my head decently covered, while he bullied the Senate into glorifying Vitellius' few, rather vague policies. I walked with him on Mars Field, where he was saluted and cheered and made much of. And in all these public places I let him put his square, brown hand on my knee or my breast whenever the mood took him, possessing me before the whole world, telling everybody, 'This woman is mine.' A few months ago I'd been Galba's great-niece, promised to a man who was descended from Pompey the Great, but now I was Fabius Valens' woman—no more.

I listened to him, not always with pleasure, for he could be boastful and arrogant and crude, as he told his tales about Germany and Gaul and dropped hints about the wild British women he'd tamed. I heard him speak to men twice his age and a hundred times his rank as if they were beggars at his gate, yet, although his greed and his cynicism and his occasional flashes of cruelty distressed me, there was a directness about him that I couldn't dislike. I had been hamstrung all my life by the conventions, by my mother's enormous preoccupation with what was 'done' and what must not be done. But Valens had no rules at all. He ate when he was hungry, said what he had to say, took whatever he could lay his hands on, and when I tried again to question him about Vespasian—about the future—all I could gather was that he saw no cause for alarm.

Vitellius, as one of his first acts on entering Rome, had upset the list of consuls so that Valens and Caecina could take office immediately, and although neither of them had ever set foot in the Senate House before and had no idea how to proceed, Caecina, at least, had tried to learn. But Valens found the processes of government a dead bore. When he wanted something done he took his sword and an armed escort with him and was so irritated by political life that I could only conclude he didn't intend to be involved with it for much longer. He was waiting, although he wouldn't say so, for my mother to make her mind up about Vitellius. And as soon as she did and Vitellius agreed to abdicate then Valens would dispose of the troublesome Caecina, lay down his own emblems of office, marry me, and live luxuriously, for as long as he could, on what I brought him and what he'd grabbed for himself. That, I believed, was his bargain with Sextilia, and it presented me with problems I couldn't resolve, for, as my ears grew accustomed to the harsh note of his voice and my body relaxed in his energetic embrace, I found that the gulf between what I wanted and what I knew I ought to want was widening.

He was necessary to my house, no more. But my body—far ahead of my mind—fell into the snare Nature had set for me. I discovered that pleasure awakens need, and, when he wasn't there, my breasts and the pit of my stomach and the whole eager surface of my skin soon learned to ache for him. I was ashamed and tried to deny it but when he went out of town with Vitellius and I didn't see him for three days I hungered and thirsted. And when he came back the mere touch of his hand on my thigh, scorching through the silk of my dress, released physical sensations that shattered me. "So," he said, grinning complacently, "it seems you're the kind of girl who can't be left alone for long. I'll take you with me next time." And so he did.

We went to my father's house at Ostia and spent ten days by the sea, days when my joy was as intense as the hot sunlight, when I was dizzy and enraptured and enslaved, and the world ended at the foot of my bed. He took me, dangerously, into the sea or scrambling up some rocky pinnacle to make love surrounded by blue air and blue water and the odours of salt and sand and wild summer flowers. And when I came back to Rome, after those few days of careless, perfect freedom, my body at least was not the same. I could feel the sleekness of my own skin and the muscles rippling beneath it, I felt light and strong and powerful, and my ears were full of the music Valens' hard hands released in me. I felt ripe and luscious and beautiful. But my father was still with Vespasian and if he returned, with Vespasian's armies, and stabbed Valens to the heart, what would I do then? And what would I do if it was Valens—with his keen eyes and his steady aim—who drew his dagger first and killed my father?

My duty was to my family. I had no doubts about it. And so I tried to justify what I was doing with Valens—what I was starting to feel for him—by calling it another name.

"It seems—sometimes—that we're friends," I tried to explain to Fannia, but Corellia, who was sitting with us, brooding over her own fate in a mirror, suddenly burst out, "Friendship—that's a new name for it. And we'll see what happens to friendship when the war starts again. Your father and your brother are with Vespasian, darling, or had you forgotten? So what are you going to say to your friend when he has them executed for treason, or when he arranges to have them quietly murdered on their way home? And he will, you know, because then he can take Clarus' share of the money as well as yours, can't he? My share. Don't imagine he hasn't thought of it because I'm damn sure he has. It was probably part of the bargain." And I covered my face with my hands and said, "Oh God—don't say it." Because I'd thought about it too.

I had just come from the palace where I'd seen them throw a man down at Valens' feet and then drag him off to execution because he'd picked up some smattering of news concerning Vespasian—that he'd denounced Vitellius, proclaimed himself emperor and entered Egypt—and the man's face still lingered in my mind. His face and Valens' face, grinning at me and refusing to answer when I'd pleaded, "Is it true? has Vespasian refused to negotiate—?"

"Do you care?" he'd asked me tauntingly. "Tell me, darling, tell me true—whose side are you on?" And although I couldn't answer him I'd gone with him to his room at the palace, to make love, scandalously, in the middle of the morning, and even now, in my mother's house, I could still feel his hands on me, still remember that nightmare sensation when, for an instant, his insolent black eyes had changed into my father's warm, brown ones, asking me that same question, "Whose side are you on?"

19

VESPASIAN HAD INDEED entered Egypt. His brother, Sabinus, brought my mother the news and had no reason to believe us anything but overjoyed. "It won't be long now," he said. "The ordeal is almost over. From Egypt my brother can cut off Rome's corn supply and we shall see the Vitellian cause crumble away now under the threat of starvation. Responsible government—law and order—we shall see all these things again. You can be very sure of it."

But Vitellius' birthday celebrations went on, in early September, just as planned, beginning with a memorial service to Nero out on Mars Field at which Vitellius sacrificed a hecatomb of prize beasts, and continuing throughout the day with so much feasting and frolicking that the mob began to cheer Vitellius with a right good will, hailing him as Nero's true successor and a man after their own fickle hearts. Valens and Caecina tried hard to outdo each other in the magnificence of their contributions, but so much was given away that day that neither of them emerged a clear winner.

Vitellius showed himself everywhere, at the races, the amphitheatre, at public banquets, where he chatted genially to everyone who wanted to say a word to him, exchanging racing-talk and bawdy-talk and sentimental reminiscences of days gone by, letting his people touch him, kissing a few pretty girls and every child in sight, listening carefully to all the old ladies and letting them see the tears in his eyes when they told him of the boys they'd lost in the fighting, or of their old husbands who'd served under him when he'd been governor of Africa, and who were ready now to serve him again. And that day at least Vitellius was emperor of Rome.

The palace was feverish with gaiety and the official banquet, begun at noon, went on all day and far into the night. Everybody was invited, everybody came, everybody got drunk, while the hostess—Vitellius' sister-in-law, Triaria, since neither his wife nor his mother were well enough to attend—spent the day changing her clothes, appearing in green silk with emeralds, white with pearls, blue with sapphires, and finally a purple robe so covered with precious stones, and with so much jewellery on her thin arms and around her scrawny throat, that it was both a comedy and a disgrace.

"That's her husband's share of the loot," Valens murmured in my ear. "If the enemy get to the gate all he has to do is pick her up and run."

"And what do you have to do?" I said, but he avoided an answer by raising his cup to Caecina, who had just come scowling into the room with his untidy wife. I saw him put an arm around her shoulders, while she leaned against him, abandoning herself to him as she always did, and suddenly it seemed to me that she was not so much embracing him as huddling against him like a frightened child. He stroked her cheek gently, pressing her head against his chest as if to shield her from whatever dreadful thing was approaching, and I said urgently, "Has something happened?"

"Yes—as always when I get close to you—of course it has—shall we just slip away—"

He would say no more, but later, alone and in that vulnerable time after making love, he asked me, "Do you know that Vespasian is in Egypt?"

"Yes."

"Well, fancy that. And just how do you know?" His insolent eyes laughed down at me. "Don't you know such knowledge is dangerous—it carries the death penalty. Shall I kill you? I've killed everybody else I could catch who admitted to knowing the bastard's whereabouts—where he is and just what he could do to us."

"Don't," I said, my mouth dry, "don't make it into a joke—tell me the truth—is it all falling apart—?"

He got up to pour himself a cup of wine and then sat down on the bed, his naked back hard and brown in the lamplight.

"I don't know about that," he said. "But I'll tell you what I do know. Vespasian is in Egypt all right, which is a shrewd move because Egypt's our corn supply and he can starve us unless we can get him out. And since he also controls Syria and Asia, and possibly Africa as well, getting him out won't be easy. In fact I doubt if it can be done. That's what I know. And now I'll tell you what I think. Vespasian was in Judaea, and a man called Mucianus was just next door to him, governing Syria. And I think they got together and worked it out between them. Vespasian is going to call himself emperor, because only one of them can do that, and Vespasian has the bigger reputation. But what they're really planning is a partnership. So—they leave Vespasian's son, Titus to finish off the war in Judaea. Vespasian goes to Egypt to secure the corn supply and be on hand if somebody like the governor of Africa has a change of heart and decides to back Vitellius after all. And Mucianus sets off to bring the war into Italy."

"How long?" I whispered. "How long before Mucianus gets here?"

But suddenly Valens gave a shout of laughter. "Yes, how long? The legions do twenty miles a day—they don't hang about, even over that kind of distance. But what both Vespasian and Mucianus have forgotten is that there's a man called Antonius Primus in Pannonia. He's just persuaded the Balkan armies to desert Vitellius and declare for Vespasian—and he can get here a damn sight quicker than Mucianus. So if Mucianus isn't careful somebody is going to pinch his laurels—and then we'll see whether Vespasian remembers they're supposed to be partners."

I sat bolt upright and shouted at him. "Don't you care? You're making a joke of it again, and it's not funny—it's not funny at all."

But he ignored me. "I know Antonius Primus," he said. "He's the kind of man I would know. He was convicted of forgery once. A real bad lot. Beats me why someone hasn't done him in, years ago. But he always manages to climb back somehow. He was Galba's man, and he tried to be Otho's, and Vitellius' man too, and now, for as long as it lasts, he's Vespasian's. He'll get here before Mucianus—you can put money on it. He's not much of a soldier and he'll have a wild bunch with him. He won't be able to frighten them, and he sure as hell won't be able to make them love him, so he'll have to buy them. After all they're in it for the money, just like he is. So he has to get here first, doesn't he, to get the richest pickings. I don't doubt he's got his orders to wait until Mucianus catches up with him. But he can't afford to obey them—and in any case, the men won't let him. They won't want to share the loot with Mucianus' lot, and there'll be plenty of it."

"Stop it!" I yelled. "Stop it. You're talking about people—about killing and dying—and you think it's funny."

I struck out, a random blow that couldn't hurt him, and, very much as Caecina had done, he put his arms around me and pressed me against his chest.

"Where was your mother tonight?" he said, his mouth in my hair, and I shivered.

"Does it make any difference now?"

"I suppose not. But Vitellius did very well today. He really looked like an emperor. I could have cheered him myself, if I hadn't known better. And if he gets to like it—being imperial—then not even your mother will be able to stop him. And he wasn't supposed to like it—we didn't bargain for that, did we?"

"I don't know. I don't know." I shook my head, still pressing tight against him, holding on while he was still there for me to cling to.

"No, Antonia, he wasn't supposed to like it. But life's like that—up and down, full of surprises. Sometimes you win and sometimes you don't. Who'd have thought, this time last year, that I'd have been here, a consul, in a house like this, with a girl like you trying not to cry all over me? I forget who this house belonged to, but whoever it was had damn good taste —your kind of taste."

"But you'll fight?"

"Oh yes, I'll fight. I got the poor bastard into this, so I'll have to get him out of it. Or try to. But it may not be necessary. Caecina wants to fight. He knows Vitellius is sick of him, and it gives him a chance to try and slip a knife in my back in the confusion. And Antonius Primus certainly wants to fight because that's the only way he can pay his troops and make something of himself again. But Vitellius doesn't want to fight. And I expect Vespasian, and Mucianus as well, would rather have the empire handed over to them intact, than have it torn to pieces. The main problem is the soldiers. There's no profit for them in peace. You may not know this, but if a city is taken the booty goes to the troops, if it surrenders everything goes to the commanders—so—peace treaties and soldiers don't see eye to eye. And if Primus can't, or won't control his men— But I can control mine. And Caecina's not a bad lad when it comes down to it. He thinks a lot of that skinny wife of his, and he'll want to come back to her in one piece. The question is, Antonia, what do you want?"

"No," I said, denying with one word everything that was inside me, and then, in utter despair, I threw my arms around his neck and sank my mouth into his with all the force I possessed, so that he fell back against the pillows, chuckling, allowing me for just a moment, to hold him down, until his desire became urgent and he had no time for games.

"If I let you go," he said, "how far would you run?" And I couldn't tell.

Perhaps I wasn't expected home that night for our doorkeeper looked quite astonished, and let me in gingerly, as if he thought I might be an impostor. No one but my maid should have been awake. Corellia and Fannia would still be at the palace—everyone of consequence would be at the palace on a night like this—and my mother should have gone to bed hours ago, wishing, perhaps, that she was at the palace too. But lamps were lit deep in the body of the house, as far as the garden-court, so that I knew someone still sat there.

"Who is it?" I said to a servant, who had appeared from somewhere just behind me, but the woman, murmuring some disconnected words, glided past me and I saw, with surprise, that she was my mother's personal maid, and that she was moving so quickly, with such determination, that she could only be going to deliver a warning. "My lady, someone—an enemy—your daughter—is coming."

Vitellius, I thought. Was he here, at last, to plead or to compel? But the air was too quiet, too cool, for Vitellius, and even he could hardly leave so many guests unattended. But, as my mother came hurrying to meet me, the man behind her was the elderly, respectable Sabinus, Vespasian's brother. Sabinus—and, in the distance someone else, a lamp quickly extinguished, a door closing, as my mother's maid whisked whoever it was out of sight and then came back to bar the escape route with her own, devoted body. And yet, for all her efficiency, when I managed to get into the garden-room where they'd been sitting, there was a scarf, a trailing wisp of green silk, across a stool, and, on the floor, a hair ornament in emerald and gold that I recognised.

My mother stood just a few steps away from me but now she was no stranger. The vague, dreamy woman who had been living in her body only this morning, was gone and she had returned to herself, the woman who had raised me to do my duty and who, it seemed, had now decided to do hers. The small space between us widened into a gulf that could never be crossed and, showing her the ornament in my hand, I looked straight at her and said quietly, "I always knew that untidy woman would lose her jewels one of these days."

There was no doubt in my mind that the diadem and the scarf belonged to Caecina's wife. And if Salonina had been here, in my mother's house, talking to Vespasian's brother, then she could only be acting for her husband, brewing treason and death for Vitellius—for Valens—and in that moment my mother and I were deadly enemies.

"So," I said, hating her, knowing she despised me. "You've made your decision then—about which side you're on—about which men to support?"

Her eyebrows lifted in their old, sardonic line, and she had no pity for me. She was a woman who had made her choice and who had chosen right. I was a girl who couldn't bring herself to choose at all, who was still desperately trying to keep faith with both sides, with both men, although I knew it couldn't be done. And my plight failed to move her.

"My dear girl, there was never any decision to make. Did you really expect me to betray your father? Did you want me to betray him?"

"No, of course not—how could I?"

"How indeed. And could you betray him yourself?"

I shook my head.

"Well then—having made that point quite clear—there's really no reason to make such a fuss about a hair ornament, a trinket that is really, well, rather cheap. Not our kind of thing at all."

And, taking the jewel from my hands, she walked away.

Sabinus remained, just a moment, his smooth, pleasant face full of pity, for he knew of my relationship with Valens and yet, just the same, he trusted me. I was my mother's daughter and he knew I wouldn't betray my class.

"We are called upon to bear such burdens sometimes," he told me gently. "But it will soon be over now. My brother is a good man, Antonia. He will be a wise and generous ruler—and your own future, my dear, concerns us all. My brother will find you an excellent husband—a splendid match—in recognition of your father's great services to him. And you will be content."

Yes, I thought bitterly, content—with your dreadful, spiteful nephew, with that moody boy who pinches me until I bleed and stares at me with his odd eyes as if he could see into my head. And I couldn't bear it. I wouldn't have it. Yet, throughout the bleak remnants of that night, as my mind frantically sought an escape, every path I took had my father at the end of it, smiling his warm, hesitant smile, trusting me too. And no amount of weeping could wash that trust away.

20

ANTONIUS PRIMUS ENTERED Northern Italy with his Balkan armies well ahead of Mucianus, as Valens had predicted, and, after a great deal of hesitation, Caecina marched out of Rome one warm September day to meet him. The sky was streaked with gold, the autumn sun glinting on polished armour just as a spring sun had shone for the Othonians, and a pale, winter light had illuminated Galba—an age ago—when he'd planned to make me Empress of Rome. And now, as I watched the German auxiliaries straighten their backs and sniff the air, shaking off their dissipations because they were heading North again, to the grey sea and the green breezes Valens had told me about, I felt so desolate, so full of pain, that I could have died of it where I stood.

I went home after the parade and walked past my mother in the atrium without speaking to her, hating her so much that the bitterness of it choked me. And yet, what she had done was right. She had allowed Sabinus and Caecina to use her as a go-between in some scheme of theirs to destroy Vitellius. And how could I call her treacherous when she had chosen to support her husband—my father?—rather than a man whose advances she'd rejected twenty-five years ago? There was no answer. Two men loved my mother and, wanting her to keep faith with them both—for I loved my father and pitied Vitellius with all my heart—I hated her for not being able to do the impossible, for not being able to do what I longed so desperately to do myself. And, more than that, I hated her because she made me treacherous too. Every time, now, when Valens took me in his arms, the memory of Salonina's jewel and her trailing, green scarf came between us and sometimes my mind screamed out a silent warning. Yet I couldn't speak, for I didn't know how deeply my father was implicated, and those few words, 'Beware of Caecina. He'll betray you', could well be his death-warrant. And how could I do that? Like my mother—how could I?

Valens left for the front a few days after Caecina, and I dined with him the night before his departure, dry-eyed, yet with the ache of tears in my throat so that I couldn't eat and had little to say. But Valens, in his flowing, lawn robe, with his curly hair gleaming and his body fragrant with expensive oils, seemed not to have a care in the world. He wore a fortune in rings on his powerful, brown hands, a ruby at his shoulder that my grandmother would not have despised, and he had the same pleasure in his possessions, a frankly sensual enjoyment of fabric and precious metal and rare wood, that he'd shown that first evening, four long months ago—a world ago.

"It's better than the military prison at Bonn," he'd said to me that night, and, remembering his voice and all his careless bravado, I couldn't bear my silence any longer, and said abruptly, "Don't you want to marry me before you go?"

His eyes lit up with their insolent black sparkle. "Do we have time—between now and tomorrow morning?"

"No," I almost shouted, angry because anger is a safe emotion. "You know perfectly well there isn't—and that's not what I mean. You could have married me weeks and weeks ago—Vitellius wouldn't have stopped you—but you didn't because you knew the war was going to start again—and so, instead of making sure of me before you go, like any sensible man would do—you're leaving it to chance, like you leave everything—because you're a gambler—and because you think you're not going to win—"

He got up and stood for a moment with his back to me. "Is that what you think?" And then, serious, almost intense, for the first time since I'd known him, he sat down on my couch and took my hands.

"Don't yell at me," he said, "I'm a superstitious man and I've never known a run of luck like this to last. I'm not saying it's over now, because I'm a determined man too—I hang on to what I call mine—but it doesn't do to tempt the Fates by taking too much for granted. So—I'll tell you what I want you to do. For as long as you think there's a chance I'm alive, bear me in mind. But as soon as you hear, from a reliable source, that I'm dead, then forget me. It's much the best way."

His hands were warm and hard, and, returning their pressure, I looked him full in the face—because it wasn't a time for tears—and said steadily, "I'll never forget you. That may sound foolish and girlish, but it's true. I don't mean there won't be another man, because I suppose there will. But I'll never forget you, Valens. You can believe me."

"Well, then," he said, squeezing my hands quite painfully, "that's something to take away with me—"

But my control broke and my emotion released itself in violence, in the shower of useless blows I rained against his chest, until at last he took me in his arms in a grip that crushed me into stillness. And there, with my face pressed against him, and my eyes tight shut, I muttered, each word a dead weight on my tongue, "I have to tell you this—and God knows how I'll live with myself afterwards. Because I'm betraying my father, and there is no worse crime—I'll never be clean of it—but Caecina's wife was at our house, talking to Vespasian's brother—and so Caecina must have made a deal with Vespasian—oh, damn you, you're worth nothing compared to my father—and I'm worthless too—"

"No," he said, stroking my hair, rocking me. "No. You're lovely. And I even made you fall in love with me, didn't I? And that was more than I'd hoped—much more—"

"Have I at least told you something you didn't know?"

"Look at me," he said. "Stop crying and look at me, because it's done now. That's better—you even cry elegantly—but there's no need for it, darling. No need. Perhaps I didn't know it, but I'm not surprised. I expected it—thought about it—I'm prepared for it. Telling me or not telling me makes no difference. You've done your father no harm, and me a lot of good, because now I am sure of you—and that's what I wanted. Antonia—Antonia—don't let them marry you to anybody else until you're certain I'm dead. And even then I may come back and take you. How about it—dead or alive? Whether Vitellius wins or loses? How about it? I'd have to hire myself out as a mercenary to some barbarian prince at the back of the North wind, or somewhere—if there are any left. That's something you can do while I'm away. Try and find out if there's a king somewhere in the world—or a queen, I'm good with queens—who's not subject to Rome, and who could use a man like me. And if Vitellius loses I'll take you there. Will you come?"

"Yes," I said, "I'll come." But there was no barbarian prince, no place in the world for him to shelter in, no corner where Vespasian wouldn't find him.

"What went wrong?" I whispered, through the pain in my throat, and he shrugged and smiled, the sparkle back in his eyes.

"You mean to our famous deal with Vespasian? Well—Sextilia's a shrewd old bird in her way. She had my measure all right. She knew I could be bought and she knew how to buy me.

But she somehow never found the right coin for Vespasian. And her own dear Vitellius was difficult too—more difficult than we'd thought."

"Why? Was it my mother?"

"I doubt it. He may use your mother as an excuse, later on, if things don't work out and he has to justify himself. But no—not really. If Vespasian had actually made an offer—a villa at the sea and enough money to live in the style to which he'd grown accustomed—then perhaps Vitellius would have been tempted, whether your mother was willing to share it with him or not. But we couldn't bring Vespasian to the point—he just wasn't enthusiastic. He's too far away to spot a double-cross, you see, and he didn't feel strong enough to take the chance. And we could hardly ask him to trust us, could we now? But I tell you when he will deal. If Antonius Primus or Mucianus ever get as far as Rome, that's when he'll offer to buy Vitellius off. He can't very well let his lads take Rome, can he, because he has to live here, afterwards, and he wouldn't exactly endear himself to his subjects if he let that bloodthirsty crew loose on them. We had our fun in Gaul, I don't deny it, and Northern Italy paid us our price too, but even we had to draw the line at Rome. And Vespasian will have to do the same."

"And will Vitellius accept—so late in the day?"

"I expect so. If he's on his own—without me and Caecina—he'll be scared, and what else can he do? But even then—well—it's still risky and I'm not sure they can really let him live. It could work out for a while but the first time Vespasian introduces an unpopular measure, there's sure to be somebody who'll start shouting 'Up with Vitellius. Let's have him back.' And Vespasian can't allow that, can he? I know I wouldn't allow it—so, goodbye Vitellius."

And suddenly he laughed. "I just hope the poor bastard has enjoyed himself as much as I have these last few months."

"You're talking about people," I told him desperately, "about human sorrow— " But his body came down on mine, crushing everything from me but my great need for him, and the pale light of approaching day was in the sky before he released me.

"You're a beautiful woman," he said. "A lovely, warm, beautiful woman. Be very sure I'm dead before you let them give you to somebody else."

And as his head came down on my shoulder and his body relaxed against mine in sleep, I held him in my arms, easing him through his troubled dreams, aware, for the first time, of my own strength and endurance. He was reckless and callous and unafraid, but he didn't want to fight any more, didn't really want to go adventuring again, and my only thought was, "Come back and I'll look after you. You don't know how strong I am—Perhaps I didn't know it myself until now. But I'm stronger than you. I'm as enduring as the earth. Rest on me. I can bear your weight and the weight of your weaknesses and your selfishness and your crimes. And there's healing in me too—just as there's healing in the earth. Here, or at the back of the North wind—anywhere—somehow I'll save you.'

And my new, woman's courage lightened that bleak hour, so that I believed it could be done.

21

For a long, slow time there was no news.

I didn't watch him leave the next day. I went home, and met my mother's eyes without shame because I'd made my choice too and, right or wrong, I'd stand by it.

"I told him about Caecina's wife coming here to see Sabinus," I said steadily, and she lifted her shoulders and eyebrows in her own, special gesture of contempt.

"The choice was always yours, Antonia. We must simply hope that you told him too late. If not, then I trust you will be able to find a way of living with yourself—of coping with your disloyalty—" And, bitterly, distinctly, I told her, "I imagine so. There's enough of you in me for that."

Caecina and Valens were heading separately for Cremona, the scene of their past triumphs, putting themselves between Rome and the army of Antonius Primus, and, as once before when the Vitellian hordes had been approaching, the city was full of rumours. The Germans, once so terrifying, had grown comfortable with familiarity, and it was the men from Pannonia we feared now, and after them, the men from the East, Vespasian's own troops who were as stern and fierce as their master, and would punish us for loving Vitellius, or Otho, or Galba, or for attending that spectacular memorial service for Nero. But, whether they came from the East or the North, once again Roman soldiers were being drawn up to fight each other, and it was only a matter of chance—of being in a certain place at a certain time—whose side one happened to be on. The city was full of families who had a son with Antonius Primus, a son with Caecina, a son who had died fighting for Otho, families who prayed simply for peace, for an ox or an ass to rule them if it meant an end to the slaughter.

The city mob were still hysterically pro-Vitellian, but a strong senatorial party was forming against him now, substantial men who knew Vitellius was no politician and were more than willing to open the gates for Vespasian. They came often to see my mother, senators I'd known all my life, considering our house a safe meeting place, and she excluded me from all discussions, refused even to let me meet them sometimes, because I was no longer to be trusted. I was a thief in my own home who stole words and gave them to the enemy, and I had to be watched, apologised for, despised.

I had made my choice. If Valens lived I would go to him anywhere—a villa in Campania, or a hut at the back of the North wind, anywhere, and I'd cope. But the waiting hurt me. When I entered the house I could no longer look at our household gods, those friendly little guardians of our hearth and our store-cupboards, who had watched over my childhood from their shrine just within the hallway. As a child I'd always had a smile for them, knowing they loved me because our family was their special care and I was a part of it, but now, although I knew they were images endowed only with the life we gave them, it seemed that they watched me sorrowfully, and as I passed on down the atrium, the marble heads of my ancestors drilled holes of accusation into my back. One night, as I slept, they came and stood around my bed, disembodied heads staring at me with silent menace, so that I woke screaming and Fannia had to spend the rest of the night with me, murmuring, as if I'd been a child, that she wouldn't let them come again. And the next day, when my mother heard of my nightmare, she smiled.

If my mother was suffering for Vitellius, or dreading my father's return, she didn't show it. She was, once again, the paragon who'd ruled my childhood, and now that her vagueness was gone, now that she'd finally strangled her other self—the girl who'd let Vitellius kiss her all one summer long—she took the reins of the household firmly back into her hands. Everything was shining and clean again, the food eatable, the servants efficient and polite, and—because if Vespasian found it necessary to hold up the grain supply he'd be obliged to starve his friends as well as his enemies—she set about buying corn wherever she could and storing it in huge bins that were guarded day and night. If my father came home he would find her unchanged. There would be no warm welcome, no fuss, but at least she'd be here. And he'd never had more than that.

Corellia, who for months had come home only to change her clothes, began to slow down, preparing instinctively for Clarus' return. Most of her friends had gone off with Caecina in any case, but there was more to it than that. Her body was finally so weary that there were times when it wouldn't obey her, when her limbs were a dead weight and she could do no more than curl up in the autumn sunshine and doze like a sick animal. Her eyelids were blue-veined, her cheeks hollow, yet, incredibly, her dissipations had not coarsened her. She looked exhausted but very lovely, and I knew that my brother would find her new frailty very much to his liking.

We sat together in the garden almost every day, Corellia and I, as that golden September mellowed into the smoky fragrances of October, and it seemed that we were both waning with the year, coming to the end of our separate ways. The world we knew was teetering on the brink of destruction, the men we knew were bracing themselves to claw one another to death, and so we sat and talked about small things, about the bland days of our childhood and, hesitantly, about love.

"Do you remember Camerinus?" she asked me abruptly one day, and when I nodded she smiled awkwardly, as if her mouth hurt her. "Yes," she murmured, "good old Camerinus. Who could forget him?"

She sat brooding for a while, bruising herself on her memories, and, after a long time, she said, as if she had to convince herself rather than me, "I was in love, you know. Fannia makes fun—and I know you thought it was just a spring dream—but I was in love with him, really and truly. I've always had an ideal man—even as a child I used to dream about someone beautiful and sophisticated and elegant—and a little crazy too—and Camerinus was all those things. The first time I met him I felt I'd known him for years, because I'd been thinking about him for years. I'd known him for less than an hour when he put his hand on the nape of my neck and said 'I want to make love to you', just like that—straight out—and I said 'Yes', and we did, then and there in some kind of a store-room up at the palace while Galba was counting his money-bags, and Clarus wasn't even out of Italy. And it seemed right. But real life's not like that. The beautiful men one falls in love with turn out to be poor and get themselves killed, and the good, solid men one marries stay alive and multiply. And so I made my decision, just like your mother has. And I want you to know, Antonia, that I'm going to stand by it. I haven't changed my mind and I won't change it. I'll be waiting when Clarus comes home."

I nodded. "Yes, I know. And I know you don't care what I think about it. But it's wrong. You'll be burying yourself alive.

And what about Clarus? His life is short too, like yours and mine. You don't love him, but there are other women who could, if you'd leave him free to look for them."

"He doesn't want anyone else," she snapped. "He's like your father. Everybody knows he'd be better off without your mother—but he doesn't think so." And then, with a sudden, unexpected note of pleading in her voice, "Antonia, you wouldn't really go away with Valens, would you? If he loses everything and wants you to join him in some godforsaken hole somewhere? You wouldn't really go? It's just romantic talk, darling, isn't it? Oh Antonia, listen to me—I know that look on your face—you mustn't even think of it—you can't do that to yourself. Darling—don't you see—it would have to be some dreadful place, you'd have to go among savages—to a German forest or right into the wilds of Britain where they still offer human sacrifices and eat them—oh darling—living anyhow in cold and danger—and there can't be love in such conditions. And when you stopped loving him—and you would, you would, believe me, you would, I've thought it all out—what would be left then? You'd die of it, Antonia. Just as I would have done, with Camerinus. You wouldn't have to kill yourself—you'd just die of shame and mortification—darling—you couldn't go."

"But I could. And I intend to. Yes, I'll go to him, and it's the simplest decision I've ever had to make. Because—to know that he's alive and not go to him would be unthinkable. It's as simple as that. The problem wouldn't be whether or not to go, it would be how to get there. And I could cope with the rest."

"No," she said fiercely, "No, you couldn't. Because love would wear out. And you can't really love him anyway. He's not even a good man. He's a gambler and you'll never get him to leave other women alone for long. And he's coarse and worthless—"

"Oh yes, I daresay he is. But Camerinus is pretty worthless too, isn't he?—and Vitellius—and what has that got to do with love? If we only fell in love with worthy men you'd be perfectly happy with my brother. And my mother with my father."

And although she shook her head, denying the whole of it, she was silent and very pale for the rest of the day.

No news, and then suddenly so much of it that it rippled through the streets like a hot, hurrying tide. The Vitellian cause had been crumbling away, as province after province declared for Vespasian, and as first Aquileia and then Verona were occupied by the invading Flavians, but at last there came a glimmer of hope. We knew that Caecina had established himself with a strong force at Hostilia, after sending the rest of his army on to Cremona, some thirty miles away, near enough to the Flavians, who were based at Verona, either to fight them or to attempt to negotiate some kind of a truce. But what we didn't know was that on his way north Caecina had gone to Ravenna to meet the commander of the fleet and, following some plan which may have been proposed and paid for in my mother's house, it was agreed that on the same day—the 18th October—both the fleet and Caecina's troops at Hostilia would denounce Vitellius and go over to Vespasian. The sailors deserted willingly but then—and it seemed a miracle—when Caecina tried to make the army at Hostilia swear allegiance to Vespasian they refused, threatened him, and when he insisted—for he'd gone too far to be able to draw back now—they tore down the pictures of Vespasian he'd had put up all over camp, arrested him and his suite and sent the lot of them under guard to their mates at Cremona.

"Valens?" I asked desperately, as Corellia came running in, bubbling over with the news, and she put her arms around me and hugged me as she used to do when we were children.

"No one knows. Perhaps he's at Cremona too. And if he's not then he jolly soon will be. He must be heading there as fast as he can because he can't leave the army without a general. Vespasian's forces are at Verona, within striking distance—and I suppose now that Caecina has made such a mess of things they'll have to go ahead and strike. I suppose they'll try to take Cremona—but at least Vitellius' soldiers seem to like him, which means they'll fight bravely, and Valens is a good soldier. I've been talking to people, and they all say he's a professional and he knows what he's doing. If he gets there in time he'll lick them into shape—or whatever—whereas this other man, this Antonius Primus who is leading Vespasian's army, seems not to be much of a soldier at all. They say his men are quite wild—just a gang of thieves—and if Valens can't beat them he may be able to buy them. He'll know what to do, darling. Everyone is cheering Vitellius in the streets and garlanding his statues, and how splendid for him, really, that all those men refused to desert him. I'll bet he never expected anything like it."

Vitellius, who without Valens and Caecina, had been moving through his official duties like a man in a dream, suddenly awoke. There was a party at the palace that night, and he seemed his old, genial self, laughter booming out of him as he went the rounds of his guests, hugging and kissing people whose names he couldn't remember, pressing gifts into eager hands, making promises as if he thought he'd have the time to keep them, his eyes full of tears whenever anyone mentioned Hostilia and his loyal troops.

Yet even as the celebrations reached its height, somewhere in the city the rumours began, the first horrified whispers—hastily suppressed—of what Vespasian's army had done to Cremona.

22

Caecina's plot had failed but, just the same, he'd managed to split his men up and leave them in a vulnerable position—part of them at Hostilia, the rest at Cremona, all of them without a leader—and Antonius Primus was enough of a soldier to know that the time to strike was now, while the Vitellians were separated and uncertain, and before Valens had a chance to catch up with them.

He attacked Cremona early on the morning of the 24th October, and, although they were leaderless and confused, the Vitellians resisted him all day, holding out until the men from Hostilia—who had marched thirty miles in one day—arrived, exhausted but determined to see the thing through. They fought again through the night, Romans butchering Romans, some from loyalty to a cause, some for money, and when the Flavians wavered, someone—and who could it have been but Antonius Primus?—pointed to Cremona and told them it was theirs if they could take it. We didn't yet know the details of pain and torment, how the walls were breached and who was the first through them, but we did know that the city of Cremona and all its people had been given to 40,000 armed men as a toy to play with. The game went on for four days—the killing, the rape, the looting, the torture for profit and the torture for pleasure—and when it was done, when they'd bled the city dry and turned it into a reeking nightmare, they burned it to the ground.

Cremona was no more, and all I could say, in a strangled whisper, was the one word, "Valens?"

"No one knows." Corellia told me again, and I knew she'd been all over the city to enquire. "No one has seen him alive, but no one has seen him dead either."

"If he's alive—if he's alive—what can he do now?" I pleaded, and Corellia gave me an unexpected kiss on the cheek.

"Antonia, there's a rumour—just a whisper—that he never got to Cremona—that he heard about the defeat while he was still on the road and that he got on a ship heading for Marseilles or some such place. And if he did then he must be trying to get to

Gaul and overland to Germany, either to escape, or to raise the Northern provinces for Vitellius. That's what they're saying—certainly the soldiers I've spoken to believe it. And it could be true. It would be like him, wouldn't it? An adventure?"

It was hope, a straw to cling to. And it was like him. I closed my eyes and saw him on that ship, laughing into the wind, and then making a crazy gambler's bid for freedom, or even for fresh glory. And it was like him. I saw him on the road, taking his chances, and then throwing down his challenge lightly in the first auxiliary camp he came to. 'Come on, lads. There's been a right cock-up down there. Let's go and get Vitellius out of it.' Or else, and far more likely. 'There's a native queen up in the north of Britain who pays good wages. How about it lads?'

And I found I had clasped my hands so tight that I had drawn blood.

"Whatever they say against him," Fannia said quietly, "he has shown that he can be loyal—while Caecina—"

"Yes, but Caecina's alive," I said, and the bitterness of those few words burned my tongue.

Caecina, who had been held prisoner at Cremona by the men he'd tried to betray, had been rescued by Antonius Primus and sent to Vespasian in Egypt. Salonina too had left Rome, presumably to join him, and it seemed likely that they'd be back one day to enjoy their country villa and their riverside mansion, to make love and raise children on the wages of their treachery. And I decided—one unbearable, sleepless midnight—that if Valens died I'd kill them both.

My mother sent for me a few days later. I hadn't been in her room for a long time and it struck me afresh how virginal it was, how utterly unlike the room of a married woman. I couldn't imagine any man, not even my father, disturbing that narrow bed with its spotless cover—white embroidered on white—couldn't imagine any man ardent enough to survive the chill in the air. Her maid was with her, getting out her silver combs and mirrors and an assortment of pearl hair-pins, making preparations, in fact, for a journey, while she herself was already dressed to go out.

"Where are you off to so early?" I asked, not really caring, and she smiled and clasped her hands together as if—incredibly—she was nervous.

"Yes. I shall be away for some days—I can't say how many—but not too long."

"Oh?"

She smiled again, a swift, excited movement of the mouth I didn't recognise in her.

"Antonia—I feel I must explain—we have never been close together, you and I, but perhaps—?"

And suddenly lightning flashed in my brain and I said harshly, "My God, you're amazing. You're going to Vitellius, aren't you? You've helped them betray him and now you're going to him—in charity—just like you go visiting our tenant-farmers after a bad harvest—to offer him your crumbs—I hope he throws you down the palace steps."

She sat down, abruptly, as if her legs couldn't take her slight weight, yet she was smiling and she seemed frail and faraway again, not my mother at all, but that quiet stranger, slipping back into her summer dream.

"How intolerant you are," she said. "But you're young and I suppose it's a fierce time of life. He knows I'm coming. He's waiting for me. And it's not charity. You see, my father was right, all those years ago—my father was always right. I couldn't live with Vitellius. I know exactly what he is and what I am—and I know that the end, in the long term, could only be disillusion for us both. My father assessed my character accurately. He knew I would always do my duty, and so I have. I allowed myself to become involved in a plot, hatched by my husband's friends and my lover's enemies—which was only right. But now it's done. Vitellius' cause is lost. He knows that very well. And until your father returns I really have no duty to anyone. And so, I'm going to set myself free, just for a little while. And if it's charity, then perhaps I'm the beggar—not him. You've never been close to me, Antonia, because I've never allowed it. Children die so easily. And I wasn't going to risk being hurt again. And then, you belong to your father, and he could have taken you away from my care at any time he wished. So I kept my distance, and we have grown very far apart. But—in these strange times—perhaps we can help each other now—Antonia?"

She smiled straight into my eyes, offering me not a mother's tenderness and care, for it was too late for that, but an alliance, the friendship one woman can give to another. And although it wasn't enough, it was more than she'd ever offered before.

"I don't know," I told her. "There's one thing you must understand. If Valens survives and if he manages to contact me, and I can get to him, then I'll go. No family politics or pressures will stop me. I love my father but if he stands in my way I'll get past him somehow. I won't sacrifice myself, as you have. This is my life and I'll live it as I choose. I don't expect you to approve, but if you want my help then I'm entitled to yours."

"Yes," she said. "You're entitled to that." And as she got to her feet I saw that her mind was so filled by Vitellius that I was just a shadow to her, just a part of that long, waking dream that had kept them apart.

"Just think," she said, "if I'd had your kind of courage—if I'd gone to Vitellius when he first wanted me—you would never have been born."

I accompanied her to the palace, obeying a summons from the lady Sextilia, who was unwell and wished to see me, and although the distance wasn't great, it was an agony to her. She had waited twenty-five years but now every moment away from him was too much to bear. She wanted to jump out of the litter and run to him on her eager feet, arriving flushed and breathless and laughing, as perhaps she'd done all those years ago at Luceria. And Vitellius was eager too for when we reached the palace precinct he came rushing down the steps to greet her, scattering his guards, his face pale, his eyes bloodshot and one of them half-closed as if there was pain behind it. He looked overweight and unfit—he looked old—but his whole, flabby body was blazing with delight. And as she stretched out her hands to him he scooped her up in his arms and carried her—his prize, his treasure—up those shallow steps as tenderly and as touchingly as a young bridegroom.

I followed quickly behind, painfully aware of the soldiers smirking and winking at one another, of insolent palace servants peering around pillars to watch their master make a fool of himself, and suddenly my mother's role and mine were reversed. She was the child, I the parent, and I was horrified at the thought of what this hot, heavy man was going to do to her. But, as he slid her to her feet, she leaned against him, her fingers eagerly drinking in the feel of his freckled, hairy arms, and I could only suppose she was seeing him as he'd been twenty-five years ago, in the days before his belly started to sag, when he'd been wicked and sophisticated, and not at all ridiculous.

"Dear child," Vitellius said to me, "it grieves me to shock you—and it must shock you—indeed—" But my mother shook her head as if to say she'd take care of all that later. Her cage was open, her spirit free for the first time in her life, and as Vitellius saw her radiant, loving smile, his face flooded with so much unmanageable emotion that nothing else existed for him.

Hugging her to his chest in a tremendous embrace he lifted her again and carried her away, and as a door slammed shut behind them I leaned against the wall, fighting the nausea in my stomach, wanting nothing more than to sink to the ground and stay there, covering my eyes and stopping my ears, so that I didn't have to see, didn't have to know, about tomorrow, or the day after.

Eventually, when I could, I went to Sextilia who was back at the palace again, for her health was failing, and Vitellius, like any good son, had wanted her in his care. She was lying in the middle of a wide, soft bed, propped up with pillows and was surrounded by her own people, who had moved to the Palatine with her. I knew she was ill, could hear the wheezing of her difficult breath, but her cheeks were rosy apples, her eyes bright, and she looked very much as usual.

"Now then," she said comfortably, "I'm glad your mother has seen reason at last. She's been so stubborn—quite naughty—but they're together now, bless them, and that's the main thing." And I understood that their elderly passion, which had disgusted me, was in her eyes young and whole and wonderful.

"Don't worry about her—you silly child—she's going to be so happy. People don't always know what's best for them. But Sulpicia has always wanted Vitellius, and now she's got him. And we'll make it up to your father, somehow, when he comes home. You'll see. He may growl and grumble for a while, but he's a handsome man and he'll find his consolation."

She beamed, a happy little woman with not a cloud in her sky, and it came to me that the brightness of her eyes and cheeks was not health, but fever.

"Oh yes," she said. "Everything is going to work out beautifully. I am expecting letters from Vespasian any day now, offering my son the honourable retirement we agreed upon—Vespasian and I. He's perfectly reasonable, the dear boy. People have whispered to me, you know, that he's not to be trusted—Vespasian, I mean—that he'll promise this and that, and agree with all I ask of him, and then go his own sweet way. But he's not like that at all. I wrote to him, you know, telling him what was the best thing to do—and, of course, now that your mother has come back to us, my son won't hesitate to agree. I think they should settle at Aricia—I've told him so—he has a nice little villa there, near the city, so he can come and see me. Because I don't care for country life, you know. Aricia will do very well.

Although I must say I'm getting rather cross with that scoundrel of yours—that Fabius Valens. Will you tell me what he thinks he's doing, running off to Germany to raise troops for my son? We don't want troops any more—we've had enough of them—and he promised me he wouldn't interfere. And that's one thing I can't bear, a broken promise. 'Buy me', he said to me, the young scamp, when I first spoke to him about it. Buy him, indeed. And that's just what I did. 'Give me something I can't get for myself' he told me, and I did that too. He could take all the money and the property he wanted, I knew that, but an alliance with a noble house, legal title to a fortune like yours, that was something he'd never even thought of. But when I suggested it to him he knew, all right, how much he wanted it—and he promised me. 'Give me that girl', he said, 'and I won't do anything to stop Vitellius going into retirement. I'll even have a go at talking him into it.' And we agreed. I showed you to him that first evening you came to the palace—no, I didn't dine that night, but the palace is full of spy-holes—and when he saw you and I saw the look on his face, I knew I had him. But now—you must call him back and tell him to stop this foolishness. I really must insist that you call him home. It escapes my mind for the moment—but did you marry him? Because if you didn't, and he continues to misbehave, we shall have to break the engagement and give you to someone else. So you'd better call him home."

"Yes," I said gently, "I'll do that."

"Good. And do it at once. We can't have him spoiling things, because everything is going to be all right now."

She closed her eyes for a moment, her breathing laboured, and I understood that if she knew about Cremona at all, she had blocked it from her mind, hidden herself away from it, so that now, at what may be the ending of her days, she could believe her own cheerful words. "Everything is going to be all right."

She lay for a while in silence, until I thought she'd fallen asleep and I was about to leave, when her thin, flushed eye-lids lifted and she said, "Your grandparents were not good people. They are to blame for all of this. Oh yes, they were full of what society calls virtue, and they knew all those long speeches about tradition and class-loyalty—but your grandmother cared for nothing but her own comfort and your grandfather only valued his pride. And they sold your mother to pay for it. Your father took her almost without a dowry, and they made him pay through the nose—oh yes—poor, innocent lamb—" She began to cough but when I made a gesture of concern she brushed it aside.

"I have loved my children," she said, "and that is something your grandmother never did. She thought me foolish because I forgave them when they behaved badly. And she thought me extravagant when I gave them what I had. But that was my pride. My sons could have the garments from my back and leave me naked if it served them. What else is a mother for? I never required them to be brilliant or successful. I just wanted them to be happy. And happy in their own way, even if their way wasn't mine. And your grandmother thought I was foolish. 'Naturally Vitellius is wild', she used to say. 'What else would one expect from the son of that foolish woman.' But my son loves me. And did her daughter love her? Her daughter was afraid of her—that's how she was able to break her spirit and take her away from Vitellius. And I'll never forgive her. He should have got Sulpicia pregnant, as I told him, or abducted her, and then we'd have been at peace now and there'd have been no need for all this. Don't blame my son—it's not his fault, poor child. There was a skirmish at Cremona—I suppose you know about that?"

I nodded and, as she took my hand, her touch was a dry flame. "They'll blame Vitellius for that too, I daresay—so I must write to Vespasian again, to explain to him—and tell him that Aricia is the place we have chosen—Aricia—" She smiled, her eyes closing again. "You'll like it at Aricia—yes—I thought of you when I suggested it to him. 'Take her to Aricia' I said, 'She likes trees and woodland plants and those little singing streams—she'll be happy there'. And you mustn't be afraid of him, my dear. He's changed, I admit, and he'll be ardent and he may even be rough sometimes, but it's only because he loves you, and he's waited so long. And you're not so innocent as you seem, are you child? I used to say to my husband, 'She's a deep one—there's more to her than we think.' And who else would have waited so long for you to make up your mind? Take him to Aricia, and you must do anything—anything—that pleases him, you owe him that, and between us we'll save him. I'll stay here and talk to Vespasian, when he comes—and you must stay with my son, never leave his side—be a good girl, at last. That's right—a good girl—dear Sulpicia, I never liked your mother, but you're a good girl, and we'll keep him safe. And when I'm gone you'll know how to take care of him—take my place. That's all I ask—care for him"

And abruptly she was asleep. Her head sank into her pillows, her colour drained away, and, with this relaxation of her mind and spirit, her body was shrunken with defeat. Awake she could pretend that all was well, believing her own lies, but asleep her body knew what had happened at Cremona, knew that Antonius Primus was heading south with Mucianus somewhere behind him, and that with the Flavian armies in Italy and Vespasian himself in Egypt, her son's cause—if there had been a cause—was lost. And perhaps she knew too, with a knowledge buried deep beneath her love for him, that Vitellius would have to die. Vespasian may promise that villa at Aricia, if it enabled him to take Rome without bloodshed, but once the city was his, it was a promise no one could compel him to keep. In Vespasian's place Valens would not have kept it. And, looking down at Sextilia's fighting, loving, dying face, I didn't believe she would have kept that promise either.

23

October suddenly became a biting, sparse November, the city streets full of the raw winter wind and men's most primitive fears. What had been done to Cremona could be done again, here, to us, and it seemed that the North wind—the wind that came from Cremona—carried the screams of women in torment and the blind panic of dying children sewn up in its skirts.

The city was silent, as I had never known it. We moved on quiet feet as one moves around a death-bed, and, we drew our garments around us, huddling into them as children hide in corners, settling already into attitudes of grief and despair. It was a season for tying up loose ends, for doing what had to be done while there was still time, and, as always happens when one comes to the end of hope, every man was alone to find his own solution. But however much one prayed or cursed, or, like my mother and Vitellius, tried to cram a lifetime into a few desperate days, when it came to it there was really no way to prepare oneself for rape and torture and famine. And we were all afraid.

After Caecina's desertion and Valens' disappearance—after Cremona—there seemed no hope for Vitellius anywhere. His army was crushed, the imports he needed from Egypt and Africa and Asia were in Vespasian's hands, and as the fickle wind blew province after province away from him, it also fanned the sparks of local discontent—local opportunism—so that there were rumours of native uprisings in Britain and Germany and Pontus which, if allowed to escalate, could topple both Vitellius and Vespasian and the whole of our civilisation with them into chaos.

Antonius Primus, still approached from the North, on fire to get here before Mucianus caught up with him so he could take full credit for the campaign. And perhaps it was time now for Vitellius to step down, to sacrifice himself in the interests of peace as Otho had tried to do. Certainly the Senatorial party were itching to be rid of him and prepare Vespasian a hero's welcome, but the ordinary people had taken Vitellius to their hearts and, after generations of not caring who was in power so long as they got their regular shower of lottery tickets and gladiators and free food, they had decided that no one but Vitellius would do. He still had troops stationed North of Rome, at Mevania, ready to block the Flavian advance, there was the city garrison, the imperial bodyguard, and if that wouldn't suffice, then the people themselves would take up arms and fight for him. They had given their love to no other man. They'd said 'good-riddance' to Galba, hadn't cared either way about Otho, but to Vitellius, who had created himself emperor because it had seemed like a good idea at the time—and not even his own idea at that—they offered a devotion he hadn't expected and which, in the end, would kill him, for it was the one thing Vespasian wouldn't be able to tolerate. Loyalty blinded these staunch Vitellians to the truth so that they began to see the whole, world-wide upheaval as no more than a local problem. "We've just got to smash Antonius Primus and keep him out of Rome." And it was useless to say to them, "What about Vespasian who holds Egypt and Asia and probably Africa too, and can cut off our imports without which we can't live? What about the armies of Spain and Britain and Gaul who have declared for Vespasian? We have lost the fleet at Ravenna and the fleet at Misenum. We have no ships, nothing to back up the troops at Mevania but civilians with sticks and stones. And we have no general." It was useless, because Vitellius had become a cause, an ideal, and the city, which had been without ideals so long that it had forgotten its need for them, grasped at this one with the crazy courage men find sometimes at the end of the road, when it becomes necessary to do at least one splendid, foolhardy thing before all is over.

The soldiers Corellia spoke to still insisted that Valens had got through to Germany and would be coming soon with a new army to take the Flavians from behind. But, although I prayed with the back of my mind every moment of every day for his safety, I knew he was too much of a realist for that. It had to end now, the sooner the better, and if Valens raised the entire German province for Vitellius it could mean no more than a diversion, something to halt the day of reckoning that was bound to come. Perhaps Valens wouldn't care about the death and destruction but he wouldn't want to lose, and I prayed simply that he'd save himself, that he'd cut his losses as any gambler would, and make his escape. And the rights or wrongs of it didn't concern me. I didn't want him to be heroic, or honourable or merciful. I just wanted him to live.

Winter, and the bleakness of rain and wind filled every room of the house, defeating the shutters and the charcoal burning beneath the floors, so that we were cold all day and shivered into fitful, inadequate sleep at night. Fannia took to her bed, or huddled all day over a brazier, wrapped in thick, woollen cloaks, one on top of the other, coughing as the charcoal fumes hit her chest, while Corellia and I went around the city, listening, talking, gleaning what news we could. It no longer mattered which side we were on. If the Flavians took Rome as they'd taken Cremona, the common soldiers wouldn't know, or care, that my father was with Vespasian, that his brother was our friend, and we'd be in as much danger as anybody else.

At the beginning of December the furnaces at our house on the Esquiline—that imposing residence of the Sulpicii—ceased to function and there seemed nothing to do but move across the river, to the villa where I'd hidden Camerinus and let him make love to me in what now seemed an absurd and sentimental dream. The rooms were no warmer, the garden colourless and bare, and when the upheaval was over, all I'd gained was a little extra weariness which enabled me, for a night or two, to sleep.

Every morning our hall was full of clients, coming to us as clients always do in times of crisis, for advice and support but, more particularly, for bread. Vespasian's occupation of Egypt had caused panic buying so that there was no grain to be had anywhere, and I opened our massive storage bins and recklessly distributed their treasure to anyone who could prove they owed service to our house.

Fannia, from the depths of her cloak and her depression, told me bluntly, "You're taking the food from your own mouth—and mine."

But I cut her short. "No. Because it can't last much longer. Once Antonius Primus gets here he'll have to feed his men and Vespasian will lift the blockade. So, if we're alive, we'll eat too."

But just the same, there was panic in the city and warehouses where corn was thought to be stored were broken into and torn apart by angry, hungry mobs. And men were killed.

I worked all day. The servants, in my mother's absence and in their own fear, were hard to control, but I controlled them, setting them to clean and polish and cook and sew as they always did at this time of year in preparation for the Saturnalia, the festive season we had no hope of celebrating. And when a job was ill-done, although we could all be dead tomorrow, I saw that it was done again. Like my mother, I accepted no excuses and was unmoved by tears. I needed exhaustion to stop my mind from following Valens' every step of his way, to stop myself hoping and planning and dreaming and hearing his voice on the wind, and so I drove myself hard and the household with me. I became cool and sharp and my face, when I took a moment to glance at it, gave me no pleasure at all.

Only in the evening, sometimes, when I sat with Corellia in the small, winter dining-room, with all the lamps and braziers burning, could I relax and allow myself to think about him. He had told me about the frozen, Northern winter, about ice and sleet and damp wind that tore the skin and splintered the bone, about feet bleeding on iron-hard pathways and a world swimming for day after bitter day in a vast, frozen fog. And I shivered, now, thinking of him in that white wilderness.

"He's been there before," Corellia consoled me. "He'll be able to stand it."

"Will I be able to stand it?" I whispered, and when she made no answer, when she just smiled at me sadly, pityingly, I didn't know if it was because she thought Valens was dead, or that he'd already forgotten me.

And he could forget me. I knew it, grappled with it, told myself brutally that what had attracted him to me here, in Rome, would no longer apply if I was a refugee, stripped of rank and fortune, with no skills at all to cope with life in those rough lands. Did I even seem real to him now, as he galloped through the thin, grey air into the ice, or was I just something he'd had to leave behind, with his gambler's nonchalance, like his villa and his garden on the river—something, perhaps, he'd known all along he wouldn't be able to keep? Yet, when my despair was keenest, I heard him tell me, 'Be very sure I'm dead before you let them give you to somebody else.' And I knew that, at least, he'd wanted me then, when he'd spoken those words, and that it had grieved him to let me go. Perhaps I had become unreal to him, perhaps there was a native princess somewhere who could be of more use to him now than I could, but he was real to me. His eyes sparkled just as they'd always done. Somewhere he sat, laughing, beside a camp-fire, eating whatever was put before him, telling his bawdy tales, living—and that had to content me. My own future was uncertain, painful, because when it came to it they'd give me to somebody else whether I wished it or not. But at least I could think of him alive and free, and, if nothing else, I'd be a part of his camp-fire tales—the patrician girl who'd loved him and had been willing to sacrifice her father's gold for his sake. And if no one else believed him, he and I would always know it was true.

A biting November and then a December that seemed to have been sent to us from the North itself. Grey mornings freezing into sombre afternoons, driving rain and wind and my one, everlasting prayer that it would end. And the end seemed near for war was closing in all around us. Mevania—our last barrier—had fallen. Antonius Primus was already as far south as Carsulae, a mere ten miles from Vitellius' remaining forces at Narnia, and, to the south of Rome, the defection of the fleet at Misenum had induced the greater part of Campania to declare for Vespasian too. We were hemmed in, surrounded by those vicious, greedy men who had sacked Cremona, men who had been allowed to run riot on their way through Italy, just so long as they made haste about it and got their indulgent, desperate commander—Antonius Primus—to Rome first. Yet now he called a halt. Cremona could perhaps be explained away, forgiven, but if he did the same thing to Rome could Vespasian possibly let him get away with it? He rested for a while, waiting for orders, his army so near the Vitellians that, since they were all Romans and some of them brothers, cousins, fathers, sons, best mates who hadn't seen each other for years, they could get together and exchange views. His plan, obviously, was to show the dispirited Vitellians the enormity of what confronted them so that wholesale desertion would make combat unnecessary. Some men at the end of their tether, crossed over the line, but, in spite of all Primus' blandishments, the majority stood firm, refusing with more courage and loyalty than any one had dreamed of, either to be bought or persuaded.

"Why won't they give up?" I raged, furious with them, ready to break heads myself. "Why won't they see reason? It's no longer a case of winning or losing. It's just how to lose with as little bloodshed as possible."

But only the senatorial party, led by Sabinus and joined now by a great many army officers—cool men who dealt in facts not emotions—shared my view. The soldiers and the ordinary people meant to fight on and when volunteers were called for, men who'd never held a sword in their lives rushed forward as eagerly as if there had been a marauding horde of Parthians at the gate, or Hannibal come back again to remind us of the virtues of our ancient past.

Vitellius' brother, Lucius, had gone with six cohorts and some cavalry, to Campania to try to contain the situation there, but

Vitellius himself stayed in Rome, calm as some men are when they can see their own death, and, although he was at the very centre of the storm, it hardly seemed to touch him. More than ever now he was just a straw in the savage wind that had been blowing him this way and that, all the way from Germany, and he had no resistance left.

"He should abdicate," Corellia said. "He should end it now—do it with dignity before they do it for him."

But Fannia shrugged. "I wonder if he can? The people want him to stay where he is. Can he let them down?"

December, a morning when the maids lost their wits and bungled their work, when the house was full of people asking me for things I couldn't give, hanging on my skirts like children, amazed that I too could be cold and hungry and had no magic touch to heal their anxieties or fill their store-cupboards, or bring their men safe home. A morning when my head throbbed and my back ached and I was so peevish with small, domestic concerns that when Corellia came running into the house I didn't immediately see the tears streaming down her blanched cheeks. She didn't like the touch and smell of other women but now she threw her arms around me so roughly that she almost knocked me over, and her anguish was so evident that my mind went to Camerinus—to Clarus—to my father.

"Darling," she sobbed, "oh darling—" And she was in such distress that I began to make the gestures of comfort that were becoming automatic in these dangerous days, and I didn't see, at first, that the grief was not hers but all my own.

"He's dead—oh Antonia—they killed him yesterday—I've just found out—and I have to tell you and tell you quickly before you hear it in the street or from a maid or somebody—oh and I can't—but I must because it's only right, and there isn't anyone else—oh Antonia—it's the hardest thing I've ever had to do in my life."

"Yes?" I said distantly, and she swallowed hard, avoiding my eyes.

"It was because of the soldiers, you see. They were so sure he'd get through to Germany, and because of that they weren't deserting fast enough—but he never got through to Germany. Oh darling—can you hear me? Are you taking it in? If only I could keep it from you, I'd give anything—"

"Tell me," I said harshly and my voice hurt my own ears.

"Oh yes—darling—he never got anywhere near Germany. His ships had to put in somewhere near Marseilles because of the bad weather—and they arrested him—the imperial agent, Valerius Paulinus arrested him, oh I've never liked that man—and they've had him with the army all the time, coming south, all the time when we thought he was getting away, going north."

A flood of tears, her pity for me, gushed from her eyes, and then, looking at me almost fearfully, she said, "They've been holding him at Urvinum—so near, you could have reached him there—and they killed him yesterday morning because he was the Vitellians' last hope, and now they know he's dead they haven't any hope at all and the soldiers are deserting just as quick as they can—"

She wavered, stopped, and before I could feel pain, Valens' voice said it to me, very clearly, 'Be sure I'm dead'. And I answered him, not Corellia.

"No. He's not dead. It may not have been him. We can't know—how can we know? Just propaganda—for the soldiers, like you said."

Her face went completely grey and she shuddered violently, but then, with far more determination than I'd ever given her credit for, she said quietly, "We know, Antonia. The soldiers were slow to believe it too. They needed proof, so they cut off his head and displayed it to them—and that's when they first began to desert. There's no doubt. He's dead."

And even then I heard a hysterical voice—my voice—babbling dreadful things. "They displayed his head, did they? And what does that prove? They displayed a head, any head with black hair—and there must have been plenty of them—heads—all over the place—and who looks at the face?" But then, on the instant before I had to look at that face myself and know it and go mad, an iron hand crushed itself around that deep, inner part of me where emotion lives, squeezing me until I was dry and numb, and I said, "There's something I have to attend to—something to do—"

And Corellia said, "Yes—there's some kind of a panic in the kitchen about the bread."

I kept on my feet all day, moving like some mechanical device, because if I stopped I may never find the strength, nor the desire, to get started again, and it was far into the night and the night after that before, at last, I was able to turn to Corellia, who had stayed up with me and whose face was drowning in fatigue, and say "He's dead." And even then my eyes wouldn't cry and the iron claw that gripped me seemed only to fasten itself tighter still.

24

EIGHT DAYS, TEN days crawled by, blank days that had no face for me to tell them apart, and then a messenger came from the palace to say that Sextilia had died and my mother wished to see me.

I didn't care about Sextilia, or my mother. I existed, it seemed, because the blood still flowed in my body and air still filled my lungs, because my brain and my hands still functioned and performed their tasks, but the feeling part of me was encased in ice, and if I had no pain I had no pity either. The palace, a house of mourning now, looked neglected and cold. There were soldiers stationed in every doorway or marching in determined twos and threes down passages which the servants, sensing a change of ownership, hadn't bothered to sweep, and there was candle-grease on the walls and unpleasant, unnameable stains underfoot.

My mother was alone, in a gaudy, octagonal room that had a brazier burning fitfully in a corner, and as she held out her hands to the warmth, dipping her face in the glow, she looked younger than I felt, frail and lovely, with dreaming eyes and a smile I'd never seen before.

"Are you cold?" she said and I shrugged, her own gesture of intimidation.

"Yes. But the fire won't help."

"You know that Sextilia died in the night?"

I shrugged again. "Yes. What do you want me to say. She was old. She knew she was dying. And she had nothing to live for."

"I'm sorry," my mother said and because the tears in her eyes may have been for me and Valens, and because I wasn't ready for her sympathy. I said harshly. "Is it over then? Is he going to abdicate?"

"He's going to try. He waited until his mother died. She clung so firmly to her belief in Vespasian's good faith, and he didn't want her to know that it had all been an illusion—that she'd lost. He didn't want to give her any more sorrow. They have offered him an income and an estate in Campania, if he helps them to take Rome without bloodshed. And today he's going to try to accept their offer. Sabinus and the rest of the senatorial party have been informed and, by now, they must have got word to Antonius Primus that he is going to surrender the city. But it is my belief— and Vitellius' belief— that they cannot let him live. We think, he and I, that some accident will befall him, something that can be explained away. And so he is going out to sacrifice himself, as perhaps any king should be prepared to do, for the sake of peace."

I could doubt neither the nobility nor the depth of her sorrow, I should have pitied her, admired her, but suddenly Valens' head came just within my vision, bleeding and dancing grotesquely on the end of its spike, and I said bitingly, wanting her to bleed too. "That's noble— a little late in the day— but noble. And it's very convenient for you too— since my father may well be with Mucianus. He'll be coming in one gate as Vitellius goes out of the other— what could be handier? But if Vitellius manages to stay alive, what will you do then?"

I could cope with her hostility and her disdain, perhaps I even needed these things now to keep that dreadful, dancing head at bay, but instead of allowing me to fight her, she said simply, "I am farther along the road than you, Antonia. They haven't cut off Vitellius' head yet, but they may well do so tomorrow. And so perhaps we can help each other now— you and I?"

And when I said, "I doubt it," she smiled.

Vitellius left the palace on foot, dressed in deep mourning, heading for the Forum, to address his people for the last time and surrender his insignia of office. The men of both the urban and praetorian cohorts had been confined to barracks to keep them out of mischief, and Sabinus, as Vespasian's brother, was ready to take control. Vitellius was planning to say no more than a few words, nothing to arouse any undue sympathy, and, had he been a wicked man or a cruel man or simply a nondescript man, this handing-over of authority would have gone smoothly and he may even have kept his life. But the people had decided to love him and that love was his death-warrant. No emperor of Rome had ever abdicated before and so, there being no accepted procedure, he simply asked to be remembered kindly and offered his ceremonial dagger to one of the consuls standing beside him. The man refused to take it and so— with that one foolish gesture — unleashed a flood of devotion that carried Vitellius like driftwood on the tide, out of the Forum and back, in crazy triumph, to the Palatine. We heard the roars and the cheers and the stamping of military heels in salute as the soldiers joined the throng, and I saw my mother's face turn the colour of cold ash.

"The emperor," they shrieked. "Long live the emperor." Yet when he came back to my mother's room there was nothing in his face but an immense sadness. "They wouldn't allow me to go" he said. "It's just as we thought, love. I shall have to see it through to the end." And they clasped hands in a gesture of total love and understanding that had nothing sensual about it.

There was nothing more, it seemed, for Vitellius to do but wait. They had refused his abdication but he had abdicated in his heart and now he sat down beside my mother, devoting the last moments of his life to the woman he had always wanted. Silence wound itself around them so that they were an island set in the middle of a quiet water, so separate from the real world that when messengers arrived they spoke first to me.

"My lady, would you inform the emperor—?" And when I told him that there had been a clash between his own supporters and the senatorial party and that Sabinus and Domitian and a crowd of their adherents had occupied the Capitoline Hill, he simply sighed and nodded his weary head.

Sabinus, I thought, smooth and bland, a kindly old man who wanted me to marry Domitian and thought I should be glad to do it. What was he doing now, with a sword in his hand, fighting in the streets? It wasn't like him, and yet it seemed it had been expected of him, men had wanted him to do it, had told him he'd be a traitor to his brother's cause if he didn't. And so, like Vitellius, he too had been carried by the tide and was now under siege, washed high and dry on the Capitoline Hill, wondering perhaps what on earth to do next.

The night passed and with it a transference of power not from Vitellius to Vespasian but from Vitellius to any tribune or centurion or any strong-minded soldier who could persuade a few others to follow him. They still believed they were fighting for Vitellius but they were doing it now in their own way, without any clear direction other than the urge to kill Flavians, and it was their tragedy and ours that the only Flavians available were the inoffensive Sabinus and his noble friends who, by knocking down the statues which had stood for generations in the temple area, had barricaded themselves into the Capitol.

Perhaps, in the time that it took to root them out, the Vitellians forgot just who they were fighting and saw no further than the limit of every knife-thrust, or the tossing of a fire-brand, And, since fire was a weapon of terror they always used at the storming of an alien city, the Vitellians brought it with them as they came yelling and stamping up the Clivus Capitolinus, and when the buildings began to burn and the flames to run on ahead of them, they simply followed, yelling the louder. The Flavians, with their backs to the wall, resisted hard but there were few real soldiers among them and, in all that horror of blood and smoke and flame, as the Vitellians forced their way in and started to round up their fellow-countrymen as if they were naked savages destined for the slave markets, no one noticed—for a moment or two, until it was too late—that the ancient temple of Jupiter, that immortal monument to our national glory which no foreign enemy had ever managed to destroy, was burning too. And as it crumbled away to smoking dust, to smoking shame, the Emperor of Rome sat and held my mother's hand and stared at something in the far distance, a quiet couple whose love was old and true and wouldn't fail them now.

They brought Sabinus, in chains, to the palace steps, a grimy, greedy crowd of soldiers and city loiterers, dragging that mild-mannered pleasant old gentleman as if he'd been a murderous Parthian warlord. His face was blackened with smoke, his garments dirty and torn with rough handling, and even in this desperate plight I could see it worried him to be less than immaculate. They were bringing him to Vitellius as a cat comes to lay a mangled mouse at its owner's feet, expecting praise, and when, shaken at last from his reverie, Vitellius lifted up his arms in horror they were too far gone even to notice.

"No," he cried out. "No. This must not be." But no one in that crazy throng, except perhaps Sabinus himself, heard him, and before he had finished speaking the first knife-thrust went into the old man's side, and then another, and there, on the palace steps, before the sick eyes of their emperor, they hacked Vespasian's brother to pieces and then dragged the carcase away, cat-like again in their joyful cruelty. We didn't know the names of his murderers, wouldn't remember their faces afterwards if anyone sent to enquire, but not one among them would ever understand that the knives which had killed Sabinus had killed Vitellius too. There could be no villa at Aricia now, for the man who had watched this butchering of Vespasian's kin, and I saw Vitellius straighten his shoulders and heard him heave an enormous, echoing sigh.

"So," he said, "I can expect no mercy now. But I expected none—and it may be easier to make an end now, than to be allowed to hope—" Taking my mother's narrow head between his hands he kissed her eyes and her mouth and then held her gently, briefly, against his chest. "You must go home now. Take your daughter and go home." And I understood that they had already said goodbye.

We walked, unattended for the first time in our lives, through a hushed and desolate city. The pale winter sky was stained with smoke, the air foul with the stench of burning, and every empty street held the presence of death in it, the memory of life bleeding away into the cobbles and the terrible knowledge that there was more to come.

My mother had nothing to say to me. Her back was straight, her step light and sure, her face the face of the woman who had raised me. But as she entered my father's house she stumbled slightly across its threshold, averting her eyes from his household gods, and for a moment it seemed to me that she was going to turn and run wildly, like a bird seeking frantic escape. And then she composed herself and walked quietly back into her prison.

25

THE FLAVIAN SOLDIERS came the next morning, some of them to avenge Sabinus, some for plunder, some because they had been caught up in events greater than themselves. But they came, and the Vitellians couldn't keep them out. There was desperate combat, young men with all their green lives before them dying horribly, stupidly, some of them even honourably, but I didn't care, and the city mob who had never seen street-fighting on this scale before, didn't really care either. They went out to stare and cheer and take bets, as they would have done at any other gladatorial show, and, as soon as the outcome was decided, there was money to be earned by selling hastily sketched maps of the city to the invaders and showing them where Vitellian officers were hiding.

Men were dragged outside and butchered simply because someone pointed to a doorway and shouted 'Vitellian' and, as households dispersed, running for their lives, men who were neither Flavians nor Vitellians nor anything else, slipped through abandoned corridors and began, systematically, efficiently, to pick the empty houses clean. We barred our doors, closed our shutters, held our breath, hoping that our isolated position on the riverbank would be a protection, but it could be dangerous too—for who would hear our screams, who would help us?—and by noon I knew that we hadn't a male servant left in the house. And by evening we had no servants at all.

"It's Cremona," Fannia moaned, her nerve gone. "They'll do what they did at Cremona."

But my mother said quietly. "It won't be long now. It can't be long. Like childbirth, it has to end—and we can only wait." And, amazingly, through my despairing pain, she smiled at me.

Vitellius died that afternoon, as Sabinus had died, hacked to pieces by an unruly mob, but the essence of him had died long before they touched him and my mother, who had been mourning him in her heart for days, heard the news without flinching. He would perhaps have done better to have taken his own life, instead of allowing them to hunt him through the deserted passages and halls of the palace and then drag him to his brutal, untidy end, but it seemed to have happened as my mother had foreseen and all she would say, in a voice that could have been Sextilia's, was, "He was an honest governor of Africa once, and, for a time at least, he was an emperor." And when she said it again, and then a third time, I realised it gave her comfort.

We waited until evening and only Fannia seemed concerned about the realitites of pain and humiliation. The rest of us sat in a stillness that was a terrible thing in itself, and the early winter dark brought no respite for, although Vitellius was dead and the Praetorian Barracks, the last centre of resistance, had fallen, the city was still full of hungry, men who, now that the blood was drying on their hands, had time to spare and other appetites to kill.

"Surely they'll sleep—eventually," my mother said and, with the words hardly spoken, there came the sound none of us could bear to hear, the arrogant hammering at the door that tore away our status and our privileges and made us victims, like everybody else. I'd never before heard the noise of hinges being forced apart, of wood and metal shattering, giving way, hadn't realised how it could chill the blood and dry up every fluid part of me so that my mouth was parched and my throat burned. Yet, for all that, we stood in a tight little group, the four of us, even Fannia remembering she was a patrician woman who had been taught to master fear, determined to make a decent end.

There was the noise of a cohort, a crude rampage of armed heels and deep-chested laughter, the indignity of things being over-turned and smashed, the rape of our household by mindless brutes who had been men a few days ago, with hearths and children of their own, and would be men again—next month, next year—when it was over. I'd thought all our servants had fled but I heard a woman's scream, and another, and the screaming entered my head so that my mind was screaming too, for there were many of them and we had no hope. But someone called from outside, offering some fresh excitement, and after a long time, only two of them finally kicked open the door of our frail concealment and came swaggering into the room—two ordinary soldiers, one middle-aged, one young, our masters.

There was blood on them and dirt, and they had rings on their fingers and huge grain sacks bulging with loot in their hands. One of them had a chain of emeralds around his neck, and they were both leering and preening, men no longer, but walking appetites, far beyond the edge of reason or compassion, stuffing themselves to satiation point before someone called a halt. There was a moment of silent confrontation—of sheer outrage when I refused to believe this was happening to me, although I'd been thinking about it all day—and then the older man grinned and began strutting around us. "Yes," he said. "Noble ladies. That rounds it all off very nicely. We'll stay the night, Marius—eh? Two each—and I get first pick. This one."

And with one stained, brown hand, he traced the outline of Corellia's frozen body appraisingly, feeling her breasts and buttocks as men do in a cattle market.

"And I'll take this one," the younger man said, staring at me, slashing at the air with the sword in his hand, and although he didn't touch me there was something in his eyes—the same odd, blank gaze Domitian had—that flicked my stomach to nausea. He smiled, licking thin, pale lips, and I knew that he was a man who would hurt me and take delight in my pain.

I could not have forced my tongue to speak, not even to cry uselessly for help, but my mother said, without a tremor in her voice, "I must tell you that you are putting yourselves at risk. My husband is a close associate of the Emperor Vespasian, and any damage you inflict on his property, or on his daughter, will have to be accounted for. You would do well to leave quietly—for your own sakes—and at once."

A nervous spasm flickered across the younger man's face, some remembered conflict with authority, with women like my mother who, all his life, had been telling him to run along and remember his place, and the sword in his hand bit into the air again, his face full of nervous movement as if his body needed more than sex to relieve it of tension.

"Is that so?" the older man said, his hands leaving Corellia and his body turning in swift excitement to my mother. "Well now—we're just common soldiers, madam, and Vespasian may be a friend of yours but he doesn't know our names, and you won't remember our faces. We'll see to that. We've had a hard winter, madam—it's a bloody long march from Pannonia—and you should thank us—thank us. You're the real thing aren't you? A real patrician woman outside and a bloody tart underneath, I'll be bound. You could teach me a thing or two, couldn't you? Vespasian's friend—noble lady—couldn't you?

Breathing heavily, his coarsened fingers began plucking at my mother's dress, ready to strip her naked where she stood, until, suddenly, Fannia took a step forward and said with authority. "Leave her alone. If you want to learn something—well—I've been to bed with Nero and Otho and Vitellius too, and just think what a good story you can make out of that—if you're man enough, that is, to stand the comparison."

She stopped him, almost comically, in his tracks. He gave a low whistle, his eyes coming out of his head, and putting a steady hand on his arm, she said, "Yes, dear boy, I mean it."

The shivering, complaining Fannia of the past few weeks was gone and in this hour of degradation—perhaps our last hour on earth—she was her old flamboyant, compassionate self.

"Oh Fannia," my mother said, with love in her voice, and Fannia shrugged her splendid shoulders, determined to do the whole thing with style.

"I won't die of it," she murmured, pressing herself against his chunky, grimy body, reminding him of the delights in store, reminding us that now we had only one man to deal with.

But the other man, feeling he was getting the worst of the bargain, stirred restlessly with the disgust nervous men can easily feel for women. "I'm dirty," he said, almost in tears. "They'll wash me and feed me first—they'll behave like women for the first time in their lives—they're just whores—your noble ladies—legalised whores who don't even earn their keep."

Hatred spilled out of him, filling his mouth with bile, and he went thrashing wildly around the room—frightening us because we didn't know what drove him—his face drained, his eyes red-rimmed and out of focus as he fought the screaming torment of his own nerves. And then abruptly the heat was out of him, his face emptied itself of humanity, becoming blank, unreachable, a face in a sick dream, and I felt in him something I'd never met so close before, the need to kill not for gain, not even in hate, but simply to watch someone die.

"You," he whispered. "You." And his arms were so cold that I seemed to be held in metal, helpless, as he began to drag me away to find a lair where he could bind me, like a giant spider binding its prey, and play his atrocious games.

"No," my mother said. "No." But I was a woman drowning, disappearing, and she was on dry land, fading from my view, until, through the nightmare, Corellia was coming towards me like a flame, leaping and clawing at the soldier with all her desperate, young strength so that his grip on me relaxed and I could fight him too. We went down, all three together, an obscenity of arms and legs and screams and heavy gusts of breath, and then there was a knife in Corellia's hand, scratching, stabbing, not knowing where to strike until the blood came—a great, hot spurt of it—and our young, wild-eyed, pitiful enemy rolled aside choking with pain and amazement, his own blade in his throat.

There was blood everywhere, an ocean, filling my eyes, and then, through the red-flecked mist, the other man, older and harder, advancing with a professional's cautious step, laughing and saying "Come now, ladies, that's enough." But he was more alarmed than he cared to admit, and as he came on to kill us—because what else could he do now that we'd killed his mate?—we fanned out instinctively, splitting his concentration, annoying him like flies on a bull's hide. Somehow my mother got behind him and, snatching a heavy bronze candlestick from one of the abandoned grain sacks, struck him a hefty blow on the back of the head. It didn't knock him out but he blinked, couldn't quite see straight, and suddenly, sickeningly, we were all at him, Corellia, Fannia, my mother and I, with heavy objects in our hands, battering, striking, screaming, women no longer but mad dogs worrying a rat, our humanity suffocated by blood and fear, and it was only exhaustion, when our arms could no longer strike and out throats burned from that dreadful screeching, that we stopped and saw that he was dead.

I have never known a silence like the one that fell on us then—a silence that pulled us to the ground in attitudes of despair and held us so motionless that—bloodstained as we were—it was not easy to tell the living from the dead. Fannia, slumping beside me, suddenly got to her feet looking for a place to be sick and her stiff, awkward movements awoke us all.

"It's not over yet," my mother said, moving her mouth with difficulty, "We can't leave them here. Other soldiers may come, and if they see this—"

"The river," Fannia muttered, her face yellow, "Tip them in the river." But my mother shook her head for the river was unreliable and could bring back what it took away.

"No. Not that. But we must do something and we must do it now, because if we wait, none of us will be able to touch them—and I can't—I can't—have this—this—on my floor—"

Hysteria crackled briefly in her voice and then she said, "The garden. We have to bury them in the garden—until Lucilius comes home. Antonia—please—we must have something to wrap them in."

"Yes," I said. "At once." And as I walked through the house on aching limbs there were things in the shadows that pointed and whispered at me and tried to grab me by the hair.

I brought the first things I found, a bundle of my father's togas, bordered with the purple stripe of the senatorial order, and, not looking at them and not looking at one another, we parcelled the two men up in wrappings far nobler than any they had worn in life. Parcelled them up until they were men no longer but merely corpses, anonymous and somehow more terrifying than they had been before. We dragged them one by one through the house—Corellia and I—trying not to know what they were, trying not to think beyond the heavy folds of white cloth, but there were places where the blood seeped through, reminding us like a sinister whisper, that these things had once been human, like ourselves—if we were human still—and although we had to be rid of them couldn't stand not to be rid of them, although they were unbearable and unspeakable, we had begun, crazily, to mourn for them too, finding it terrible that life could be disposed of in this way, tossed into a hole without a word or a prayer, a nastiness to be covered up and somehow explained away when father came home.

"Is there a shovel?" Fannia said and for a moment I didn't even know what a shovel was, much less where one could be found, but eventually we found them and, scraping away at the rock-hard winter soil, frantic now with haste because our breaking point was very near, we didn't hear the soldiers again until it was too late and they were already swarming through the house.

I ran forward, I don't know why, hoping, perhaps, on some mad impulse of self-sacrifice, to delay them until the others got away, into the river, anywhere, just away. And I had almost reached them, almost thrown myself stupidly across their path, when my eyes cleared and instead of the regiment my fever had imagined, there were just three of them and an officer close behind who suddenly cried out a word of command. They halted, shuffled their feet, there was some growling conversation as they agued about whether to obey him, words which I was too deep in shock to understand, and then they slouched away, leaving me with a man who said, "Antonia?" And when I looked up it took me a long time to realise he was Camerinus, so completely had I forgotten his face.

He didn't ask me why there was blood and soil all over me, why I stank and trembled and couldn't speak. He walked past me, down into the garden, his red cloak swirling around him, the plumes on his helmet unbearably white, and when he got there he stood for a while looking from face to face, at Corellia and Fannia with shovels in their hands, at my mother standing straight and pale, at the shallow pit and the ghastly bundles lying beside it. And then, taking the shovel that I'd abandoned beside that inadequate grave, he began slowly to dig.

No one spoke, no one except Camerinus seemed to move. The ground was hard even for an officer of the Pannonian hordes, but he tossed his cloak and helmet aside and went on digging until the sweat ran down his handsome face and the curve of his back was weary, ready to break. We waited until the pit was deep enough and then we rolled them in and waited again— in that agony of silence— while he covered them over.

"Well," he said, leaning on the spade, "I expect they were my lads. But then— I've been killing Romans all year, so what do a few more matter. They were all 'my lads' weren't they?" And, throwing the spade away from him so that it bit deep into the earth, he turned his head and walked quickly back into the house.

26

I HAD NEVER seen so bleak a January, bringing in the New Year, and yet I was alive, I ate and slept, and having faced that ultimate horror—having learned to live with the memory of Valens' severed head and my own murderous hands beating a man to death— I had nothing more to fear.

Domitian, in his father's absence, moved into Nero's gold house, the corn began to flow into the city again and, as the men from Syria and Judaea drew near, we heard that my father and Clarus were safe and would soon be home.

"Surely," I asked my mother, "You won't say anything to Clarus about Corellia? Not now, after all that's happened?" But I saw by the lift of her eyebrows that I was wrong.

"My dear girl," she said. "Corellia may have been brave and resourceful— she may even have saved your life— but does that really excuse her conduct these past months? And will it make her a better wife to Clarus in the future? I think not. One must not fall into the trap of making emotional decisions. One lives in the present, and hopes to see the future, and I cannot feel that Corellia has any place in Clarus' future at all— I am thinking of his good, not my pleasure. He must be told." And I looked away because I'd wanted her to be different, wanted the woman I'd glimpsed in her once or twice in our most difficult moments, and it grieved me to see her so totally the same.

I took the news to Corellia but her maid had got there before me and I found her sorting through boxes of clothes as one does before a journey.

"Clarus will be here in three days," I said and she nodded, biting her lips.

"Yes. And I shall be gone by then."

"Gone?— with Camerinus?"

"Oh no. Oh Antonia, are you so blind?" And as she smiled, with a new, astonishing sweetness, and put her arms around me, I realised Camerinus meant so little to her that she could hardly remember his name. "Yes— yes— I know I've told you over and over again how much I loved him. But it was never true. I see that now. I wanted to love someone like him—someone like Otho, I suppose—someone dazzling and dangerous—and he was there, and I was there, and the whole thing happened inside my head. I made it up. And then, afterwards, I was determined to keep on loving him because otherwise I'd have looked a fool—and I didn't want Fannia laughing at me and telling me she'd known it all along. And perhaps it gave me an excuse for all the other things I've done since then. But he faded—faded so that I had to make an effort to see him—and I kept on pretending because I had nothing else to put in his place. That's been the trouble all the time. I've never known what I wanted and so I've kept on inventing things, getting into scrapes. Don't look so sad. Perhaps we'll meet again. You told me, didn't you?—you put the idea into my head—that without me Clarus would find a girl to love him, and that I may meet someone too. Well, you're right, and don't say anything about the money and how I can't bear to be without it—because, somehow, when you've killed a man with your own hands and seen how fragile life is, everything seems quite different. No, darling, don't try to stop me. I've made up my mind and I don't want to fight you now, when it could be ages and ages—I could throw myself at Clarus feet, but I'd be destroying him, wouldn't I? I've always known that and I didn't care, because I was more important than him. Perhaps I still am, but life is so short—so short—darling—and I've made such a mess of mine. Everything in my life so far has been false. And it may always be so. No way has ever been right for me. But I have to try. Antonia, I have to find myself before I can find anyone else. You understand that. And so I'm going to my aunt, my father's sister, in Toscana. There's always been a home for me there—although I never wanted it before—but now I have to get away, to think. Make it easy for me, Antonia, like you always do."

She came to my room before she left, resolute and smiling her new, misty smile, her hands clasped around the ornate silver box that contained her jewels.

"Please give these to Clarus for me," she said. "It may be an empty gesture—I know he can buy all these things ten times over—but I don't want him to think I just took everything I could grab and ran away before your mother got the chance to tell him—whatever she'll tell him—" And without a word to her mother, or mine, she clasped me tight in her arms and went away.

Camerinus called that night—to see me or to see Corellia I

wasn't sure—and we stood awkwardly for a while, making painful conversation, for things were uneasy between us.

"Corellia has gone away," I told him at last, hoping perhaps that he would go away too, and he showed no surprise.

"Oh, she finally got on her way then, did she? Good. It's what she wanted, and she'll like Toscana." And I didn't know whether I was glad it meant so little to him or sorry that he was so shallow.

He was shaved and curled again now, living up at the palace with Domitian's rowdy young men, smiling at all the rich old ladies, but there were lines in his face, marks of strain and weariness and bitter memories, and an odd expression in his eyes when he looked at me that made me uncomfortable. There were bodies buried now in the garden where we'd made love and I didn't want him to remind me.

The house was quiet and strange with twilight, my mother and Fannia long asleep, no servant anywhere to see when he took my hand. And because there was an enormous pleading in him I sat down and allowed him to hold me very close, feeling the trembling of his body with nothing deeper than sympathy. He was thin, fine-boned, light-weight, and all these things were alien to me because they were not Valens, but I had once almost loved him and, because I loved him no longer, my vision sharpened and I could see, with my pain-scoured eyes, that beneath his sophistication he was timid and kind and eager for love, and that he was very close to loving me.

"I did as you told me," he said, smiling shakily, "I cleaned my wound and put on dry clothes. And although I didn't get to Judaea—which you never expected me to do anyway—I did get a command from Antonius Primus. Did I do well?"

"Did you? If it was worth it to you—How can I tell?"

"Don't," he said, and the pleading was back again, flowing from his trembling hands to mind, calling to my pity, to the female part of me that knew about rocking and holding and making the world right again with a kiss. And although I didn't love him I cared about him, I wanted him to be warm and safe and well, and he was beautiful.

"I came back as soon as I could, Antonia. It was all I thought about—coming back—and I hoped you'd want to see me. You do want to see me don't you? I worried—thinking I'd left you in a delicate situation—although I know you're strong, stronger than me—and I couldn't stop thinking about that lovely night—our lovely night. Am I wrong to think about it? Don't tell me to stop because I need that memory. And I need you, Antonia. Do you believe me?"

"No." My voice was friendly, amused, hurtful. "You may believe yourself—but you're just speaking words because you like the sound of them."

"No," he said, gritting his teeth, his hands tightening around mine. "Don't hurt me. You've enjoyed doing it in the past, but not now. Listen—take me seriously—I know you loved somebody else. Corellia told me about it, told me I hadn't a chance with you and that I shouldn't pester you anymore, and I was upset, but I can stand it. Let me help you. Share it with me, and help me too. Antonia—I was at Cremona. Make me forget."

Valens, suddenly, came through the air, disembodied, hideous, and I said harshly. "Forget? Why should I help you to do that? I forget nothing. Why do anything—why suffer, why struggle—if you're going to cancel it out by forgetting? So you were at Cremona. So were thousands of others. At least you're alive, and however bad your nightmares may be, it's better than being dead."

"Yes," he said, letting my hand fall into my lap and swallowing several times, very quickly. "If you say so. I was at Cremona. I saw them die and I saw them burn—and I can smell it and hear it—but I'm alive. And you're alive. And I need you. Not for money—not for anything except that with you I feel right and calm and safe—and I've never felt like that before. I've been in and out of love ever since I could talk, and this isn't the same thing. I need you, and whatever your parents say, if you want me I know you'll manage it somehow. I'm not much, but whatever I am, I'm better than Domitian—and he thinks of you— He likes to pull the wings off insects and pluck live birds, and when he's emperor he says we'll have to address him as 'Lord and God'—and he thinks of you."

Domitian was something which had to be faced, but Valens still lingered around me in the dark, his voice in my head saying 'Be very sure I'm dead before you let them give you to somebody else'. And I said, "You were at Cremona. Were you at Urvinum when they killed Valens? Did you see him die?"

His face, dipped in the shadows, looked pale, easy to hurt, but his voice was steady. "Yes. I'd like to say no, lie to you, but you'd find me out, and I couldn't bear that. Remember—I don't want to tell you, but yes, I saw him. He laughed at them. I suppose he knew, as soon as they picked him up at Marseilles, that he hadn't long to live and he kept on laughing at them when they pretended he was just a prisoner, and they'd release him as soon as Vitellius abdicated. He was rather magnificent, wasn't he? I felt his charm, although I couldn't like him. He was the kind of officer I'd be afraid to serve under, the kind who'd take his men into every hot corner he could find, just for the hell of it—yes—I'd have been afraid of him and he'd have thought me effeminate—he'd have made jokes about me and bullied me, I expect—it's happened before—and there's no way to convince a man like that, that courage isn't necessarily muscle and sweat and not giving a damn. I cried at Cremona. I couldn't help it. I'd fought in the battle, stood my ground, and I'd got on with the men all right on the way there. But once inside that city they were animals—I look at them now and I shudder—and I'll never go to war again. I'll starve before I'll kill anybody else, believe me. And that's courage too—the courage to refuse what you know can't be right. Anyway, you wanted to know about Valens, not about me. We brought him to Urvinum in a reasonable state—throwing dice with his guards all the way and winning their money—but once there, in sight of the Vitellians, he laughed once too often and so they shackled him. They said it was to stop him from escaping or being rescued but he knew there was no escape. He was a gambling man, wasn't he? And perhaps it was easier for him than it would have been for you and me. They killed him honourably with a knife in the heart, but then they needed proof—for the soldiers—and he understood that himself, expected it. It's what he would have done to Primus or Vespasian, given half a chance. He didn't seem to blame anybody. He didn't say much before he died. They asked him if there were any messages, and all he said was something about it being better than the military prison at Bonn. Does it help? Darling Antonia—I was afraid of making you cry, but you're not crying."

"No," I said and turning my face I kissed him, in friendship and gratitude and something more, for Valens' ghost had receded a little, telling me to make the best of what life still offered me, and the spectre of Domitian raised its head, those odd, excited eyes stripping me bare, those pinching fingers humiliating my skin, so that all my strength, born of loss and hardship, awoke in me and I knew I'd never submit to that.

Camerinus' mouth found mine again and as he began to cover my face and neck with kisses, I said, "Really. Whatever are you thinking of? Not on a couch in a reception room where a servant may come in at any moment. And where have all your romantic notions gone? Carry me to my bed like a bride. And this time you have my permission to get me pregnant. Vitellius' mother, Sextilia, always thought it a shrewd move, and in our case, she could be right."

27

THE EMPEROR'S SON— the emperor-to-be— Domitian, invited us to dine on the anniversary of Galba's murder, a macabre celebration I had no wish to attend, and it was on that day I told my father I would never be Domitian's wife.

He had been home for ten days, rushing to clasp his own cool wife in his arms, and love for him had pierced the hard shell around my heart bringing me the blessing of tears. I'd sobbed in his arms— for Valens, for Otho and Vitellius, for the girl my mother had been and the woman she might have become, for Corellia, and for Clarus who was stunned by her loss and wanted very much to cry too.

My mother had taken him immediately aside to perform her patrician duty, and afterwards he'd done all the things expected of a man in his position— got drunk and into a fight, gone to bed with a whore, brooded and sulked, thrown things at the servants and at me. But his suffering went deep and I ached with him. "I expected it of her," he said. "She was always a bitch— a mercenary, bloody bitch— I'm better off without her." But he wasn't, and although my mother began to give dinner-parties again, now that the corn was flowing, and invited a great many girls, he went back night after night to the Subura, to the lowest women he could find and made an ugly scene when my father protested.

"Poor lamb," Fannia said, but her own position was more precarious than usual, for Clarus refused to speak to her and when we moved back to the Esquiline, leaving that haunted, riverside garden behind, it was only on my insistence that she was invited to come too.

My mother clearly wished to block the past year from her mind, to pretend it had never been, and although there were times when she was kinder to Fannia, and I thought she remembered how she had been saved from rape, she was so very much herself, so engrossed in the petty details of domestic life, that I couldn't be sure. Stewards and upper servants waited, once again, outside her door, secretaries submitted menus and guest lists and accounts for her approval, and my father, only ten days after his return, slipped out into the night again to look for the brown-silk actress who had smiled and winked at me one night—long ago—in Otho's time.

"Does she ever think of Vitellius?" I whispered to Fannia, but Vitellius, who had died for her twenty-five years ago, had died a second, final time, and her real life, her real thought, continued locked away inside her head, excluding us as it always had.

"You'll never be like her," Camerinus told me. "Never. I'll never let you go away from me like that. We'll live in the real world, darling, in the sunshine, not shut away in dreams."

But until the anniversary of Galba's death, when Domitian wanted me to share a couch with him, I wasn't sure that I would be living with Camerinus at all.

There was never any question of attending the party. My mother's ill-health came to our rescue and we spent the evening making uneasy conversation, talking around the things that really mattered, until my father said, "Antonia—you know how Piso's death grieved me, and as for those others, if they grieved you then I regret it. But we must look to the future. The most splendid marriage of all escaped you—Piso would have made you an empress and a happy woman at the same time—but much may still be achieved. The Emperor Vespasian and I have become close friends. He has spoken to me of you, and when he returns there is every reason to hope that your future—his younger son, Domitian, is a charming boy—"

He paused, smiling at me, loving me and wishing me well, doing his best for me, and I said very clearly, "His younger son Domitian is a savage little brute who likes to pull the wings off flies and get his hand up my skirt—and I can't marry him, not even to please you."

And I got up and walked out of the room, leaving my father to his confusion and wondering—not for the first time—which side my mother would take.

Clarus was waiting for me, hovering on the edge of the battle, heavy with his misery, and he came with me to my room and threw himself down on my bed, looking tanned and fit beneath his sulking, older and more attractive than before.

"She's a bitch," he said, meaning Corellia. "She's impossible. And how dare she leave her jewels behind as if she thought I needed the money? She's the one who needs the money. What's that aunt of hers like? Does she have a decent place? I never heard of her before. You know, I've a good mind to go to

Toscana myself and throw these damned jewels right in her face. That's all she deserves."

And then, after a long, brooding time. "Antonia, you know her better than I do. If I went out there, just to clear things up—just so that we could part friends—do you think she'd see me? I wouldn't ask her to come back—naturally—but it would ease my mind to know she's all right. I haven't been blameless. I took her and thought I owned her because she didn't have any money. And she's proud. I understand how she could have resented it. I tried to buy her because I thought I couldn't have her any other way—and perhaps I couldn't. But I don't know her, really. I never saw beyond the way she looks. And I'd like to get to know her."

And all I could say was, "Give her time."

My door opened sharply and my mother stood there, unreadable, immaculate, a woman with right on her side.

"Your father is in great distress," she informed me. "He feels—and I must agree with him—that he hasn't deserved this. He finds such conduct in you, unbelievable—and shocking, and you may consider yourself fortunate that he chooses to take a charitable view. I was able to persuade him that our troubles, during the past months, have afflicted your nerves, and I think a short holiday—Praeneste perhaps—is indicated. I'm sure you'll see things differently after a few weeks of good food and mountain air. Vespasian is not a young man. His elder son, Titus, has no children. Domitian may well be our emperor one day, and whether you marry him or not—which is by no means decided yet—I cannot allow you to slander him."

But I shook my head, free because I was no longer afraid. "No mother, I'm sorry. The last thing I want to do is hurt my father and so I'd better tell you this—there are reasons why I can't marry Domitian, reasons why I can't marry anyone but Camerinus—Sextilia's reasons. I know you'll understand and make your arrangements accordingly. It would be best, I think, in order not to offend Vespasian, if we could be married immediately before any other proposal can be made. You'll know how to convince father that I am right."

And, amazingly, instead of scorn and punishment, there was a brief softening of her face and a smile hovering at the corners of her mouth. "I suppose you realise you have broken your father's heart," she said, but we both knew I hadn't. He wouldn't like Camerinus, but he'd love the child I may, or may not, be carrying, and he'd never know how often, in my heart, I journeyed somewhere behind the North wind, to look for Valens and tell him I'd kept my promise, that I'd made sure he was dead, and that, like him, I'd made the best of it, that I'd decided to take what I wanted while it was still there to be had. I hadn't let them give me away. I'd given myself to a man I'd almost loved and could love again—a good man who needed me to show him his own goodness—and if a part of me remained closed to him I'd give him everything I could, everything there remained in me to give. And when I went on my lonely journeyings only my mother would ever know.